THE

APPOINTED HOUR;

A ROMANCE OF VENICE.

"I stood in Venice on the Bridge of Sighs
A palace and a prison on each hand."—BYRON.

London.

PUBLISHED BY E. LLOYD, 12, SALISBURY SQUARE, FLEET STREET, AND SOLD BY ALL BOOKSELLERS.

PREFACE.

———

THE signal popularity which has attended the publication of the Romance of Venetian Life, entitled "The Appointed Hour," is probably mainly owing to the truthfulness of its incidents.

All who are familiar with the domestic policy of the State of Venice under the Government of its Doges, will at once acknowledge how easily naturally the events detailed in this romance might occur, strange and wonderful as they appear to the ears of modern Englishmen.

Indeed, the slight glance that is in "The Appointed Hour," given of the Bridge of Sighs, affords but a trifling commentary upon the horrors which the dungeon of that building really have witnessed, at a period when Venice was called the Queen of the Adriatic, and was carrying her acts and her arms throughout Europe, and most of Asia.

The insidious attacks of Flavius upon the enormous treasures of the Doge, which were kept in the dungeon like recesses beneath the Palace of St. Mark, is an historical fact; and after some years of incarceration as a lunatic, the Lord Treasurer was led forth to public execution, surrounded by every mark of opprobium.

Grateful for the marked interest which the lovers of Romantic Literature have paid to "The Appointed Hour," the author returns his best acknowledgements.

London, December, 1848.

THE APPOINTED HOUR.

A ROMANCE OF VENICE.

GORDONI RELATES TO THE ABBESS FLORANTHE'S ATTACK UPON HIM.

CHAPTER I.

TWILIGHT ON THE ADRIATIC. — THE VESPER BELL. — THE APPOINTED HOUR

"HE loves me—he loves me! Yes, he loves me. Was there ever such a heart as his? Did there ever beat in human bosom so kind a spirit? Yes, yes, he loves me—he loves me!"

Such were the words which the young and beautiful Floranthe breathed in cadences soft and low, her face lit up with joy and love, by the casement of her apartment in the palazzo of her father, in Venice, she, with a throbbing pulse watched the dying sun upon the Adriatic.

Sunset at Venice! Can anything be more beautiful—more absolutely enchanting?

The meanest habitation in the city of the sea now looks a palace, fit for an emperor, as the sunny radiance of the descending majesty of day falls upon it in long streaks of golden fret-work, while from the canals are uplifted with sparkling lustre the beauty of that sunset which only can be seen in such a city.

The heat of the day is past, and thousands of persons, who, in the cool shade of their closely veiled apartments, have waited for the delicious hour of twilight, now sally forth to enjoy the soft breeze upon the surface of the waters.

The sun is lower still, and now and then steal over the surface of the before bright and beautiful sky long shadows, and the gorgeous tints of the sunset turn from gold and azure to a deepening purple, which each moment, too, seems itself to be fading to a black hue. The twilight has come, and the night is slowly but surely creeping on.

Floranthe looks again from her casement. The evening breeze fans her cheek. Ah! how beautiful she is, and what a dear privilege of that soft, zephyr-like wind to kiss so fair a brow!

She gazes down upon the waters of the grand canal, upon the heaving bosom of which many a gay and streamer-decked gondola is winding its way through that mimic ocean. She looks above to the blue vault of heaven, with the sweet kindred blue of her eyes, mocking the beauty of things that are immortal with the exquisite radiance of those innocent orbs.

"A star!" she murmurs; "a star! Yes, I see a star! The appointed hour is coming, and I shall listen again to those tones that linger with a faint echo in my heart like music. Stralani, I shall see thee once more—once again I shall feel the soft pressure of that hand—once again look upon that face which to me seems to have an angel's likeness—once again I shall hear that voice make its magic music, as it tells me that I am beloved."

The night crept on.

One by one came out the lamps of heaven, and like angel's eyes they looked down upon the green earth, while a soft, gentle dew fell, with a shadowy effect, upon all objects.

"Yes," she murmured again, "the appointed hour is coming!"

Again she looked out upon the beautiful eve—again she marked all those signs and indications of the coming night, which was so sweetly stealing over the romantic city.

With rapid strides the dark clouds began to cover up the few remains of twilight that yet lingered on the scene, and shortly not a trace of that fading beauty would remain to tell the gazer that there had been so glorious a day in Venice.

But it was only a change from one beauty to another. If the daylight, which had made all objects so full of glory and brightness, was fading away, it was but to give place to magnificence of a different description; for if anything, the night in Venice is more glorious than the sunlight.

Myriads of stars began to peep out from the azure sky, and soon, with a bright glow, and a halo of great beauty around it, there arose the moon, tinting with silver the stately edifices and the sparkling, murmuring waves of the Adriatic.

Again the beautiful Floranthe took a long and earnest gaze from the casement of her father's palace; and while her eyes wore a still softer expression, and a more roseat hue spread itself over that fairest of faces, she again whispered gently,—

"The appointed hour is come!"

She moved two steps towards the door of her apartment, and then she paused, and with a sweet coquetry gave utterance to her maiden thoughts.

"Shall I," she said, "hasten so quickly to keep the assignation which I have so longed for? Shall I shew even to Stralani how strong a hold he has upon my best affections? Is it wise that even he should fully comprehend how much he is my heart's treasure, and how I have panted for the hour to come when we should whisper to each other the words of the fondest affection?"

Again she moved towards the door, but it was again to pause, and murmur to herself the rapid rising thoughts which were not the results of her own imaginings, but particles of the cold wisdom of others.

"I have been told," she said, "that love will grow cold if it meet with too ardent a spirit to return its tender aspirations. I have been told by those of more wisdom than myself in the heart's tumults that maidens should be coy and distant, feeding themselves with but faint hopes; but oh, how can I be cold to Stralani? Does he not love me truly?"

Was there ever a maiden in all the world who did not believe her lover to be a very paragon of constancy?

Floranthe now began to feel quite angry with herself for the part she was playing towards one in whose truth she really had every reason to rely; and she hurried to the door of her apartment, to seek the small garden of her father's mansion, where she was to meet her adventurous lover.

We say garden, and to those who have been accustomed to consider Venice as a mere collection of houses and water, it may appear somewhat strange that we have done so, but the fact is that even in the city of the sea there are some green spots.

The principal edifices are built upon islands, and care has been taken to preserve any small spot of ground which would give even the semblance of a garden to the sight, so that there are both trees and flowers in Venice.

The garden attached to the palace of the Count Syracuse, the father of Floranthe, was one of the largest in the whole city, and it was within its precincts that the fair girl had promised to meet her lover.

And now, having first reasoned herself into thinking that she ought to keep her lover waiting, and then reasoned herself into a belief in the cruelty and injustice of such a course, Floranthe was as eager to seek the place of rendezvous as she could possibly be, and hurried to the door of the apartment accordingly.

Her hand was upon the fastening, and she was in the act of opening it, when it was gently tapped from without, and Floranthe heard the harsh tones of Bianca, a sort of confidential servant and general spy of her father.

"Floranthe, Floranthe," she cried, "you are wanted in the grand saloon."

The young girl's heart sunk as she heard these words, and it was a minute or two before she could summon resolution to reply to them, during which interval they were again repeated in more vociferous tones than before.

Floranthe was scarcely aware that she had not yet actually drawn the bolt upon the inside of her chamber door, and that, therefore, the duenna had no resource but to entreat from without.

When, however, she recovered sufficiently to be aware that such was the case, she thought it was a state of things which might as well be maintained, and she acted accordingly.

"I am sick, Bianca," she said, "and wish not to be disturbed."

"But your father, signora, is waiting."

"My father cannot wish me to leave my chamber if I am indisposed."

"Nay, I don't know that. I am commanded to desire your presence in the grand saloon, where a young gallant expects you."

"A young gallant?"

"Yes, to be sure. Oh, I warrant me you will come now."

For the moment the blissful idea came over Floranthe that Stralani had adopted the bold course of avowing his attachment to her, and soliciting her hand of her father; but then again the improbability that he would take so important a step without her connivance was so great that the first feeling of joy subsided, and again she felt desirous of retaining the use of her chamber for the present, and yet each moment that kept her from her appointment in the garden was an age of agony.

"Tell my father," she said, "that I keep my chamber from indisposition."

"And you do not ask who the gallant is?"

Floranthe was silent, and the old woman, finding such to be the case, and that let the curiosity of Floranthe be what it might, she would not ask the question of her, added,—

"Well, I will tell you. It is no other than —— Are you listenin·?"

"I am."

"Well, then, it is the noble chevalier. Do you hear me?"

"I do."

"Gordoni?"

"What, my cousin Gordoni? You could not have told me of a name that would sound more harshly in my ears. I know him as a man without courage—without any of that high-souled principle which should make up a perfect gentleman. I have heard, too, that he would stoop to the basest of crimes to accomplish any of his wild designs."

"And yet he is a fine gentleman, and as your uncle left him large estates, and your father has but one small one, he thinks that an union of the cousins ——"

"Peace!" exclaimed Floranthe, her dove-like nature exhibiting for the first time an appearance of anger. "Peace, I say! My father could not—would not insult me by such a proposition, and I am not disposed to endure it from you."

As she spoke she flung open the door of the room, and with a noble and beautiful indignation, faced the duenna, who gazed at her with both surprise and anger depicted upon her countenance, as she replied,—

"It is none of my business, signora, to quarrel with you, but I will report to your father."

"Yes," said Floranthe, "that is your fitting office—to report to my father. I long have known you as my father's domestic spy."

"What is this?" said a harsh voice, and the Count Syracuse himself appeared in the corridor which was just beyond the apartment of Floranthe.

CHAPTER II.

THE THREAT AND ITS EFFECTS.—THE GARDEN BY NIGHT.

FLORANTHE could defy the inuendoes and the insults of such a person as Bianca, but the sight of her father, from her earliest childhood, had always been severe and harsh to her, at once brought terror to her bosom, and she shrunk back in alarm.

"My lord, you are come in good time," exclaimed Bianca. "Your lordship's daughter refuses to obey your orders to repair to the saloon."

The Count Syracuse bent his haughty brows upon Floranthe, and in a voice of half suffocated passion, he uttered the one word,—

"Refuses?"

Floranthe was silent, and after a slight pause, the count gave so furious a stamp upon the floor that she started with terror, and he exclaimed,—

"Speak! What is the meaning of all this? Speak!"

"I am indisposed," said Floranthe, "and do not wish to leave my chamber."

"Being well enough," said the count, with mock courtesy, "to wrangle with

Bianca upon the threshold of your room, you will excuse me for thinking you may possibly manage to reach the grand saloon."

Against this there could be no appeal. To be sure, had such a speech come from any other lips than those of her father, Floranthe might have cut the matter short by a flat determination not to leave her room, with or without reason, but now she could only cast her eyes confusedly to the floor.

The count placed her arm beneath his, and led her along the corridor, and as she went down the magnificent staircase to the saloon, she could not help repeating to herself, in low, mournful accents,—

"The appointed hour is come!"

"What say you?" cried the count.

"Nothing—oh, nothing."

"I do not like these mutterings," said the count. "But matter of moment calls now for your consideration. Yet, why should I say consideration? You will, of course, obey me."

"I have been dutiful in all things in which a child might obey a father."

"In all things it is right to be dutiful. I will have no qualification. You will meet in the grand saloon the Chevalier Gordoni."

Floranthe shuddered.

The count proceeded, without seeming to notice her emotion.

"You will meet, I say, the Chevalier Gordoni. You know who and what he is?"

"I have heard."

"'Tis well. It is time that the family estates should be in our branch of the family, so that the dignity of all should be kept up becomingly. That is a thing that can and shall be accomplished by your marriage with your cousin, the Chevalier Gordoni."

A kind of mist seemed for a moment to come over her eyes, and she could not reply, but the count was much mistaken in translating that silence into anything in the shape of acquiescence in the proposition he had given utterance to. In the course of a minute Floranthe recovered.

The first act of the beautiful girl, which partook of the character of resistance to the stern decree of her father, was certainly one that took him considerably by surprise. She twined her small, delicate arm in the gilt balustrades of the staircase, and in a firm voice, she said,—

"I will not go to the grand saloon."

The count was sufficiently surprised to fall down the stairs, had he not supported himself by the wall, and then he rubbed his eyes, to be quite sure he was awake; and in a tone of suspicious calmness, he said,—

"Repeat those words."

"I will not go to the saloon," said Floranthe.

The count drew a long breath, as he added,—

"Do you remember who I am?"

"I do."

"And yet ——"

"Yet I refuse to go to the grand saloon, under the supposition that I can ever be brought to consent to become the wife of Gordoni."

The purple hue of passion showed itself in the count's countenance, and he even went so far as to place his hand upon the hilt of a small poignard that was dangling at his girdle.

"Yes," said Floranthe, "kill me. Death would be far preferable to such an union!"

"No," said the count, making a great effort to appear calm; "no, no. And yet—yet I—I ——. Wait a moment; I give you even now a few moments for reflection. You were for the instant crazed, and knew not to whom you spoke, or what you said."

"No, no, no."

"No! You—you really persevere? To your chamber, lest in my just rage I take a life that I can never again look upon but with passion. To your chamber, minion,—to your chamber !"

These words were uttered in tones that made the vaulted roof echo again, and were accompanied by such violent gesticulations of passion, that Floranthe might well tremble as she did at the possible consequences of having drawn down upon herself such an ebulition of rage from one whose anger was generally but the prelude to some direful act.

That the command she received to retire to her chamber was more welcome to her by far than that which would have heralded her way to the saloon ; and feeling that any word of remonstrance to her father, in his then excited state, would but fan the flames of his wrath, she sprung up the stairs, and rushing along the corridor, was soon in the privacy of her own apartment.

She flung herself upon a couch, and burst into tears.

For a time she felt compelled to give herself completely up to her feelings, and it was quite impossible for her to stay their current ; but this was a state of things which could not last, and soon as her tears changed to sobs, she was able to speak.

"Oh ! how cruel is my destiny," she exclaimed, "to have so harsh a father, and yet to love so truly one whom he can never love. I would that I were dead !"

She rested her head upon her hands, and was silent, but during that silence there crept over her imagination dear and blissful remembrances of the past. She recollected each word that, at their last happy interview, had been uttered to her by Stralani. She told herself with what an utter abandonment of all shadow of suspicion she could rely upon his love ; and then she looked up, with a faint smile upon her lips, and said, in low, soft accents,—

"I will yet be calm and happy."

The night had deepened, but a glorious moonlight fell upon the city ; and although the appointed hour was past, yet well she knew that Stralani would not leave the gardens of the palace without an attempt to see her, and that if she could now, without observation, steal to the appointed spot, she might yet pour into his ears the tale of her father's cruel commands and threats.

If there be anything in this world which can make affliction bearable, and even unite it with a sort of graceful interest, it is being able to find some kindred bosom which will share in each hope and fear that agitates our own ; and well did the young and beautiful Venetian girl know that Stralani's was for her such a bosom.

She rose and approached the corridor to listen. All was silent, and then, with gentle, timid steps, she made her way along the gallery, towards a suit of apartments seldom used, but which terminated by a flight of marble steps leading to the garden.

In her passage through these rooms she did not at all expect that there was the remotest probability of her meeting with any interruption. They were the apartments which had been occupied by her mother, and in one of which she had died, and since that event the count had never, to the knowledge of any of the domestics of the palace, set foot in them.

Report, indeed, went so far as to say that the harsh conduct and absolute cruelties of the count had had more to do with sending his lady to the grave than any ordinary decay of nature, but those reports had not yet reached the ears of Floranthe.

To the fair girl, therefore, the suite of apartments only possessed that melancholy interest which was attached to them in her mind, along with the dim memory of her mother.

She never passed through them without uttering a prayer, and she did not on this occasion neglect the sad and solemn duty of appealing to Heaven for the repose of her mother's soul.

The apartments had a cold and gloomy aspect, and the moonlight, which before had rendered all objects singularly beautiful as it shone through the windows, now seemed to add melancholy and sadness to the place.

The tapestry hung in long, mournful folds—the furniture was covered by the dust that had collected, and gave all there the appearance of mourning, and recalled to her mind the parent she had lost, and it seemed as if this spot wore perpetual memorials of the past.

The moon's rays fell upon the table at which she had often sat to embroider; the couches, too, which had once been the seats of festive guests, were now unpressed, and had been so for a long time—the soft carpets, too, became softer from the accumulated mouldiness of years, reminded her of death and of sorrow.

There was a stillness in the apartment that could almost be felt—so deep, so entire was it, that Floranthe, for a moment or two, felt almost overpowered by it, and she paused, and looked round the apartment she was in.

All was quiet—a quiet, a stillness that appeared to have reigned from time immemorial. Not an article had been removed—everything stood as it had been placed for years; but she turned her eyes towards the moon, and an inward emotion urged her departure.

Floranthe passed on with a shudder.

The last room was gained at length, and she could, by the moonlight, see the door which led to the marble stairs, at the foot of which she hoped and expected—indeed, knew that she should meet Stralani.

This thought quickened her footsteps, and she laid her hands upon the door, with a flush of pride and pleasure upon her countenance—pride in the consciousness of having won such a heart as Stralani's, and pleasure at the blissful idea that the day might arrive, despite all present clouds of evil fortune, when they should meet to part no more on this this side of destiny.

"Yes," she said, "yes, he loves me. Ah, how well I know that he loves me. Has he not whispered the truth to me with all the fervent eloquence that so well becomes him? Yes, yes, Stralani, you do indeed love me, and you are well worthy that I should love you."

The small door was opened, and she was upon the topmost step of the marble flight, at the foot of which she was wont to receive her lover. Often, too, as she had descended those stairs, she had heard the soft, tinkling notes of his guitar.

She paused to listen if she could hear them now.

All was still, and with a faltering voice, she said,—

"Surely he is there. The appointed hour is past, but surely Stralani is there. Oh, yes, yes. He would not leave without one word from me, although he should have to outwatch the stars. I know that he is there; and when I come to think, I have often chided him for those notes of music that might, by attracting the attention of some unfriendly ears, bring mischief upon him."

She paused to listen, for a slight sound had met her ears; it was not a note from the guitar of Stralani—it was not anything that she could torture by her imagination into being the sound of a human voice; and yet there was a strange sadness in it that smote her to the heart, and she was compelled to lean heavily upon the marble balustrade to recover some appearance of composure.

"What was it?" she asked herself; "what was it?"

Again the sound came upon her ears, but it was weaker and fainter than before, and again the blood seemed to chill about the heart of Floranthe.

She made an effort to shake off the fears that were rapidly crowding upon her, and to do so, she made use of the few words which she generally found a charm against all unhappy thoughts.

"Stralani loves me!" she said.

The bloom returned to her cheeks—once more the light of joyous serenity was in her eyes, and with renewed confidence in the happy future, she again resumed her descent of the marble staircase.

Already she began to feel the fresh pure air from the garden fanning her cheek

—already the fragrance of the flowers came up as if to greet her, the fairest flower of all.

"Yes," she added, "Stralani loves me, and I am happy."

Thus, in maiden meditation, she passed on, and yet never had her progress down those marble steps been so slow. It seemed as if a thousand busy sprites were doing their utmost to retard her speed; but yet she paused not until upon the last step, when she called, in a low tone,—

"Stalani! Stralani!"

There was no answer.

"Cruel! cruel!" she exclaimed. "He has gone! Ah! can it, indeed, be true that a maiden's love should be a secret even. No, no. He must be here."

With such a holy, trusting confidence in the object of her love, did the fair Floranthe still continue the descent of the garden steps. That he whom she expected and wished to meet was there she would not permit herself one moment to doubt.

And now a few—a very few more steps must bring her into the garden, and a slight noise, as of some one moving gently among the leaves of an acacia that grew even to the foot of the steps, at once sufficed to convince her that she was not mistaken in supposing that her lover was there, and that the only reason of his not appearing to her, was that he wished to surprise her by his sudden presence.

"Yes," she exclaimed, "yes, it is so. Ah! dear, dear Stralani, do not longer preserve yourself in ambush. Do not longer hide yourself from me, dear Stralani!"

She paused and listened, but no answer was returned to her, and then she began to think that if he had so abjured her to speak, she would have answered him forthwith, and there came a feeling of sadness across her heart, to think that she should love him better—aye, far better, than he should love her. But Floranthe scarcely yet knew that—

> "Man's love is of his life a thing apart,"

But that it was

> "Woman's whole existence."

She had yet a dreary time to come

CHAPTER III.

THE HORRIBLE DISCOVERY.

ANOTHER step, and Floranthe was actually in the garden.

She paused for a moment, and leant her hand upon the marble balustrade. Her heart beat violently, and an universal terror came over her, which she could neither account for nor repress. In vain she pressed her disengaged hand upon her bosom to endeavour to still her heart's tumultous beating. It seemed to her as if the hand of death was upon her.

Oh! how happy would it have been for her had such really been the case, and she had then and there at that moment

> "Rejoined the stars."

But her destiny was not yet accomplished. A soft light spread itself over the garden. Some light, flucy clouds were between the green earth and the secret moon, but they were not sufficient wholly to obscure its radiance—they only softened the lustre of the glorious planet.

Floranthe had no eyes for the scene before her, she sought but the one much-loved object. The moon now gave a clear, though somewhat subdued light, which was thrown directly upon the buildings and palaces around. And thus all things above, below, and around her were visible, and in a half-choking whisper, she said—

"Stra'ani, Stralani! Where are you hidden, my Stralani?"

Then gathering strength of heart from reflection, although it was but the reflection of a moment, she moved on a pace or two.

"How wrong—how very wrong of me," she murmured, "to be thus full of foolish fears. Surely, oh, surely, heaven itself would, with a special act of its great providence, protect its creatures who love each other as Stralani and I love."

And now she stepped on another pace, and a strange feeling of having trodden into something horrible came over her. She glanced at the small satin shoe that her foot adorned. It had been white, but it was now of an ensanguined hue. With horror-stricken eyes she looked to the ground. What was it that she saw? A strange black-looking pool. She stooped nearer to it, and then it changed its hue, and she saw that it was blood!

"Blood! blood! Oh God, no, no, no, no!"

She rose and clasped her head with her hands, while she repeated the word no with frantic vehemence, and then decreased her tones to a low plaintive whisper, as she added,—

"This is a dream!"

It was a consolation to her to think, even for a moment, that the scene around her was not a reality, and yet, could a dream present its spectres in such vivid colours? Could a dream be of such a texture, that during its continuance she could say, "This is a dream?"

"No, no. Oh, God, no, it is—it is blood!"

She stooped to the ground, and carefully looked at the partially congealed mass, and now she, with a courage one would hardly have thought it possible for her to possess, she submitted to a horrible test, which consisted of dipping the point of one of her delicate and tapering fingers in the ensanguined fluid, and holding it up between her and the sky.

"Yes," she exclaimed, with a shudder, "yes, it is blood!"

Floranthe did not faint—she did not scream. Perhaps, under the impulse of some ordinary terror, she might have fallen into the one or the other excess, but this was no ordinary terror, to be expressed by ordinary impulses; and she rose up from her examination of the pool of blood, and clasping her hands, she remained for a few moments in an attitude of speechless woe.

And yet, although blood it was, she could not take upon herself to say it was the blood of Stralani, but some demon seemed to whisper in her ear that it was.

The question, however, of what she was to do—of how she was to remove her doubts, next rose up to the imagination.

"I must follow it," she said.

In another moment, crouching down, and pointing with her finger to the pool, she, with tottering footsteps, took the course it had taken along the grass plat, close to which it was now evident some dreadful deed had been recently committed.

What was that deed? Fearful question!

By the stooping position Floranthe had assumed, in order to follow the horrible marks of the blood upon the ground, her vision was necessarily limited to a small spot, and thus it was that she came most unexpectedly upon some streaming locks of hair soaked with blood. Then there was a head—an arm—a hand—she knew the sparkling gem that glittered upon one of the fingers. It was, indeed, Stralani her lover, who lay there weltering in his blood!

*   *   *   *   *   *   *

Iow shall any words sufficiently expressive of human emotions suffice to tell the feelings that came over the soul of Floranthe at that most horrible and most dismal moment of her existence? How is it possible, in all the vocabulary of woe, to find expressions which shall sufficiently define the sense of desolation that crept over her?

Alas, poor Floranthe!

Dreadful fate! cruel destiny! Is there no means by which you can be spared from so awful a mental prostration as that which has come upon you with its deadly blight? Must, indeed, the iron enter your pure soul?

We must return to that dismal picture.

A little further—yet a little further she gently creeps, and with trembling fingers she lifts the masses of hair thickened with blood. They rest upon the face of the victim—she feels that that victim is Stralani; and yet, while there is room for the shadow of a doubt, she will not permit herself to be quite sure. She has just sense and perception enough to feel that she can do a something to—

"Make assurance doubly sure."

That something can only consist of an examination of the face of him who lies there, so cold and sad, and so bedabbled in his gore.

Was ever young maiden set so horrible a task? And yet it must be done—it must be done.

"I will not go mad for a shadow," she said, gently.

Then she placed her hand upon her head, and moaned as though she felt that her reason was going from her, and the night of the intellect was coming.

With a slight violence, now she sought to turn the head aside, so that the features might be exposed to the faint rays of light that spread themselves through the silent and balmy air. Oh, how adverse to all her feelings and sensations was the calmness and serenity of that night!

And now she cannot see the face of the dead, that it actually turned towards her, for a gush of tears have come to her eyes, and well nigh blinded her. She is as one looking through a mist—all objects are dim, obscure, and dazzling. But with the hem of her robe she wipes away those pearly drops, and then she looks upon the face.

"'Tis he!"

Floranthe rose, and stood silently gazing up to heaven. It seemed as if some mental blight had come across her faculties, and that for a time she had even lost the perception of her own misery.

From her contemplation of the blue vault above her, she looked down upon the earth again, and then her glance wandered round at all the familiar objects in that garden.

She wondered that they retained their accustomed appearance, while to her the world and all upon it were so changed.

She spoke.

"God," she said, "it cannot be. Oh, no, it cannot be that heaven has looked upon this deed unheedingly of its horrors! Oh, no, no. I have been taught to think there surely is a heaven above us—a heaven of love and of joy. How the soft music comes by fits and starts."

She turned again to the corpse, and without a shudder, she knelt by its side, and kissed the pale cheek.

When she rose up again a remarkable change had come over her countenance, and those who had known her best would now be almost foiled to recognize her whose child-like beauty had often charmed them.

Alas! the wild fever of madness was beginning to cause riot in her brain, and she so good, so pure, and so beautiful, was about to become a melancholy wreck—a mere remembrance, like some fair ruin, of what she once had been.

Let us watch her.

Again she looked around her, and in doing so, it was with a strange air of surprise, as though the place were completely new and strange to her. Memory had received a shock from which it could not readily recover itself. Heaven only knows what the issue may be.

Once or twice she passed her hand across her face, as if to clear away, if she could, the mists that oppressed her intellect. Perhaps that action might be considered a proof that her mind, although it had received a severe shock was not all gone.

After a few moments, then, in a low, plaintive voice, that had much of absolute witchery, and the very eloquence of music in its tones, she spoke.

"Where are the flowers?" she said. "The bride is waiting, and the garlands are not ready. Where are the flowers? Hush, not so loud, or you will awaken the sleepers. Hush, hush, hush!"

Then with her finger upon her lips, as though enjoining silence, she looked timidly around her, and approached the clustering roses, which bloomed in nature's own luxuriance on that sweet spot of earth amid the waters.

She plucked a number of the buds, and entwined them together into a rustic garland, repeating to herself as she did so,—

"The bride is ready. Where are the flowers? Let us have roses, although the colour may be like unto blood!"

A shrill scream burst from her lips, and she crouched down in an attitude of fear, as with accents of terror, she added,—

"Blood! blood! Who spoke of blood?"

That fearful word, although uttered by herself, had fallen upon her heart with a terrible distinctness. Yes, something of a remembrance of what had happened had that moment been turned up in her mind, but it was only like the fleeting sunshine of a winter's day, seen but to be seen to vanish.

The night of the mind had come again.

She wove the flowers into a chaplet. With nimble fingers she arranged them, although in sad disorder, for the fine sense which would have imparted taste to the arrangement, was wanting, and all was chaos where had once reigned the most exquisite order. Then she smiled—Oh! God, that smile was sufficient to have melted the stoniest heart. Her tears were sad enough, but her smile was the very scene of woe.

"A brave and happy wedding," she murmured. "The guests are coming. How they throng around us, Stralani! And so my father consented at last, did he?—and without a murmur, too, and my bad cousin Gordoni is banished from the house! That is well. How the plumes wave to and fro in the soft, sunny air! Does this bridal chaplet become me, Stralani? Ah! you smile. Well, we ought to smile upon such a happy day as this."

The odorous wreath of flowers was placed upon her fair brow, and folding her arms gently across her breast, she, with that melancholy smile still upon her face, took her way to the garden steps again.

How ghostly pale she was, save one spot upon her cheek where blood from the face of the corpse which she had stooped to kiss had left its horrible trace —perchance it was that ruddy spot which made her look so pale and wan.

Up the steps she moved slowly. Along with that prostration of mind there appeared likewise to have come a complete prostration of all that life-like springing energy of movement which had made up a portion of the grace of such a beauty as Floranthe.

Oh, what a frightful shock was preparing for whoever might meet her first in that mansion!

And yet if it were impolitic or wrong to disturb the natural order of events, and

And yet if it were impolitic or wrong to disturb the natural order of events, and so save Stralani from the poignard of the assassin, we may consider that there has been some mercy shown in the fact that Floranthe is no longer able to appreciate her own griefs. That stunning shock which her mind had received was scarcely preferable to the acuter suffering of despair.

It took her at the pace she went some minutes to ascend the steps, and during her progress, she pulled to pieces, leaf by leaf, a rose that she carried in her hand, and that same smile, so quiet and so full of woe, which had before lit up her face with its truly ghostly radiance, was still manifest in all its perfect beauty.

Suddenly she paused, for she heard a voice pronounce her name.

"Floranthe! Floranthe!"—

The tones were harsh · they were those of the Count Syracuse himself.

"Floranthe! Floranthe!"

The tone was angrier still. She paused again, and then with the same quiet smile, as she pursued her course up the steps, she said,—

"They call me to the wedding. All ready—all is ready. Ah! Stralani, how happy we shall be—how very, very happy!"

At the top of the stairs the count appeared. A servant was behind him, bearing a large flambeau. The glare of light fell upon the face of Floranthe, and the haughty count started back, like one who suddenly confronts a spectre.

CHAPTER IV.

THE DEED OF VILLANY.—THE UNHOLY COUNCIL.

It was some twelve hours before the events occurred, the particulars of which we have related, perhaps, at painful length, that a muffled figure appeared in a gondola upon the grand canal of Venice.

The boat was one of those with an awning, which when drawn precluded almost the possibility of any one seeing who was within, and he who occupied its inmost recesses had either the strongest necessity for keeping himself concealed, or it was his taste to do so.

The occasion upon which he came into sight was to direct the gondolier, to whom it would appear he had spoken in vain from the interior of the canopy.

"Do you not hear me, knave?" he cried, as he bent forward. "Hilloa! Are you as deaf as the column of St. Mark?"

The blood rose to the cheek of the gondolier, as he replied,—

"I am no man's knave."

"Peace! Do you dare to bandy words with me?"

"Aye, with the doge himself, if needs were."

The cavalier muttered a curse between his clenched teeth, and then in a more subdued tone, he said,—

"Do you know the palazzo of the Count Syracuse?"

"I do," replied the gondolier, who was now evidently disposed to be as brief in his replies, and as churlish as possible to his customer.

"Land me, then, at the steps of the mansion. Your reward shall be ample."

The gondolier made no reply, but he plied his ponderous oar with activity, and the boat shot along the waters with more than the usual amount of speed.

"There is nothing like threatening and speaking harshly to these fellows," muttered the cavalier to himself, as he retired back beneath the awning again, where he was so completely secluded from all observation by the massive folds of drapery that hung around it.

Scarcely had he given utterance to the sentiment, when a sudden jolt flung him violently forward upon his face, giving him a severe bruise.

The gondola had, by some mismanagement on the part of its proprietor, struck against one of the piles of a bridge, and thus by the shock the passenger had been thrown down, although the gondolier himself retained his position with all the nonchalance in the world.

To spring to his feet and draw his sword was the work of a moment to the angry cavalier; and probably the gondolier would have felt the weight of his resentment, had he not, with the quickness of thought, produced a long, shining stiletto from his bosom, and shown by his attitude that he knew well how to use that too popular weapon.

The cavalier seemed to think discretion to be the better part of valour, for he sheathed his rapier again, and only muttered curses between his clenched teeth.

The gondolier had had his revenge for the slight that had been put upon him; so now, without further stop or molestation, the gondola proceeded rapidly under his skilful guidance to its place of ultimate destination, the palace of the Count Syracuse.

There were many marble steps reaching to the palace, the lower ones of which were always reached by the waters of the Adriatic; and the gondola was soon moored to some of the tall piles that are to be found established for such a purpose at all the principal landing-places in the city.

The cavalier threw a piece of silver to the gondolier, saying as he did so,—

"'Tis more than your desert. Think yourself fortunate that you have escaped the consequences of your folly. The weight of my resentment would have been serious to you."

The gondolier made a gesture well known in Venice among the lower orders, and which was indicative of the most supreme contempt of the cavalier, and at the same time he tossed into the water the small silver coin which had been presented to him.

The cavalier knew sufficient of the independent feelings of the gondolieri of Venice to feel that such an act boded him no good, and the colour for a moment fled from his coward cheek, as a thought of the possibility of some midnight assault came over him.

He would gladly, by a couple of pieces of gold, have made his peace with the man, but the gondola had glided away down the stream, and the opportunity was lost.

"Curses on the fellow!" muttered the cavalier, as he ascended the steps conducting to the grand entrance of the palace of the Count Syracuse. "Curses on the fellow! I would that I had not, as I have, angered him, or that having done so I had now an opportunity of killing him."

A train of hurried attendants who had seen the gondola stop at the stairs, and by the attire of the cavalier guessed him a visitor to the count, now made way for him as he passed through the vestibule, and a page made his appearance, with a humble bow, to know who he should announce to the count.

"Do you affect not to know me?" said the cavalier.

"The sound of your excellency's voice enables me to name your excellency the Chevalier Gordoni."

"You are right. Announce me to my relative, the count."

Gordoni—for it was, indeed, that most notable villain—followed the page closely to the private apartment of the count, and with but little ceremony, he entered at the moment that his name was announced by the boy, who it might easily have been seen visibly shrunk from coming into contact with the Chevalier Gordoni.

There was visible disquietude upon the face of the Count Syracuse, as with an awkward attempt at courtesy, he welcomed his nephew.

"Ah! Gordoni," he said, "you are a stranger."

Without replying to his uncle, Gordoni glanced towards the page, who was leaving the room too slowly to please him, and with a menacing gesture, he cried,—

"Begone!"

The page closed the door behind him, and then, without condescending to heed the look of indignation that was upon the face of the count, he added,—

"It is true I am a stranger here, and yet you can no doubt guess my errand. I come to know if it be now convenient to return to me the numerous advances you have made me hand to you from time to time, or if you prefer my displacing you, and taking up my abode in this ancient palace of our house."

"You—you would not ——"

"Indeed would I."

A crimson glow of colour came over the countenance of the count, but he evidently thought it prudent to subdue his passion; and by a great effort he such ceeded in doing s·   til Gordoni thought proper to proceed in his insulting style of conversation.

"You know I have power," he added, "and it is a power that I will not forego the exercise of, save upon one condition."

"You have a condition then?"

"I have, and as I see no occasion for anything in the shape of secrets or delicacy between us, I will at once state it. You have a daughter—her beauty has inflamed me. Give her to me as a wife, and from the moment she becomes mine all your debts to me are cancelled, and I will further hand over to you a thousand gold crowns beside."

The count's countenance underwent many changes before he replied, and then he said,—

"It is settled—you shall have her. But I much fear there will be some difficulty in bringing her to the match. She loves another!"

"I know it. It is the young Chevalier Stralani. But you have discouraged his approaches by all possible means, as I am aware."

"I have. I want no prying connections, who, if they found ought in my conduct or affairs that did not come up to their absurd notions of ideal excellence, would despise, and perchance insult me."

"Most assuredly would they. But you consent to my proposal without reservation?"

"Most truly, and without reservation."

"Your hand upon it."

The count stretched out his hand, but Gordoni thrust it aside, exclaiming,—

"No, your hand-writing is what I mean. Your hand I esteem of little worth. Give me a written undertaking to the effect that I have stated, and henceforward you will be free from all debt and all difficulty, for well you know that my means are most ample."

Yes, it was such a man as this to whom the Count of Syracuse, with all his pride, and with all his boastings of family importance, from a long line of ancestors, illustrious in the annals of Venice, would have actually sacrificed his beautiful child.

How often in the devious and uncertain course of human nature do we find the most abundant pride and the most abundant meanness go hand in hand together, and most certainly the Count Syracuse was a most remarkable example of such an union.

"Then, Gordoni," he said, "all shall be arranged according to your wishes. You will be a happy man."

"I shall strive to be so," said Gordoni; "and as for this obstacle ——"

"Stralani?"

"Yes; he shall not long cross my path. We have an useful set of men in Venice."

"Bravos?"

"Yes. One or two of them well paid will soon rid me of all rivalry from such a painted popinjay as the young Stralani. By heaven and by hell, it is my chief delight to find some occasion for ridding Venice of those gallants who think that because they have smooth tongues and faces, and well turned limbs, they may run riot with the affections of all the fairest of the fair. I say that the doom of this tinkling guitar-playing gallant is from this moment fixed!"

CHAPTER IV.

THE ASSASSINATION IN THE GARDEN.

.IT is, indeed, frightful to think that such a life as Stralani's should be at the mercy of such a man as Gordoni; and yet such was the state of society in Venice, at a time when as a state she had acquired a glory and a renown that extended over not only the whole of Europe, but was known and acknowledged throughout the civilized world.

It is strange that only in the decadence and fallen fortunes of a state, does it pretend to anything in the shape of public virtue or rectitude of principle.

The nobles of Venice—men who would have felt, or affected to feel, an imputation upon their nice sense of honour far more acutely than they would the pain of a wound, yet thought it, or affected to think it, no sort of degradation to stab an enemy in the dark, and so rid themselves of any domestic inconvenience.

And this fearful blot upon the Italian character—a blot which it will require the virtue and the glory of ages to wipe away—was divested even of the solitary excellence of courage. The persons who basely sought the lives of those whom they had injured, did not in any open manner strive to arrive at such a consummation. No, it was the assassin stab that was to do the business.

And worse still, it was the employed bravo who actually perpetrated the fearful deed.

Could it have been supposed, even by those who were always disposed to credit the worst tales regarding the infirmities, the follies, and the crimes of human nature, that men could be found, who, for a few paltry pieces of gold, would deliberately take a life.

And yet such was the case in Venice, and such is still the case in many of the petty principalities of Italy, that land of beauty, but of moral turpitude, which is sufficient to cast a blight for ever over its glories.

We return to our tale.

Gordoni by no means intimated his intention of doing more than it was his fixed resolve to accomplish, when he spoke of the assassination of Stralani as a something settled, and after some further conversation with the Count of Syracuse, who was to the full as bad a man as his projected son-in-law, he left the palace, and lingered upon the steps conducting to the water, until a disengaged gondola slowly came into view.

He was soon seated in the boat, and having given a whispered order to the gondolier, the head of the gay little vessel was directed towards the grand canal. In the course of a quarter of an hour, Gordoni was landed, and he made the best of his way towards the church of St. Lawrence.

The steps of the sacred edifice were thronged with purple, and a blaze of light from the interior, together with the solemn chaunting from within, ought to have been sufficient to convince Gordoni that such a place was signally unfitting for one of his descripti on to approach or to tarry in, unless it might be that the pangs of an evil conscience sought to be assuaged by a communion with the minister of religion.

But Gordoni was one who knew no scruples, and who had cast all conscience to the winds. What to him was the building dedicated to divinity? What to him was the fact that he made the crimes he meditated, more detestable by making his assignations with the ministers of them within the temple devoted to the service of the King of kings.

And this was a positive fact that Gordoni in most cases used a church as his places of rendezvouz, the sacred edifices throughout the whole of Italy being constantly open, professedly to religious purposes, both day and night.

Gordoni advanced into the aisle which was nearest to the door, and made his way into a part of the building which was involved in considerable gloom. He then paused within a few paces of a tomb, the rich decorations of which showed that it belonged to a family who had a vague idea that even death could be adorned.

Scarcely had Gordoni had time to give utterance to several expressions of impatience, which he did in not the most courtly language, when a person approached him,

This person was small of stature and delicate in appearance, and came forward with a trembling hesitation that was strikingly perceptible.

Gordoni bent his black brows upon the new comer, and made a sign with his hand, upon which they both penetrated deeper into the gloom of the aisle; when they paused it was Gordoni who broke the silence that was around them, and he spoke in a voice which he intended should sound fairly, although the deep villany which it strove to mask ought to have been sufficiently apparent to any one.

The companion of Gordoni, however, was but little versed in the ways of the great world.

" You are punctual," said Gordoni, " and that is a matter which few can pretend to in these degenerate days."

" When the heart speaks," said the other in a soft low voice, " the head does not readily forget. I have been waiting for you, signor, for some time."

" Oh ! am I behind hand ?"

" A little ; but it matters not."

" True, true—we do not meet here to trifle. Are your scruples satisfied ?"

" In part."

" Only in part ? What would you have, boy ?"

The lad, for such he seemed to be, was silent for a brief space, and then he said in a tone of deep earnestness, which almost approached to the pathetic.

" You know, signor, that when you sought me out, finding that I was in the service of the Signor Stralani, and wished to bribe me to reveal his secrets, I spurned your offer; but you then told me you meant him no harm, and that your only object was to break off a love suit that was pending between him and the Lady Floranthe."

" I told you truly."

" Well, I hope it is so. It happened that to break off—if it might be done—that love suit, jumped with a wish and a humour of my own."

" As you said."

" Yes, as I said. But I had my doubts, I wanted to be fully resolved of the stated fact that such and such only was your intention, and to satisfy me you proffered to meet me in the house of God, and with his holy name upon your lips swear that you meditated no harm to the Signor Stralani; but that your whole and 'sole object is as you state, to break off the match pending between him and the Lady Floranthe."

" Most fairly stated."

" 'Tis well. Will you now, signor, take the oath, pledging the safety of your immortal soul to its truth ?"

" Most freely I swear that I intend no harm to Stralani ; but that my sole intention is to give the Count Syracuse such sufficient proof of the fact that clandestine meetings are proceeding between Stralani and the Lady Floranthe as shall induce him to send the lady to a convent."

" A convent?"

" Yes. You do not object ?',

" It is sad to be so immured from the great world. It will only be for a time, though ; even the Count of Syracuse will not, cannot force an unwilling devotee to be the bride of Heaven."

" Certainly not. It will only, as you observe, befor a time, and then the lady, in the arms of some lover more approved by her family, will forget the tears that this little affair may cause her to shed."

" She will shed tears, you think ?"

" Perchance she may. She is one of those who weeps at trifles. But time presses and I wait for the information you promised me. I have duly complied with all your conditions. It is now your turn to speak."

The lad was silent for a few moments, and then in a weak tremulous voice, as though still in his inmost heart he doubted the propriety of what he was doing, he spoke.

" Since you have sworn to me, that you intend no harm to Stralani, I will tell you, that to-night he meets the Lady Floranthe, at the foot of a flight of marble steps, in the garden of her father's house."

" Ah !"

" Yes. There he will await her coming, and he will pour into her willing ears, those words of adoration, which——"

" You pause."

" A sudden spasm. Farewell, signor; you have your information. Let the Count Syracuse be satisfied by seeing the meeting of the lovers with his own eyes, and then be it your special care to protect Stralani from danger."

" My most special care. Here is gold for you."

The page spurned the proffered bribe, and gathering the short cloak which he wore about him, he walked hastily from the spot, and left the church.

" Ha, ha!" laughed Gordoni, when he was alone, " Simple youth ! And so you think that an oath uttered in a church will bind me. How little do you know me ! No doubt, however, the information is correct, whatever may be the motives of this lad for giving it to me, and soon I shall swoop upon my prey. Stralani your doom is sealed. To-morrow's sun will not rise for you, except in another region, if there be one."

These words were uttered with a sneering laugh, as though either he, Gordoni, had made up his mind there was no such thing as immortality, or was determined t o brave its terrors. Wretched man!

But there are many Gordonis in the world. How fearful must be the awakening of such men to a sense of the mistakes of their existence.

But in this circumstance which we have just related, there is another, whom probably the reader will at the first flash of the affair be inclined to visit with some amount of condemnation. That other is the page of Stralani, who we have seen give such information to the villanous Gordoni, as enabled him to perpetrate a crime so black, that it puts to shame the virtues of humanity.

We would willingly, if possible, rescue this page from any harsh opinion which may be formed of him, by those who know but little of his character.

When he left Gordoni, the first act of the page was to rush through the church door with the greatest precipitancy, and down the marble steps at the entrance; he went with a speed that threatened serious consequences to several persons who happened to be ascending.

" Jesu, Maria !" exclaimed an old woman, as she dropped her beads in her fright, and nearly fell down the whole flight of steps. " Is Satan himself pursuing the boy ?"

And so indeed, it would seem by the headlong flight which the page kept up, so far as he was able in that city of the sea. He did not pause until he reached the church of St. Geronimo.

It was strange, but the page certainly entered this latter sacred edifice as quickly as he had left the one in which he had had his brief interview with the villain Gordoni. It was not until he stood in the cool, calm, silent aisle, that he paused, panting from the exertion he had made.

A boy clad in vestments of the incense bearing children of the church was passing him.

" Hold !" whispered the page. Is Father Majas in the building ?"

" Yes," replied the boy. " He is even now in his confessional."

" Ah, say you so—many thanks."

The page stood for a few moments irresolute, and then he darted into one of the small confessionals that was close at hand.

CHAPTER V.

THE BRAVO'S HAUNT IN VENICE.

WE must leave the page to his devotions, while we conduct the reader to a scene in Venice of a very different character to any we have yet depicted.

Near one of the principal canals was a mansion, or palace called Palatza di Monthe. It was a large ruinous edifice. It had long been uninhabited and avoided by all men as something pestilential.

The rich and great avoid such places, because it indicates decay in some large house, and is displeasing to the sight—the poor because tradition was busy, and handed down a number of crimes that had been committed there, and the credulous believed the report which the courageous in Venice could not discredit, that the spirits of the wicked were let loose for a time, to plague the world as a punishment for its wickedness.

Be the cause what it may, the ruined palace, for so it was called, was by general consent deserted ; few indeed, however hardy they might be, would venture into the precincts of the place if the sun had sunk below the western horizon.

Indeed it was currently reported that strange sights and sounds had been seen and heard in the palace, that caused the flesh to creep up in knots, and the hair to stand erect.

Near one of the pillars that stood near the doorway, stood or rather lounged a figure muffled up in a large cloak ; he stood completely screened from the gaze of the passenger by the pillar. It was night, and few indeed were the passengers, who passed this ruined spot, and those who did were either strangers to the spot or else they increased their speed while in the vicinity.

Several individuals passed by, but yet the man who was upon the watch moved not, started not, he had some object in view which was not yet accomplished, suddenly he leaned forward and bent a keen glance around him, and then he fixed his eyes upon an individual who was coming towards him at a sharp pace.

A man enveloped in a cloak came towards the deserted palace, but was about to pass on when a slight and stifled shriek called his attention, he looked round but perceiving nothing, was about to proceed, when a weak female voice called out for help.

In an instant the stranger sprung up the steps, for the sound came from the interior of the old palace, but the instant he passed the stranger who was concealed behind the pillar, the latter drew a glittering stiletto, and with the quickness of thought struck the new comer in the back.

Without a sound the stranger fell with a sullen, heavy lump, upon the door step and then the old palace door opened, and another stranger appeared, clad somewhat like the first.

"Is it done?" inquired the last.

"Yes; help to bring him in, we can put him in the canal, here, it will cause an enquiry if it remains."

"Quick, before there be much blood about, his cloak will save some portion of it, there will be no traces."

"What a pity," remarked the man who had committed the deed, "that we cannot invent some sudden death which would not cause any flow of blood, it makes so much mess, and it so often causes detection."

"So it does, but I think we may as well get below, as standing chatting here, come in and let us close the door."

"Are they all in?"

"Yes, and if not, they can get in."

"I know they can—come lay hold of the two ends of the cloak, and I will take the other two—that's it—now below—have you got the trap open, eh? oh, well we can let it fall gently."

They let the body fall through a trap door which opened in one side of the passage and then, when the body had disappeared through the opening, the trap was opened, and the men proceeded towards the rear of the building when they descended to the vaults and subterranean chambers.

Suddenly a door opened, and a broad glare of light shot out, and the sound of voices in rude conversation came full upon the eye and ear, while strong fumes of wine came forth.

The two men entered, when one man seated higher than the rest, said in a loud boisterous tone,—

"Well, how fare the followers of the brotherhood."

"Well."

"And has the deed been done?"

"Yes, done, here is the proof," and the bravo held up his dagger which yet reeked with blood."

"Ah, a good sign, you've a strong arm and a sure aim, Giacome."

"I have done one or two things in my time," replied Giacome with a sinister smirk which was ment for mock humility."

"You have, here, a bumper for Giacomo of the best wine the brotherhood can produce.

"Thanks, captain, I'll swear that there's not a noble in all Venice that can vie with our wines, the vaults of the old palace afford good vintages."

" Aye, and it will last our time."

" It may, and yet methinks we do our best towards diminishing it, but the supply is good."

And must be replenished when the store fails; but no more on that head; Giacomo, to his health!"

There was a clamorous uproar of approbation—deep oaths, blows with the hands upon the table, and jingle of glasses, amidst which Giacomo emptied a leathern bag filled with gold pieces, as being the price of some evil deed he had done, or was to do—the appearance of which caused a fresh outbreak, which lasted for some minutes.

The hilarity of this conclave of assassins continued for some time, until the man who appeared to be the chief, said—

" Giacomo. Where's the body—in the canal?"

" Not yet."

" Then now is the time, before the vintage makes the the hand unsteady, let it be turned over at the water gate, it will go with the current, and then we shall learn of it, as we have done others, but it little matters."

" Well," said Giacomo, "I am willing, but I must have some help. Three ought to go with me."

" Then has the body been moved?"

" No, it is untouched, save by the dagger."

" That will do," replied the captain, " let it be as you wish; but my brothers, you can go with Giacomo, he has something in store for you, don't all go at once, and leave me alone, there will be enough for his assistance; come be quick, and then we will finish the night."

" With all my heart," replied Giacomo, who now arose, and seizing a torch, he was followed by three other confederates, who went with him to the place where the body lay.

" There," said Giacomo, " there is work for you, take hold of him gently and——"

" Yes, we know all that," replied one of the men, who was not well pleased at being called out from the carousal, and inserting his fingers in the pockets of the dead man with much skill, " but we like to do something else first—it's not worth while to throw away personal effects, that may be useful and ornamental to the living."

" True, I had forgotten that. What's he worth?"

" There is not very much," replied the ruffian, throwing down some gold doubloons and some articles of jewelry.

" We will take him away, now," replied Giacomo, when he had looked over the articles, giving the word to proceed, when they all went along the passages connected with the room into which the body had been thrown.

After going some distance through those places, they came to one that was cold and damp, and the cold air blew up it, causing the torches to flicker and cast their shadows about.

" Now," said Giacomo, " we must pause while I go on and get the water gates opened, and listen—when I give the signal, bring the body and throw it into the canal."

Giacomo went forward, and after unchaing the water-gates he listened for awile, and then he beckoned them on, when they immediately came forward, and the body was silently let down, and then the water-gates were closed, and re-chained, and then they all left the place silently, to return the the carousal of the other members of the gang.

CHAPTER VII.

THE CRIME OF BLOOD.

IT was to such an assemblage that Gordoni, after parting with the page of Stralani in the Church of St. Lawrence, bent his steps.

The object he had in view in seeking such a den of iniquity, no doubt is already sufficiently transparent to the reader, namely the destruction of Stralani, but yet it is necessary that we should trace the villain step by step, to the consummation of his crimes.

With a self-satisfied look upon his face, which was really something horrible to see, he walked to the nearest landing place and waited for a gondola. One soon presented itself, and he gave directions to be taken to the square of St. Mark, at what speed the gondolier could exert, promising ample payment.

Such a stimulus was sufficient to induce the gondolier to exert his utmost power, and he accordingly did so, making the gondola flash through the water at a most un-wonted speed for those cumbrous and hearse-like machines.

The grand square, which contains the largest portion of land in Venice, was soon, gained by the canal Orsini, and Gordoni alighted not far from the Column of St Mark.

It was the fate of this bad man to make enemies go whither he would, and in not the smallest possible transaction of his life could he possibly behave with any degree of honour or credit. In lieu of paying the gondolier liberally as he had promised, he threw to him] with an ungracious air the smallest amount which could be paid for the distance he had travelled.

The gondolier muttered an oath, which had very little effect upon Gordoni, who was always rather pleased than otherwise, at making any one angry.

"The knaves, they will all know me and hate me in time," he muttered, "as I know and hate them—I hate all the world, and my mission shall be to show that I do so."

A little to the right of one of the most magnificent buildings in Venice, was a small shop where water melons were sold. At least that was the blind to the real nature of the place. Into this shop Gordoni stalked, and sitting down with a careless air, he asked for a melon.

When one was handed to him by a woman who served in the place, she as if by accident pushed near him a small poinard, Gordoni lifted it, and struck it forcibly into the melon, while he glanced in the woman's face, to see if she understood him.

"Ah," she said, "signor, you want Orcolo."

"I do."

" Step this way, signor, if it please you, and I shall soon be able to send him to you ; I think he has before done business for you, signor."

" Not lately, but he told me of this sign if I should require his services."

"Ah, signor, trade has been very dull," said the woman, with an air as if she were speaking of any ordinary industrial occupation, instead of the horrible trade of assassination, in which her husband was considered one of the greatest adepts, and most unscrupulous hands in all Venice.

" Indeed," said Gordoni.

" Yes, signor, sometimes my poor Orcolo gets quite dull and languishing for want of a little job or so."

" What a pity."

" It is a thousand pities, signor, except that he will be in better condition to obey your commands. This way if you please. We must all live in this world some way or another."

" Precisely."

Gordoni was led by the lady of the shop to an apartment secluded from the public gaze, when having requested him to be seated, she left him for the purpose of finding her husband. In the course of a few minutes she returned to say that Orcolo was at what she called the rendezvous, and which was no other than the place we have described in the preceding chapter.

" But," she added, " if signor will accept the guidance of little Paulo, my eldest son, he will soon be in the presence of his humble servant, Orcolo."

To this proposition Gordoni made no sort of objection. He had often heard of the bravo's rendezvous, and had a great curiosity to visit it, and this certainly was a very eligible opportunity of so doing.

The lad who was not above seven years of age, walked before Gordoni towards the haunted palazzo, which we have already indicated, as being the place where the bravos held their meetings, and when they got quite close to it, it was astonishing to see the cunning with which the child peered about him, to see if any one was watching their entrance to so suspicious a place.

" Is there no private means of entering here?"

" My father gets in along with the canal," said the boy, pointing to a low archway, into which the dock-water was rushing, " but we cannot. There is a small door though, that nobody sees, and Matteo keeps guard at it, so there is no danger, for his stilletto will drink blood in a moment."

" You call that no danger?"

" None to us, signor. I will go first."

Gordoni could not forbear a grim smile, at the idea of his being protected from danger by a child like the one who was his guide, going first, but still there was reason in the remark, and the little sucking bravo pushed at a low arch door in an obscure corner of the building, with a consciousness that it was in his power to protect the man who was with him.

The door yielded to a touch, and disclosed a dark passage beyond. Well might a bolder man than Gordoni have hesitated, ere he plunged into that seeming abyss.

" You are afraid," said the boy.

Gordoni darted at the urchin a look of anger, which was returned by a grin of malice, and then the lad, perhaps recollecting that it was a customer he was introducing to his father, spoke more civilly.

" There is no danger, signor, come on. Matteo, Matteo! 'Tis I, Matteo !"

GORDONI'S HORROR AT DISCOVERING THE DEAD BODY.

"And who the devil are you?" growled a rough voice, as a grim visaged ruffian made his appearance at the door of the place.

"Don't you know me?"

"Oh, ah, you devil's imp, I know you now. What do you want?"

"A signor for my father."

"Good. Pass on, signor. We are bound to keep good watch here, to guard against impertinent and unjustifiable curiosity, but to a stranger we are civil enough, if he comes with a job. We are rough fellows, but we have a smooth side for all that. Walk on, signor. The place is dark, but as safe as a lady's chamber, though perhaps not quite so pleasant. Ha, ha! I always was accounted a great——"

"Fool!" said the boy hastily.

The ruffian would probably have resorted to some means of punishing the youngster for this piece of insolence, but the boy was too nimble for him, and darted through the door, and down the narrow passage, with a speed that would soon have distanced Matteo, even if for such a matter he would have thought himself justified in leaving his post.

Gordoni followed the boy closely.

After a few moments, the passage he was in did not present quite so dim an aspect. His eyes were getting accustomed to the light, for light there was at some distance down it, proceeding from a small lamp suspended by a rough iron chain from the ceiling.

When Gordoni reached the lamp, he found the boy waiting for him, with an arch grin upon his face, as though he would claim some applause for the manner in which he had succeeded in exciting the unavailing anger of Matteo. Gordoni, however, was not exactly the sort of person to praise any one, and with an impatient gesture, he cried—

"Lead on."

"No!" said the boy, "we go no further. This way, signor."

He turned aside, and led the way through a small arched door-way, into a room which had some pretensions of furnishing about it. There was a light, too, upon a table that stood in the centre of the apartment, and some coarse matting kept back the damp exhalations from the canal, that flowed immediately beneath.

"You must wait here," said the boy.

"Hem! Why wait here?"

"Because nobody, not in the profession, is ever allowed to go any further. This is my father's reception room. He will soon enough come to you."

This was scarcely what Gordoni expected. Indeed it was a great disappointment, for he had hoped to get into the apartment where the bravos of Venice held their secret meetings, but to complain was useless. He came upon business, and if he wished it to be transacted, he felt that he must conform to the mode in which those he wished to employ chose to do it.

"Be quick," he said.

The boy dashed off, for he expected a good gratuity, before the affair was over, and although on more than one occasion he was tempted to give Gordoni a taste of his boyish insolence, yet the hope of a piece of silver restrained him.

Gordoni looked after him with a malignant sneer as he recalled to himself how gratified he should be at a good opportunity of wringing his neck.

The few minutes of solitude and silence which Gordoni had now to endure, were to him most truly uncomfortable, for if to such a man there be one thing more uncomfortable than another, it certainly is the society of his own thoughts.

Moreover, the wicked are invariably superstitious, and Gordoni began to people the vacancy around him with horrid and alarming fancies. He fancied he heard sounds of dismal character coming crowding around him, and at length his eyes were fixed upon a door that was in the room, and through which, it seemed to him, as if some shape of horror would be seen in a short time to creep, and drive him mad.

He could not bring himself to remove his eyes from that door. They seemed to be there fixed with a horrible fascination.

At length, feeling that certainty was far more preferable, as it ever is, to suspense, he approached the cupboard, for cupboard it was, and laid his hand upon the handle of the door. It did not yield with ease, and he was compelled to use considerable force before he could make it do so.

Suddenly it gave way; Gordoni started back with a cry of horror, for a dead body, that had been placed in an upright position in the cupboard, suddenly fell almost into his arms, and then, with a heavy dab like a lump of lead, fell to his feet.

A voice behind him, cried—

" Is Signor Gordoni afraid ?"

He turned, and saw Orcolo the bravo.

" Not afraid !" he said, "in the common meaning of the term, but who would not start at such an apparition as this ?"

" Humph ! I have seen too many such, to care much about them. But to business, signor. What is it you require of me, or my friends, the bravos of Venice ?"

Gordoni with difficulty turned his eyes away from a contemplation of the horrible corpse, and said, in a subdued tone—

" I have an enemy."

" And you have gold ?"

"I have."

" Ho ! ho ! ho ! We understand each other already."

" What do you mean ?"

" Is not my meaning plain enough. You set one possession against the other, and so get rid of both. The thing you love you must part with in order that you may rid yourself of the thing you hate. You understand me, Signor Gordoni ?"

" I do."

" You have then but to name the man and your price."

" I will name the man, and you shall name the price."

" 'Tis well. You will do business with us after a princely fashion. Men call you a lover of your money, and say that you are loth to part with it, but we have found you generous. The sum of a hundred pieces of gold will not be too much ?"

" 'Tis high, but I will cheerfully pay it. Only rid me completely of this youngster, and your reward shall be even beyond the sum stipulated. He is the only one between me and the gratification of my wishes. Stralani being despatched, there will be no difficulty to bring Floranthe to a consent ; and then the day of retaliation will be mine."

" Then learn to understand," said the bravo, "that the young Signor Stralani is the obstacle you wish to remove. 'Tis enough, he dies. Before to-morrow's sun sets he will be numbered with the dead, or my name is not Oriclo."

Gordoni would have prolonged the conversation, but the bravo said—

" I know sufficient of the affair now, signor, and will be about my preparations the minute you quit our rendezvous."

" I may rely upon its accomplishment ?" said Gordoni.

" You may," was the brief reply.

" To-morrow ?"

" Yes, and according to the manner in which we execute it, so must our extra reward be ; you understand me, signor ?"

With these words Gordoni was conducted to the entrance of the den, and politely bowed out.

———

CHAPTER VIII.

THE GARDEN OF THE PALAZZO.

AT the very time that the villain Gordoni was bartering away the life of one who, in comparison with him, was an angel of light, Stralani, the young, ardent, and enthusiastic lover of Floranthe, was about proceeding to the assignation he had made in her father's garden with the idol of his heart.

He proceeded with a step as light as his heart to the garden of the Count Syracuse, where he expected to meet and embrace one of the fairest of God's creation. The beautiful Floranthe was anticipating the nocturnal visit of her lover, brave and honourable

Stralani, who came into the garden disguised, almost every evening, and exchanged with her vows of love and constancy.

The young page who had given the information to Gordoni, usually accompanied him, but upon this occasion, to the surprise of Stralani, he was not to be seen. So faithful was he in the eyes of his master, that any ordinary appointment would have been put off, to search for him, but the idea of any delay in meeting with the much loved Floranthe was not to be thought of.

It was necessary that the young lover should adopt precautions in approaching the garden of the palace of Count Syracuse, and upon this occasion he neglected nothing that could tend to cast aside any suspicion that any such intruder was about to show himself in that interdicted spot.

The young man wore an ample cloak, of pale grey cloth, which effectually shrouded him, so that in the dim light of twilight, he could scarcely be seen at all at any distance, and as he cautiously climbed the garden wall, he was so much the colour of it, that observation was completely at fault, unless it had been very specially directed.

That was not likely to be the case, and with a heart beating with the excitement of hope, the young cavalier leaped into the garden of the palace. The cloak he then left at the foot of the wall, concealed behind some flowering shrubs.

He then advanced, cautiously as foot could fall, towards the stairs that led to the deserted suite of apartments in the palace, and down which he knew that the lovely Floranthe would come to meet him in that world of flowers.

When, upon former occasions, he had had the exquisite gratification of meeting with her upon that spot, he had made his presence known by a few low notes upon his guitar, and as he now had it slung across his shoulders, he prepared by the same means to make his presence manifest to her.

He well knew that the few faint notes which he would draw from the strings could not be heard elsewhere than in the deserted suite of rooms, so that he was running no risk at all by their production.

"If," he whispered to himself, "they come upon the ears of my Floranthe, the spirit of love will add wings to her agile feet."

He touched the strings, and a few soft notes stole from the instrument into the night air, with great gentleness and beauty.

After this, he listened in a bent posture, attentively, with the hope of hearing the light footfall of Floranthe, but he was disappointed. It is known to the reader, that she met with some obstacles in her progress to her lover.

"She lingers," he said sadly. "She lingers, and yet the time has come when I ought to feel that beloved hand in mine, and be conscious of that incense breathing voice gently pronouncing vows of love, that might woo an angel from Paradise itself."

Again he listened, but to be again disappointed. All was still as the very grave, and in a voice of exquisite sadness, he said—

"She comes not. She comes not."

He then looked around him with saddened eyes upon the scene in which he was.

Such a glorious sight, even in Venice, had been rarely seen; the moon sailed silently in the air, though ever and anon a few fleecy clouds would traverse the space as if it came but to show off the beauty of the scene the more. Thousands of stars shot forth their minute but resplendent rays, the whole hemisphere was surrounded with them.

The garden, too, what a scene of quiet beauty was there! There was the appearance by that light of far greater space than in reality it consisted of. The shrubs looked like trees, and the trees cast long umbrageous shadows, that crossed the paths at all intervals.

The flowers were all of a colour, or nearly so — everything seemed like a phantom figure — a fairy life was there — the foliage looked like graceful fretted work, interlacing each other through the silvery light that floated over the ocean.

Then, too, the nightingale,—that boast of the warmer latitudes—sung her sweet melodious notes; her silvery and dulcet accents ravished the groves, giving music to the witching hour and ocean.

All else was solitude and quiet—Zimmerman himself could not have selected a scene fitter for contemplation and pleasure.

"Yes," said Stralani to himself, "yes, I shall once again look into the magic depths of those sweet eyes which have beamed in all their beauty for love and for me."

He pursued his way amid the flowers that formed a host of beauty in the garden, and slowly approached the flight of marble steps down which he expected the beautiful being, the mere sight of whom was sufficient to gladden his heart and cause him the most joyful emotions.

"I am soon," he murmured. "Yes, my Floranthe, I am soon, I know; but with that knowledge comes likewise the conviction that you will hasten to see, if no adverse circumstances stay you on your way. Oh, what joy it is even to meet you thus, my Floranthe."

He thought at this moment that he heard a slight rustling noise among some bushes, to his left, and he paused instantly to listen.

The noise, whatever it was, had ceased, and he began to think that it must be either a matter of imagination, or some bird perchance startled from its repose by his footsteps in the garden, where all around was so still and calm.

He soon divested himself of every apprehension as renewed thoughts of meeting with his Floranthe came across his mind.

"Ah!" he exclaimed, "what a charm against all evil is the thought even of the very loved one, my own Floranthe. Surely in the great world there is none other who can compare with thee in thy excellence and beauty. Do I deserve, great heaven, to be so blessed!"

Alas! poor Stralani, little did he imagine when thus thinking with rapturous exultation upon his rare felicity in being beloved by such a being as Floranthe, that he was as one walking on the margin of the grave.

But we must not anticipate. Sufficient for the hour surely is the evil thereof.

Again he thought he heard a sound, and he paused to listen.

"Surely," he said, "my nerves are unstrung to-night, and I am full of most strange fears. What can be the meaning of these repeated alarms and this anxious throbbing of my breast? Stralani, Stralani, has your ancient courage deserted you and left you a prey to unmanly tremors?"

Feeling ashamed of what he considered a weakness, he struck a few notes from the strings of his guitar and then hurried forward to the place of assignation.

In the distance he could hear the sound of music, for in that city of love and delight had already begun those serenades which are so well calculated to fascinate the ear of beauty.—Venice was awakening when other cities slept.

Even Stralani, who had been accustomed from childhood to the enchanting sounds of that city of pleasure and gaiety, could not help feeling proud that he was a native of the Queen of the Italian cities. It was known over the face of the civilized world as the resort of fashion, consequently were to be seen there the *elite* of all nations—some to inhale its balmy atmosphere to recruit the health that had been impaired in less congenial climates, but the majority to indulge in that hilarity of spirits which tend to return that vigour and cheerfulness we so much prize.

The oars of the gondoliers were heard to splash in the moonlit water, as they proceeded with their customers to view some grand scene, that possessed double effect on such a night. Indeed, all—everything enhanced the admiration of Stralani; but ever and anon a feeling of insecurity came over the senses of the young cavalier, which he could not define. When he thought of danger, his hand was instantly put upon his sword, and he was ready to defend himself. With the courage he possessed, combined with the ready use of the rapier, we may surmise that it would be none but powerful foes, though in number, that could subdue his master spirit, or even cause it to quail. He thought that if he were attacked by bravos, he would defend himself to the last. The opposition of the Count Syracuse, Floranthe's father, was strong; his principles were not strictly honourable ; and being in the power of his base kinsman, Gordoni, Stralani considered it probable that a price was set upon his head. As these thoughts ran through his mind he clutched his sword, and determined to wait events.

His thoughts would again revert to Floranthe ; his hand relapse its grasp, and his countenance assume a more tranquil and smiling appearance, proving him to be the child of impulse, either to possess the daring impetuosity of the lion, or the meekness and gentleness of the lamb.

Floranthe came not, and her lover began to despond, He said—

" What can have detained my Floranthe? Her father surely cannot have gained knowledge of our secret meetings here—no, no. I should have had a contention with the bravos of Venice long before this time had he been aware of it, but it is an idle conjecture. I will dismiss it from my mind as unworthy of possessing space. Can she be ill? Oh, what torturing thoughts, and yet I cannot dispel them from me. I am but a short distance from her, but cannot, if she be ill or in danger, render any assistance, for want of precise information as to where she is, and fear of drawing on her the wrath of the count, should he discover me on his premises."

He folded his arms, and seemed to be absorbed in conflicting meditations, as his uneasy movements indicated. He said again—

" The Appointed Hour is past, but I will wait, for I know when she is at liberty she will come."

————

CHAPTER IX.

THE PAGE AND HIS MASTER.

ALL other thoughts of the young gallant Stralani were now emerged into that one which came across with a gush of delight, and which pictured Floranthe quietly reposing her fair face upon his breast, and looking up to him with eyes of love and joy.

To him this was so extatic a picture that no wonder he forgot all the world as he contemplated it. Dreaming not of the danger he trod lightly on, and would soon have reached the foot of the marble steps down which he knew his love would come, had he not been interrupted by an incident which at the moment filled him with astonishment.

As he passed a small group of trees that cast a beauteous shadow upon the garden path, as their foliage gently undulated in the night air, there suddenly rushed out from among the leafy covert the page, towards whom he, Stralani, had always behaved with much kindness, and who, as we are aware, had betrayed to Gordoni the secret of the place of meeting of the lovers.

The boy threw himself at the feet of Stralani, and burst into a passion of tears, such as the human heart rarely exhibits.

Stralani started back in amazement as he said—

" Juan, what is this?"

" Spare me! Oh! spare me!"

" Spare you? This conduct is most inexplicable. What has happened to you? Be it what it might you know you may count upon my affection for you, upon my most efficient protection. I only charge you, considering the place you are in, that you speak to me in a low tone, for, after all, even in the fancied security of this garden, there may be spies."

" I have only one request to make," resumed the page.

" Speak on. It is already granted."

' Oh God! say you so?"

" Be assured of it. Only, my good Juan, knowing as you do my errand here, I pray you to stay here but as short a time as possible. Will not your request keep until the morrow?"

" It might," said the page—" it might, but then I should pass another night of misery and horror."

"Say you so?   Then speak at once."

"I—I will.   You have your sword, master ?"

"Truly."

"Oh, kill me—kill me at once, nor ask me why, I beg of you to do so.   Kill me, I pray you now."

"Kill you ?"

"Yes, oh, yes, I am unworthy to live, for I have betrayed you to one who I feel convinced now, is your worst enemy.   Your secret meetings here with the Lady Floranthe were confided alone to me, and in all Venice, you fondly thought, there was no safer breast in which to lodge it, but you have been deceived.   You have been betrayed."

Stralani was silent for a few moments, then he said, calmly, although with a touch of sadness in his voice—

"Juan, there is more in this affair, and in this strange conduct and passion of yours, than at present meets my understanding.   Come to me in the morning, and we will talk of it."

"Holy Virgin !   Can this be possible.   You do not storm and rage at me—you do not load me with reproaches—you do not threaten me !"

"Wherefore should I, Juan ?"

"Because of the great wrong I have done you."

"No—I will not chase one from my heart who in many things has shown that he loved me well, because of such a self accusation as this.   I can believe what you tell me, Juan; but I can also believe that in some way you have been most grievously misled. Leave me now, and we will talk of this further at some more fitting time."

"No—no—stay—oh, stay."

Stralani waved his hand, and walked on.   In vain the page called after him.   He would not be stopped by words, and Juan, therefore, with a most desperate resolution rushed after him, exclaiming—

"Hear my secret, then.   Hear the secret which I thought to cherish in my heart for ever.   I am—oh, hear me—hear me."

Stralani, whose firm impression was, that what the young page had to say to him was some matter, after all, of very small importance, in addition to the communication that he had made already, hastened on, and so prevented a revelation which we must not anticipate, but which, if he had heard, would have occasioned Stralani both surprise and sorrow.

Sorrow that his hitherto trusty page should have allowed himself to be tampered with by his deadly enemy, Gordoni.

But he was too busily engaged in his own affairs to pay much attention to, or meditate upon what he had just heard.   He walked at a quick pace, and was soon at the appointed place.

While he was waiting there he had ample leisure to revolve in his mind the words of the page ; his earnest entreaty and apparent distress.   The self-accusation was more inexplicable than all."

"That Juan should prove false to me," said Stralani, "is more than I can comprehend, since he has always shown the utmost regard to myself.   I have also treated him well ; he has been my confidant in every transaction of moment, and I have had every reason to believe that my confidence has not been misplaced, therefore I cannot think of casting him off on his own bare accusation.   I will prevail upon him to-morrow to explain all the circumstances which have led to this unpleasant avowal, and there is no doubt of Gordoni's being at the bottom of all this.   He probably has worked upon the fears of poor Juan to enable him to complete some diabolical plan."

It was not, however, to be at this juncture that Stralani was to be governed by the warning voice, or the solicitations of his favourite page—no, he heeded them not ; but gradually led himself into another train of thought which was more consonant with his elastic spirit.   He was picturing to himself the day on which he could fold his beloved Floranthe in his arms, and openly acknowledge her as his lawful bride.

In his mental calculations he swept over all the real obstacles that lay in his way, and arrived at once at the consummation of his desires. The contrast between the ideal and the real is great, much greater than Stralani at the time gave credit to.

Little did he think what his true position was. He was not aware that he was on the very verge of destruction, and that a step from the spot where he stood, either backward or forward, would probably throw him into the power of the worst bravos that Venice could produce.

What course the page took upon the departure of his master we must defer a detail of, until we have for the time finished the perilous adventure in which Stralani was engaged.

The indifference of the young cavalier to the communication of his page ceases to be a matter for surprise, when we come to consider how fully and completely his whole soul must have been filled with the image of Floranthe, and the hope of quickly seeing her. He knew that in consequence of the slight interruption to his progress, caused by meeting with the page, he was a little behind the appointed hour, and he therefore hurried forward, with perhaps less caution than he would under other circumstances have shewn in the matter; for that he was upon hostile ground he was well aware, and his opinion of the Count Syracuse was not so great but that he thought him quite capable of resorting to any undue means of getting rid of him, Stralani.

He could not, however, think of Floranthe and of danger to himself at one and the same time.

With a heart throbbing high with expectation, and an eye glistening with the triumph of true love, and every sense intent upon listening to any sound that might reach him from the stone steps at the foot of which he was to meet his beloved one, Stralani hurried on.

As he moved towards the steps he slung his guitar at his back that it might be no impediment to his progress, and to this little circumstance he certainly owed a temporary respite to the fate which would otherwise have awaited him.

Just as he passed a tall bush of roses, whose sweet fragrance scented all the garden round, there rushed out upon him a man, who, with a poniard, made a stab at his back.

The weapon no doubt would at once have proved mortal to Stralani, but for the guitar, which received it, and was partially broken by the force of the blow, while the young gallant was quite uninjured.

At the same time he heard a rough voice say—

"Curses on your folly, lad. Is this the result of all the instruction you have had? Get out of the way and let me finish."

That he was attacked by bravos who were paid to be his destruction, was now to Stralani perfectly evident, and drawing his trusty rapier, he at once prepared to defend himself completely, and rout his foes, or to sell his life as dearly as possible, should it be the will of Heaven that he should upon this occasion lose it.

The young assassin, who had made the bungling attempt upon his life, was the first to feel the keenness of the cavalier's sword, and with a deep groan he fell back into the bush, from where, with such dastardly and murderous intentions, he had emerged.

But Stralani had more foes than one, or two, or three, to engage with; and he soon found himself measuring swords with one whose skill nearly equalled his own in the use of the weapon. The young lover slowly retreated towards the garden steps, which gave his adversary a false estimate both of his skill and courage, so that when Stralani suddenly, with most unexpected energy, dashed forward, he was to some extent unprepared for so violent an attack, and the rapier of the cavalier passed through his body in a moment.

Thus two of his foes were dispatched, but the third and worst was still to grapple with. A bravo wrapped in his cloak had stolen behind Stralani, and in the course of a few moments after there appeared no enemy to contend with—he plunged the fatal dagger into his back.

"God!" cried Stralani, "God!—Floranthe!"

He tried to keep his feet. He reeled some paces further towards the marble steps

THE COUNT SYRACUSE DISCOVERS THE INSANITY OF FLORANTHE.

and with his sword he slashed at the night air. Then, with a long drawn sigh, and another effort to pronounce the name of her who was so dear to him, he fell upon his face, and lay bleeding on the earth!

*   *   *   *   *   *

"Hist! hist!" said the bravo, who had done this dastardly deed. "Hist! who is hurt, and who not?"

No. 5.

" Marco !" said a voice.

" Oh, is that Pedroni ?"

" Yes; I bleed to death, Marco. Curses on his sword, but more curses still upon the bungler who struck a guitar instead of a man, and gave him leave to draw upon us."

" Are you badly hurt ?"

" My race is run. A—a—confessor."

" Nay, I know not how you are to get one here."

" Oh, misery, misery ! Am I to die unabsolved of my sins? You know, Marco, it is one o our first agreements, that when we go together upon an expedition, we desert not each other, but carry off our wounded. Do you make an attempt to take me away. Oh, do not leave me here alone. I may live many hours in agony yet, and, bad as my wounds are, who knows but I may be put to t ie torture if I be taken, and made to confess some of the most cherished secrets of our brotherhood."

" That is worth considering, Pedroni.   Where are you ?"

" Here! here! to your left."

" Oh, yes, now I see you. The danger you speak of is one that concers me closely as you are aware."

" Yes, Marco, yes ; it is, indeed. Oh, how sick and faint I am. I never until now knew of what agony a wound like this was. Take care of me. Take me away, Marco, for there must be danger if I am taken alive, and put to the torture by the senate."

" So think I," said Marco : "and, as it behoves me to do the best I can to preserve our fraternity from danger, take the death that will seal your lips for ever, and place my mind at ease."

As he spoke, he plunged his dagger into the heart of the prostrate man, and kneeling upon his chest repeated the stroke there, while stifled shrieks from the dying bravo sounded in his ears.

Fearful, then, that the cries of the murdered man might give some alarm, Marco hastened away, and climbing the garden wall at a part which was tolerably accessible, and which was skirted by one of the canals, where a gondola was moored so close that rom the wall he could drop into it, he was soon gliding away from the scene of action, leaving his two comrades behind him in the garden.

A howling wind swept over the city for the space of about five minutes, as if the spirits of destruction and woe were rejoicing over the fall of so noble and accomplished a cavalier as Stralani, and then the moon quietly rose in the heavens as before, and all was calm and still, as though no warring human passions were in existence to distort the beauty and serenity of nature.

Oh, what a world of joy, excellence, and varied charms this might be, if man would but permit himself to take all that Heaven has given to him, without envy and un-charitableness towards those who should share with them the precious and most rarely estimable gifts of Providence.

It was during this period, when Stralani was fighting for life in the garden of the palace, that Floranthe was wending her way through that gloomy and deserted suite of rooms which conducted to the steps at the foot of which she hoped and expected to find a living lover instead of a bleeding corpse.

We are already aware of the horror that wrapped up her soul like a funeral pall when the dreadful truth burst upon her.

CHAPTER X.

THE BRIDGE OF SIGHS.

WHEN the page found that Stralani was not disposed to remain in the garden to speak to him, he stood for some few moments in a state of great irresolution with regard to what he should do. He moved two steps after Stralani, and then he paused, and covering his face with his hands for a moment, as though he wished to shut out the world while he took a thought of his situation, he murmured—

"Is it over?"

To what the self-put question referred it is hard to say, but the one monosyllable of "Yes," which he next uttered, appeared to engulph his whole imagination in a sea of horrors.

Removing his hands from before his face, he looked around him vacantly for a few minutes, and any one who at that moment had seen the lad might well have thought that his reason had gone from him, and that familiar things were familiar to him no longer.

It was sad, indeed, for such a face of sparkling intelligence to be so clouded by the mind's agony.

The struggle in a few minutes, however, seemed to be passed, and the page ran hastily from the garden, and climbing the wall, sped from the spot with great speed.

Now and then, as he went, he moaned and uttered some inarticulate words, but as fatigue rendered it impossible that he could keep up such a frantic rate of speed, what he uttered became much more articulate and easy to be understood.

"Woe! woe!" he said; "this fond heart is broken. Oh, how I loved him! But the dream is over, and the morning of despair has come. Floranthe, the beautiful, fills his heart and soul. He can see none but her. He can think of none but her, and I am desolate. Heaven forgive me for much that I have done, and oh, pardon that which I have yet to do, for it is the worst of all."

There was a small strip of land, lined on each side by tall houses of stone of a gloomy aspect. This street, if it might be so called, led to the well-known and world-wide celebrated Bridge of Sighs.

This bridge in Venice, is that on each side of which there are gloomily-looking structures, used for dungeons, in which to confine prisoners of state, and when it is considered impolitic to bring such prisoners for trial or to public execution, a trap door opens in the floor of the dungeons, and consigns them to the flood of waters beneath.

Many a noble spirit has thus been quenched in Venice, falling a victim to the jealousy and acrimony of some member of the senate.

Venice never was so unjust and so arbitrary as when at the height of its power and greatness, as it was at the period of our tale.

It was towards this Bridge of Sighs, then, as it was called, that the page hastened.

Having gained the top of the bridge, he stood close to a small parapet, over which he could look into the waters below, as they came surging and rushing with a mournful sound, beneath the single antique arch of which the bridge is composed.

Tears fell from his eyes like rain upon the stream.

"Farewell!" he cried, "farewell all who love me, and who have already mourned for me, as one lost. Farewell the bright world, and all that is fair and beautiful within it. A long, a sad farewell, too, to thee, thou noble Stralani, for I shall never look upon thy face again.

Having uttered these words, the page mounted the parapet of the bridge, and there stood clearly defined in the small and delicate outlines of his form, against the night sky.

At that moment, probably, he would have plunged into the stream, but a strange sound came from those dungeon-like places, close to the side of the bridge, on which he was.

For an instant he paused to listen.

Again the sound came—it was a strange grating sound, as though some heavy bolts were being withdrawn, or some rusty piece of machinery of some kind was being put into motion.

The page listened intently, but then, making a despairing gesture, he cried—

"Nothing now in the wide world concerns me. Nothing shall turn me from my purpose. If a star should drop from heaven to bid me live, I would not obey the behest, while the oblivion of the grave was within my grasp. It is but one pang, and then all is over. Farewell, Stralani."

There was a plunge into the stream below, and the parapet of the Bridge of Sighs was empty.

The waters rolled over the misguided and neglected one. Alas! that such a piece of work of the Almighty should be so lost.

*　　*　　*　　*　　*　　*　　*　　*

In a dungeon—one of those dungeons upon the Bridge of Sighs, the door of which was secured by heavy bolts and bars, and the floor of which was one whole trap-door—was a prisoner.

This prisoner was a man of tall stature and strong frame. Long bereft, however, as he had been of liberty, much of the power of his frame had gone from him, and his unshorn hair gave him a wild and ferocious appearance. His clothes were in tatters, and his eyes shone forth with a melancholy lustre, as though the light of hope had left them for ever.

By long experience, his eyes, too, had become accustomed to the dim uncertain light that was in his dungeon, so that while to one suddenly entering that gloomy abode all would have appeared to be positive darkness, to him each minute object in the place was clearly visible.

He sat in a crouching attitude, contemplating the fetters that bound his wrists and ankles.

"Old friends, old friends," he said, "I have got used to you at last. I little thought that the time would come, when I should look upon you with eyes of mildness. How strange it is, that I am for the first time for so many hours alone here,"

He ceased, and as far as the limits of his dungeon would let him, and the chains that bound his limbs, he paced to and fro, taking what little exercise that gloomy prison-house afforded to him.

This species of exercise, to which he had been accustomed for a long and weary period, never had to him appeared to be so full of wearisomeness and discomfort as upon this occasion. It was quite evident that some more than commonly distracting feelings had found a home in his heart.

Suddenly he paused and remained in an attitude of thought for several seconds. At length, in a low faint voice of much emotion, he broke the silence that reigned around him, for although far beneath the floor of his dungeon flowed the canal with its sullen roar, that monotonous noise rather helped to make up a portion of the loneliness of the place than to mar it.

"I know," he said, "I know it. I feel conscious that the time has arrived which is a crisis in my fate. Yes, my imprisonment is nearly over. I shall have no more visitors here."

As he uttered these words, he did what would have very much surprised his gaolers could they have seen him. That was, he, with the greatest ease in the world, divested himself of his fetters.

The fact was, that when he was deprived of light, air, and liberty, in that dungeon he had been a stout, robust man, and the manacles which they had put upon him had fitted him tightly, but imprisonment and bad diet, combined with a large amount of mental disquietude, had combined to make him quite a skeleton in comparison to what he had been, and hence he found that when he pleased he could slip his manacles off him.

This was a secret that he very prudently kept to himself, or he would soon have been accommodated with smaller chains, and he had only been in the habit of disburthening himself of these powerful and humiliating insignia of his condition, when the daily visit of his gaoler had been made, and pulling them on again in due time, so that no discovery of this small amount of freedom should take place.

Even that poor consolation would no doubt have been denied him, had it come to the understanding of his enemies.

"Free again, so far," he exclaimed. "What will happen next?"

This was a question, which, in his estimation, was much easier to be asked than to be answered, and yet it was one that naturally arose to his lips, and upon which he paused for a time.

Then, while he was still considering, he heard a strange noise in the dungeon adjoining his. Many a time he had listened, with the expectation of finding some indication of his having a neighbour, in which case he would have striven to establish some sort of communication; but he had always been unsuccessful. Now, however, he made sure that he heard some sounds.

By placing his ear close to the wall of separation, he could hear much more plainly; and then the sounds that met his ears were those of the withdrawal of bolts and the clanking of chains.

What could be the meaning of it, he was for a few moments at a loss to conceive; but there soon came other sounds, which gave a dreadful explanation to what he had already heard,

There was a cry for help, a shriek, and then a heavy, sudden splash in the waters beneath.

"As I suspected," said the prisoner—"as I suspected. Although I was brought hither blindfolded, I am, as I suspected I was, in one of the dungeons upon the Bridge of Sighs. Well I know that from these dungeons the unhappy prisoners never escape; but when nothing can be gained by preserving them in life, the floor opens by a mechanical contrivance, and they fall manacled, and so, unable to help themselves, into the stream below."

He now felt perfectly confident that such was the fate that was designed for himself; and if he had not had the rare good fortune to find a means of ridding himself of his fetters, he must drown; for the ablest swimmer the world ever saw could not have fought out for his life chained hand and foot.

Well might this prisoner, with all his bold, undaunted spirit, tremble at the dog's death he had so narrowly avoided the certainty of.

And now that he felt confident he should have to swim for his life, he was only apprehensive that long disuse might possibly have unfitted his limbs for that species of exertion which soon would be required of them, and he strove, by as violent exertion as he was capable of, to assure himself that he was still capable of stemming the waters, and making a bold effort for his life and freedom.

"Yes," he said—"yes, I shall be free. I will not—I dare not doubt but that I shall be free."

It was certainly delightful to think that, by the very means with which his enemies thought to ensure his destruction, they were opening to him the path of freedom from the long imprisonment he had suffered; and he now awaited, with an amount of impatience that was positively painful, the time when he should be cast into the water.

While in perfect freedom in Venice, he had heard much of these dungeons, and of their floors opening to the canal beneath, but little suspecting he should ever be an inmate of one of them, he had paid but little attention to the subject, and, therefore, had neglected to obtain information he might easily then have obtained, which to him, now, would have been quite invaluable.

"Alas!" he said, "such is the course of human life. In health we seek nó knowledge of that which in sickness would avail us much—in liberty we neglect acts and information which in captivity might be all-powerful means of our rescue."

He then beset himself to think upon what was the most probable mode in which the dungeon floor opened, so as to allow the unhappy prisoners to fall through; but in the absence of all evidence upon the subject, of course, all that he could think was but of a vague and uncertain character, indeed.

Besides, probabilities had very little to do with the dark and subtle policy of the Venetian Senate.

In the midst of these painful thoughts, he was aroused by the sharp ringing of some small bell.

Then, before he could ask himself for any probable explanation of what the sound could portend, it suddenly ceased, and a larger bell tolled thrice solemnly—and, indeed, so solemnly, that had he been a weak-minded man, or much unnerved by his imprisonment, it must have filled him with the most direful forebodings of his own fate.

As it was, however, the only feeling which those sounds awakened in his breast was one of curiosity.

"I know the worst," he said, "that can befall me in this dungeon—I know the full extent of the motives of those who have held me so long in bondage ; and why, therefore, should I allow any minor evils to affect me ?"

When the bell ceased to toll, the stillness returned with, to all appearance, tenfold quietude. The prisoner prepared himself for the worst.

He considered that, let the floor open to let him into the water how it might, he would have the best chance of avoiding any very serious shock, by first of all lying flat upon it, and so rolling off it, instead of being shook off his feet suddenly ; and he accordingly at once adopted that position, and waited, with every nerve strung to the utmost pitch of tension, the event which he now felt quite certain would occur.

Each second that now passed was lengthened to a minute—each minute to an hour of agony. Never in his life did he know fully what was the meaning of suspense until now ; and, strong-minded as he really was, he could not but feel that each passing moment was robbing him of some strength by the manner in which his best energies were being exhausted in consequence of his anxiety.

But he had still to wait.

Again there came the strange grating sound upon the other side of his dungeon from which it had come before.

"Another victim !" he murmured.

Again there came upon his ears a cry of dismay, as the floor gave way beneath some wretched prisoner, unprepared for an encounter with the waters beneath. Again there was the sullen plunge into the canal, and one more victim of Venetian tyranny sunk to rise no more.

The chains were quite of sufficient weight to keep any one at the bottom of the canal.

The prisoner shuddered.

"My turn will be the next," he said. "Yes ; my time has nearly come, now."

Better pleased would he now have been if the floor of his dungeon had instantly given way, and precipitated him into the stream, than to be kept waiting so painfully and so anxiously for the event. The silence that now ensued had something positively awful about it.

Vague thoughts began to chase each other through his brain, to the effect that after all he should not have that chance for his life which a submersion in the canal would give him, but that some other still more terrible description of death awaited him. Possibly, he might be deserted in his dungeon, and left to starve.

If any circumstance more than another could give a colour to the proposition that it was not intended to let him fall into the canal, it was the fact that his dungeon had been passed, while the prisoners on each side of him were precipitated into the waters.

To one so anxiously situated as he was now, the slightest circumstance seems to be a confirmation "strong as proofs of holy writ ;" and the unhappy man gave himself up to despair.

"Lost—lost !" he cried. "I am now lost, indeed !"

Scarcely had the words passed his lips, when, with a loud crash, the dungeon-floor opened in the middle, and down he went into the foaming waters below

CHAPTER XI.

THE CONVENT OF THE URSULINES.

RETURN we to Floranthe, whom we left in so melancholy and terrific a state of mind, after ascertaining the untimely fate of her noble, gallant, and generous lover, Stralani.

She moved on through the suite of rooms that we have already described as leading from the habitable portion of the palace to the marble steps, looking more like a ghost than a living being.

Indeed, had any one met her at that time, and looked upon her pale, passionless face, and upon those eyes in which there was "no speculation," they might well have thought her to be some pure spirit of another age, who, having had some joy or some woe during life in those apartments, had now visited them full of mournful recollections of the past.

She seemed to look upon many objects as she passed them by; but it was only seeming—she knew nothing, she felt nothing. Her great woe had, for the time, overwhelmed all thought and all sensation.

It was strange how, with a kind of instinct, she found her way through those deserted rooms; but she did so, and that could only have arisen from the fact of having traversed them so often in her path to the garden, to hold those blissful meetings with Stralani, which had, of late, been tolerably frequent.

The first person she encountered in the house, after she had quite left the apartments devoted to silence and solitude, was the duenna, who had been appointed by her father to watch over her. This person had sought Floranthe in her apartment by command of the count, and finding her not, had in some tribulation of spirit—for she knew that blame would fall upon her—been looking for the fair girl throughout the palace.

To come suddenly upon her thus in the great gallery—which was where they met—was a great relief to the duenna, who prepared to commence a process of scolding, until she was herself alarmed at the strange aspect of Floranthe.

Never had she seen the face of the beautiful girl so utterly colourless, and her eyes wearing so unmeaning and strange an expression as they then did.

The duenna crossed herself devoutly, as she exclaimed—

"Holy Vigrin protect us! What has happened?"

Floranthe paused, and looked her in the face fixedly, as she said—

"Have you brought flowers for the bride?"

The duenna shrunk back with a cry of dismay, for in the tones and look of Floranthe there was unmistakable insanity, and what she might next do or say might, by a possibility, not be wholly harmless.

"Where are the flowers?" again spoke Floranthe. "Are there none white? We mus have white flowers! They are not all dyed with blood! Oh, God—no, no, no! Blood blood!"

[Pauline and her Father Discover the Body of Stralani in the Garden of the Count Syracuse.]

She shuddered and held her hands over her eyes for a few moments, during which the duenna gathered strength to scream for aid.

"Help! help! help! My Lord! Help! Oh, help! The Lady Floranthe has lost her wits. Mercy—mercy!"

Floranthe stepped up to her and held her wrist tightly, as in a hissing and ear-piercing whisper, she said,—

" Did you do the deed ?"

" Oh, no, no, no !"

" Are you innocent of blood shedding ?"

" Yes, Holy Maria. Yes."

"'Tis well. God shall look upon us all. Heaven help those who have black spots upon their hearts. Evil be to them who have made human bosoms desolate as sandy deserts. But we must have white flowers for the wedding. All must not be dyed with blood. Oh, no, no, no ! Hush! what was that ?"

The cries of the duenna had reached the ears of some of the household, and the noise which now struck upon the ears of Floranthe, and provoked the enquiry that had come last from her lips, consisted of the sound of their approaching footsteps.

" Oh, spare me !" said the duenna, for she thought of little else than that Floranthe would find some means of destroying her.

Before any more words could be spoken by either, several of the domestics bearing lights made their appearance in the long gallery. The sight of them nerved the duenna with fresh courage, and breaking away from the hold of Floranthe, she flung herself into the arms of a rather corpulent major domo, for whom scandal said she had long had a secret partiality.

The major domo either really had not strength sufficient to stand this onslaught, or it was too sudden for him to put forth what power he did possess. Certain it is, however, that down he fell on to the floor of the gallery with the duenna above him.

Both parties cried " murder !" as loud as they could, and if anything had been further wanting thoroughly to alarm the whole palace, these wild cries would most completely have filled up the want.

A scene of great confusion ensued, during which Floranthe stood as calm and still as a statue, plucking the leaves from a rose which she took from a vase of flowers in a niche hard by.

And now there came a blaze of light up the grand staircase that conducted to the gallery where Floranthe was, and several servants bearing flambeaux preceded the Count Syracuse himself, who was closely followed by Gordoni. No doubt the latter had a shrewd suspicion of the real cause of the tumult that was taking place in the palace.

The villain trembled in spite of all his exertions to seem to be quite calm, and only somewhat anxious to know what the uproar was really all about.

Upon the countenance of Count Syracuse, however, there was an expression of great anxiety, he knew that he had departed from the level path of rectitude, and that honour could not be with him. He dreaded some calamity upon his house in the shape of retaliation for the evil he had done already, and the evil that he had contemplated doing, in the time which was to come.

He could not but be well aware from what had passed between him and Gordoni that some means were to be resorted to in getting rid of the young gallant Stralani, and when he heard the cries of alarm in his palace, he in his own mind connected this in some way with the lover of his daughter Floranthe.

No wonder then that the Count Syracuse came with a blanched check, and throbbing heart into the gallery from whence the cries had proceeded.

Still he made an effort to be stern, harsh, and cold as usual.

"What is this?" he cried, "who makes this unseemly uproar in the palace? let them dread my resentment."

"Oh my lord, my lord," cried the duenna, who had given the fat major-domo sundry punches, and managed to scramble to her feet, "oh my lord, my lord you will not believe!"

"What?"

"The lady Floranthe, the lady Floranthe is bereft of her reason."

The count staggered back, and but for the saving arms of Gordoni, who was still close behind him, he must have fallen headlong down the grand staircase, and perhaps ended his career.

"Peace, woman," he cried, "you know not what you say."

"Oh yes, my lord, yes."

"If it be false, dread my vengeance. If true—I—I—but no, I will not suffer myself to think so—it is not so, where is Floranthe, I will seek her if she be in the palace."

The servants who had first upon hearing the cries of the duenna repaired to the scene of action, were so standing that Floranthe was hidden from the sight of the count, but now they hastily stood aside, and both the count and Gordoni saw her busily employed plucking the rose to pieces.

"Floranthe, Floranthe," said the count, "what is the meaning of this."

"Pshaw!" cried Gordoni, "she only plays a part to avoid your commands."

"Ah, say you so?"

"As I think."

The count strode up to his daughter, after snatching a flambeau from the hands of one of the attendants. He looked keenly in her face, but as he did, all present could see that the light trembled in his hands, and that he became so much agitated that he could hardly maintain himself upon his feet.

"Floranthe!" he cried, "speak! oh speak!"

"Will the bright grass?" she said, "which is made blood red, recover its soft ver dure and look beautiful in time to come."

"What does she mean?"

The count looked at Gordoni as he asked this question, but the latter merely replied by a shrug of his shoulders, as though he would say, it is quite past my comprehension.

Floranthe continued plucking the rose to pieces.

"Listen to me," said the Count Syracuse, "listen to me, Floranthe, tell me that this is not real, and you may hope to change my lately spoken purpose."

"To the chapel, to the chapel," she said, "bring flowers for the bride, white flowers; do not, oh God, do not let all that is beautiful be dyed with the blood of the innocent. To the chapel, to the chapel, bring flowers and music for the bride."

The count stepped back with a groan.

"It is done," he said.

"What—what?" cried Gordoni.

The count did not answer him, and Floranthe walked slowly past them both, along the gallery, followed by the wondering eyes of the domestics, who were all panic-stricken by what they had seen and heard.

"Rouse yourself," whispered Gordoni to the count. "For your own sake, and for the sake of all you value, rouse yourself. Do not let your dependents see that you are thus unmanned."

"What can I do? Oh, what can I do? All is over."

"What is over?"

"All your hopes—all my hopes."

"By Heaven, you speak mysteriously; I do not understand you."

"Can you wed Floranthe now? Is she not as one out of the world? Her mind has left her—that is too evident."

"You think so?"

"Behold her."

"Come aside, and let me tell you that as yet I am not sure that this is not one of those wily tricks that the simplest maidens always understand so well in affairs of the heart, but if it be that some sudden shock has displaced reason for a while from its throne, she will soon recover; and even should she not, I am yet willing to redeem my promise."

"Oh, no—no."

"I say yes. The Lady Floranthe shall be mine. If not better on the morrow, I would recommend that she be taken to the Ursuline Convent, kept by the holy Abbess Moloni, who is kinswoman to us; and there, amid the quiet and seclusion of conventual rules, she will soon recover her mental serenity, and be glad to come forth into the world again as my bride."

"You give me hope."

"Which will brighten into certainty, if you adopt my advice."

"But yet I have heard strange tales of the Abbess of the Ursulines."

"Sheer calumny. Merit always provokes calumny; I have heard strange tales even of you."

The count bit his lips at this sarcasm, shot home to his heart, and then, after a few moments pause, he turned to the duenna, and motioning with his hand in the direction that Floranthe had gone, he said,—

"See to your charge."

"Yes, my lord. Yes—I—I will."

"Of what are you afraid?"

"Oh, nothing—nothing."

Trembling, partly from fear of the anger of the Count Syracuse, of which she had during her residence in the place seen some samples, and partly from a dread of any association with Floranthe during the period of her mental blight, the duenna proceeded after the unhappy girl.

"Let this affair go no further," said Gordoni to the count.

"No, no," he replied, and then raising his voice, he said to the servants,—

"Whoever babbles of what passes in this house had better confess his sins, for he will be in danger."

This hint was amply sufficient, for well they all knew the implacable character of the count, and that he thought little of human life. Moreover, his position and connections in the state—that state which was one of the most corrupt on the face of the earth—made it possible for him to commit great crimes without the necessary consequences following upon them.

The servants bowed in aequiescence, and then leaning upon the arm of Gordoni, and conversing with him in earnest whispers, the bold bad Count of Syracuse left the gallery, and proceeded towards the private apartment, where he and Gordoni had been drinking Cyprian wine at the moment when the alarm that something was amiss in the palace reached their ears.

CHAPTER XII.

THE PORTER AND HIS DAUGHTER.

STRALANI lay weltering in his blood in the garden.   The grass and the flowers around him were dyed with the red tinge of murder, and the air had about it the scent of gore.

The early dawn was coming, and the birds were awakening from their gentle slumbers upon the branches of the trees around the dead. In whirling flights they flew by the sad object that lay at the foot of the marble steps.

And now over the Adriatic and that City of Palaces came the light and beautiful morn, bringing with it upon its roseate and dew-spangled wings, light and life and joy to thousands.   And there was one who rose at that early hour whispering to herself as she glanced from the little casement of her window,

"It is at such an hour that the young buds are fairest. It is at such an hour that like pearls, the dew-drops spangle the leaves of the gentle rose."

This young girl, for such she was, resided with her father in a small rustic lodge situated in the garden of the Count of Syracuse's palace, and it had been her custom for many a morning to rise with the early dawn, pluck some flowers for the Lady Floranthe, by whose goodness she and her father were permited to live in peace and security within the precincts of the garden, although the service they rendered in opening and closing at rare intervals a little gate, was of small amount.

This homage of flowers however, went to the heart of Floranthe, and she was ever willing to rise and accept at the window of her chamber, the gentle and beautiful offering of the young girl.

Throwing across her shoulders a scarf, the gift of Floranthe, she with radiant smiles crossed the portal of the little lodge, and entered the garden.   The confusion and alarm in the palace, during the night, had not reached the humble abode of this young maiden, whose name was Pauline.

How little did that innocent young creature think, that such dreadful deeds as those we have had the pain of recording the perpetration of, had taken place so close to where she had slept, in all the fancied security of the shadow of a noble house. But so it was, murder had been within ear shot of her, although she had known it not, but had gone on gently dreaming of flowers and sunshine, and perchance of some one who had smitten her youthful heart, and awakened it to a consciousness of sweeter feelings, than as yet had before dawned upon its reveries.

A large bird—a bird of prey, came wheeling through the air, and with a hoarse tone startled Pauline.

She paused and looked at the strange guest. It had come from the lagunes, attracted by the smell of blood, which its rare instincts had made perceptible to it, at some miles distance.

In circles it sailed round and round one particular spot of the garden, as if it wished and yet feared to alight thereon. With some feelings both of fear and curiosity Pauline slowly advanced.

When she arrived at the cluster of flowering shrubs, from the centre of which, the bravo had made the first attack upon Stralani, she first saw in advance of her upon the grass, the young cavalier. Fear at the moment, rooted her to the spot on which she was, and she was alike incapable of advancing or retreating, had she ever such a will to do either.

This feeling however, soon passed away, and there arose the impulse to rush back to the little cottage, and alarm her father, but if ever humanity in its most glorious form inhabited a human bosom, it was this young girl's, and after she had taken several steps homewards, she paused, saying—

" Why should I fly. Is it not possible that timely aid might save a life. He who lies there in seeming death, may yet breathe. I have heard of birds having a strange sagacity, in knowing where life yet lingers in the human frame, and will circle around that which they wish to make prey of, until the last breath has passed away, ere they will alight, and begin their dreadful repast.

Another moment only did Pauline pause, and then crossing herself, and in a low tone invoking the assistance of Heaven, she walked towards the foot of the stone steps where lay the body of Stralani.

It was not in human nature to keep from shrinking a little as she came near to the spot, but whispering to herself to have courage, she did at length manage to get sufficiently close to see that it was some one in the habit of a cavalier of some rank, and at all events, no vulgar ruffian, who might have met with a just punishment for some projected crime, who lay before her.

This was encouraging, and she made another step in advance.

She now saw the guitar and something of the fatal truth began to dawn upon her mind. She knew that a young and noble cavalier was wont to serenade Floranthe contrary to the wishes of her friends, and the heart of Pauline had always gone with the lovers, although Floranthe had not confided to her the name of the noble Venetian who so often risked her kinsman's anger and revengeful feelings to pourtray to her his love.

The idea that this was the person, however, immediately found a home in the breast of Pauline.

All her previously awakened sympathies now doubly awakened, and soon she overcame the natural repugnance it was to be expected she would have to the blood-stained object before her and kneeling by the side of Stralani, she placed her small hand upon his breast to feel if life yet lingered in his heart.

Alas! all was to her perception still as death.

" It is over," she said, faintly.

To rise to her feet now was the work of a moment, and dashing the tears from her eyes, for they were blinding her, she rushed on towards the little lodge, where by th is time she hoped and expected her father would be stirring.

She found him lighting a few sticks, by the aid of which to prepare the morning meal, and rushing towards him, she breathlessly related the dreadful sight that she had seen in the garden, adding—

"Come, oh, come again with me, father. You may better know if life yet lingers in his frame. Come, oh, come."

The old man had listened to his daughter's narration with much and tearful emotion. When she had concluded, he shook his head, saying,—

"You have heard of bravos?"

"Yes—oh, yes."

"This then, is work of theirs, my child."

"But it may not be complete."

"Seldom, very seldom, my Pauline, do these villains leave their work half done They know the danger of not striking home, but yet will I go with you, and if Heave n has been pleased miraculously to preserve the life of him whom you have seen in the garden so far, he shall not now perish for lack of further aid—shew me the way , child."

With eagerness Pauline conducted her father to the spot where still lay Stralani, when she reached it she clasped her hands, exclaiming,

"He lives! He lives!"

"How know you, child?"

"He has moved. Oh! father, he has moved. He did not lie exactly as now he lies when I looked upon him some short time since."

The vulture screamed from a neighbouring thicket, and again commenced its wheeling flight round the body of Stralani.

With eagerness the old man knelt down and made a more close and accurate exami- nation of the body than Pauline, in her fright and great excitement, had been able to do. Then rising, he said,—

"My child, I am old, and not so capable of active exertion as once I was; can you help me, think you, to carry this wounded youth to our little humble home?"

"Wounded?—wounded?"

"Alas! is not his wounded state sufficiently apparent?"

"Yes—yes—but—but do you mean only wounded. Is he not dead?"

"He is not dead."

"Oh, joy—joy!"

"I have served in the wars against the Turks, and many a time have listened at a bleeding comrade's heart, to know if death had indeed claimed its prey—I ought to know the dead from the living. Help me, my child—help me quickly."

"To the palace, father—to the palace?"

"No—to our own house; I must know, by patient inquiry, more of this affair, before I say aught concerning it in the palace. Gordoni, whom I know better than he wots of, is in the palace, and it may be that I should be surrendering the lamb into the hands of the wolf by conveying this youth to the palace."

Pauline at once now understood whence came her father's reluctance to convey the wounded cavalier to the palace, and from the moment that she did so, no one could be more nervously anxious than she to get him to a place of safety where some care could be taken of his wounds.

Pauline now was a living example of the fact that we never know what we can do until we try, for if she had been under ordinary circumstances asked if she could help in the removal of a man covered with blood, she would probably have declared her insufficiency for the task, but now with her father's help she managed very well to get Stralani to the cottage.

"Now my child," said the old porter, "go to the convent of the Cordeliers while I place this youth in bed, and ask for father Ambrosio, beg of him to come to us as quickly as though I were waiting in the death agony for extreme unction, and tell him he is wanted to assist one sorely wounded.

"Yes, yes."

"He will in that case bring with him medicaments and bandages."

Pauline needed no second bidding, but darting from the cottage she hired the first disengaged gondola she saw, and desired that she should be taken to the well known monastic institution of the Cordeliers. There finding the holy father whom she had been told to seek, she brought him back with her to the cottage; nor did he forget to bring with him what might be necessary in a case of urgency such as that partially detailed to him by Pauline.

"Benedicite," said the monk, as he crossed the threshold of the cottage.

"Thanks, holy father, thanks, "here is one nigh unto death.'

The monk approached the couch upon which lay Stralani, and with a start he cried,— "Know you him?"

"No, holy sir, we do not."

"It matters little, I must see to his hurt."

With the greatest assiduity the monk now examined the wound which Stralani had received and after a time he said,—

"He may recover, but it will be little short of a miracle, nevertheless, there is no limit to Heaven's power and mercy; I will do all that human skill can do for him, the rest is with God."

Stralani was in a state of perfect unconsciousness while the monk was doing what was necessary for him in his wounded condition. When he had taken measures to stop any bleeding, he poured between the lips of the sufferer a few drops of a liquid he brought with him. The effect was to colour the features of the cavalier, and to throw him into a deep sleep.

"I will return in an hour," said the monk.

The old porter left Pauline in charge of the wounded youth, and went himself to the palace, with the view of getting some information which would guide him concerning what future steps he should take. He cautiously spoke to the servants, but none dared to speak to him about the events of the night, and he felt that his mission at present would be in vain.

As he was passing out of the palace, he had to go by a private room, where he knew the count frequently sat.

COUNT GRADUNIO AND THE PAGE RESCUED BY JEROME, THE GONDOLIER.

He paused at the door of the chamber, and as he did so, he plainly heard voices within, and the first words that came to his ears, rivetted his attention, and made him doubly anxious to hear more.

The voice was the count's.

No. 7.

"Are you quite sure, Gordoni, that your bravos did their work?"

"Quite."

"And yet, the disappearance of the body of Stralani suggests a doubt."

"Not at all."

"How do you account for it?"

"Easily! I think the bravos might have a natural wish to put aside all evidence of the deed, and doubtless, they themselves removed the body, and cast it into the grand canal; I have no doubt I shall hear as much, and then you know, we are completely rid of him."

"It may be so. At all events, he must have been killed, or else, why this shock of grief to my daughter?"

"True—true. All you have to do now is to get her quickly to the convent."

The old porter had heard enough. He quickly withdrew, and made the best of his way unobserved to his cottage again, when casting himself upon a seat, he related to Pauline what had happened.

"Gracious Heaven!" she exclaimed. "What can be done?"

"My child," said the old man, "it may be that Heaven has chosen us to be the ministers of its pleasure in this business. We are living alone, and seldom indeed do any of the pampered domestics of the Count Syracuse venture to pay us a visit."

"Seldom, indeed," said Pauline.

"Then my child we can, if we wish it, keep this wounded gentleman in safety here until perchance by Heaven's help he may recover, and be able to pass out in health and strength from among his foes."

Tears of joy gushed from the eyes of Pauline, and she flung herself into her father's arms.

"He will live, father," she said. "Something seems to tell me he will yet live to bless you for your goodness to him."

"May your words be prophetic, my child. But remember that this affair must be kept a secret from all. Heaven only can guess at the amount of evil that might fall upon us if it were known."

"Oh yes, father, I will guard the knowledge of the presence of this stranger, as I would guard the holiest secret of my heart."

"Do so, my child, and all will be well."

"Hush! Father do you hear nothing?"

The old servitor listened, and then he plainly heard the sound of voices in the gardens of the palace, and then the tread of feet. He had but just time to shoot a bolt into its socket at the door, when an attempt was made without to open it.

He placed his fingers upon his lips, and pointing to the door of the inner chamber where lay the wounded man, Pauline at once understood him, and closing that door she sat down on a low stool and appeared to be busy with a book.

A violent knocking came upon the door of the little lodge, and continued for some moments unceasingly.

CHAPTER XIII.

THE PRISONER AND THE PAGE.

IT is necessary now for the due conduction of our narrative, that we leave for awhile Stralani in the sad condition to which he was reduced, while we take a passing glance at the fortunes of two persons in whom must necessarily be concentrated some of the interest of the strange events which have yet to come.

Those two persons are the lonely prisoner in one of the dungeons of the Bridge of Sighs, and the young page of Stralani, who sought by plunging from the parapet of that gloomy structure to end "the heartache and the thousand natural ills that flesh is heir to."

The rushing stream, as it dashed and foamed under the bridge, received two bodies into its perturbed depths.

The dungeon floor of the prison gave way at the precise moment that the page took what he intended should be his last look at Venice, and the world, and plunged into the water.

The prisoner had, as we are already aware, been well prepared for what was to happen, so that his descent into the canal was by no means so violent or sudden as those who with devilish art had contrived those dungeons intended it to be.

His freedom too from the manacles which bound him, and which had he retained them would have been the instruments of his death, gave him power.

He went deep down in the water, but in a moment he rose again, and drawing a long breath he buffeted it with lusty strokes.

Then it was that a few feet from him he saw an object appear upon the surface of the stream.

To dash aside the tiny waves which were between him and it, and to grasp it tightly was but the work of a moment, he saw that it was a human form, and feeling as if Heaven had released him from a long and dreary imprisonment on purpose that he should be the means of saving one of its creatures, he felt fresh strength, and with one hand grasping the body of the page, for the page it was, he with the other swam with the stream, looking anxiously to the right and to the left, for some secure landing place.

Many good, and sufficient reasons induced him to think that some lonely spot would be preferable to land at, to any part of the city where he might have been required by the authorities to give troublesome and dangerous explanations with regard to from whence he came.

Accordingly he stemmed the current as best he might until, after passing some walls the bases of which were washed by the stream, he directed his way towards a small gate, at the top of a wide flight of steps, the lowest of which was constantly laved by the water.

He spoke but once as he sped towards this place, and then his words only were,—

"Dare I return to my own home, or has the dastardly policy of my enemies, be they whom they may, despoiled me of all that I might call mine?"

The strength with which he had hitherto been enabled not to swim well but to support the page in the water, he now found was only that impulsive energy which at a moment will be lent to some one who naturally possesses much physical power. Long imprisonment, bad food, and want of exercise had broken completely down one of the strongest frames.

The prisoner began to think that he should never be able to reach the landing place to which he bent all his efforts.

"Alas!" he cried, "I shall yet suffer the death that was meant for me by my enemies."

He was yet some distance from the stone steps upon which he fixed, in the dim light, his longing eyes, when he felt his strength rapidly going, oh, what a moment of bitterness and anguish was that for him who had but so short a time before exulted not only in his own freedom, but in the blessed chance of being the instrument in the hands of Heaven of snatching from death another.

Summoning all the power that yet remained in him, he made a desperate plunge forward towards the landing, but it was too far from him, and he felt that that was his last.

It was with the instinct of despair he cried aloud,—"Help! help!"

"At hand, signor," replied a voice, and the dark shadow of a small gondola glided across his eyes.

In another moment, with such a grasp as those only who are clutching at something that holds them up from the grave, was the prisoner clinging to the side of the boat.

But in the midst of his own sadness, in the midst of his own despair, and of the horrors that had thronged across his mind, he had not forgotten the youth he had hitherto kept above the stream, and now with that nobility of soul which belonged to him he said, to the gondolier.

"Whoever you are, friend, I pray you in the name of the Holy Virgin, to lift this lad into the boat first, as I have yet strength left to hold on for a brief space."

"Master, master!" cried the gondolier.

The prisoner dashed the water from before his eyes, as he said,—

"Great God, who is it?"

"I—'tis I—'tis Jerome, oh! master is it really you or a spirit?"

The gondolier trembled so excessively that he could hardly give the necessary assistance to getting both the prisoners into the boat, but yet he did continue to do so, and the prisoner lay so still, and so motionless, and so silent, that he seemed to have fainted.

Such, however, was not the case, it was only that from sheer exhaustion, he was incapable of saying another word just then, but the gondolier was alarmed and hastily directing the head of his boat to the shore steps, he audibly prayed for the recovery of him whom he called his dear master.

In the course of a very few moments the landing place, was gained, then the gondolier having made fast the boat to a stake which was there for such a purpose, himself landed, and was ready to assist from the little vessel, the two passengers he had so unexpectedly become possessed of."

By this time the prisoner had a little recovered, and he said in a low faint voice,—

"I think you are Jerome?"

"Yes, honoured master, I am he, indeed.—Did you not know me, my lord. Oh, what a weary time it has appeared since my eyes were blessed by a sight of you, and there are many besides myself in Venice, who have much missed the Count Gradunio."

"Hush, Jerome, do not breathe my name and title, there may be danger in it."

"Danger, my honoured lord?"

"Is it possible, Jerome, that you do not know what befel me?"

"We all heard, my lord, that you had gone on an excursion to the sea, by the lagunes, and perished in a storm. But who is this lad with you, my gracious master?"

"You recall me to a first duty," said the Count Gradunio.—"Do you and your wife still occupy the house in the garden?"

"Yes signor. Yes."

"Then take this poor boy at once home, and see if life be in him. Let me remain here for the present. Rest will be of service to me, and I can as well take it in the gondola, just now as elsewhere. Take the boy in your arms, I think you can carry him, and give him into the care of your wife, who I know has the heart of kindness in her to do the best she can for him."

"Who is he, my master?"

"That I know not."

The gondolier saw that his master was really in earnest about the page, so taking the fragile, light form in his arms, he strode rapidly through the garden, towards a little cottage-like building, in which he and his wife resided, so as to be always ready when required with his gondola, for the service of the noble family to whom he belonged.

In the course of ten minutes he returned, and by that time the count had in a great measure recovered from the fatigue of swimming so far in his debilitated state.

By the assistance of Jerome, he got from the gondola into the garden, and leaning upon the arm of his old faithful servitor he said,—

"Now tell me, Jerome, as we go to your cottage, where for a time, I shall crave your hospitality, what changes have taken place during my absence from my home, an absence which I think has exceeded six long, weary months."

"Great changes, signor."

"As I thought,—as I thought. I shall be able, if you relate them to me, to judge who are my enemies.—Who resides here now?"

"The palazzo is in the joint occupancy of the Grand Treasurer, Flavius, and the Chevalier Gordoni, your nephew, as I think."

"No, only a cousin, Jerome; and a bad man, as I believe. Does he claim my palace?"

"He does signor, as your next of kin."

"And Flavius?"

"The Senator Flavius and he are good friends, residing here together, and making great revelry from day to day. The senate has confirmed Gordoni in the possession of all that was yours, subject to security in case you should reappear, and that security Flavius the Grand Treasurer and Senator has given."

"And you have heard nothing further concerning me?"

"Yes—a—something."

"Which you seem unwilling to mention."

"I am unwilling, my lord.   You may be offended."

"Nay, how can I be offended with you, if it be ever so unwelcome a piece of intelligence? well I know, Jerome, it is communicated to me by friendly lips, when it comes from you."

"Then, my kind master, I will venture to tell you, that they accuse you of plundering the doge's treasures."

"Plundering?"

"Yes, that is the name they give it."

"But upon what grounds can such an accusation be made against me?   Surely you mistake?"

"Ah, my noble master.   I thought that you would not be able to believe the story even when you heard it."

"Tell me all.   Tell me all."

"Nay, that have I already done, my noble master.   I know no more than that, as the story goes, you were accused of plundering by some secret means the doge's treasury, which is in the vaults beneath the palace of St. Mark.   After that it was said, that for fear of discovery, which would result in disgrace to you and yours, you preferred death—that you wilfully cast yourself away, on the occasion of a storm."

"The villain!"

"What villain?"

"Flavius!"

"Ah, signor, it was he who made the accusation I am told, and a halberdier of the palace, who is friendly with me, said that the council sat in secret upon it many hours and after that the Three who rule Venice, wisely or not, it is not good for me to say, visited this place, and remained an hour or more."

"Indeed?"

"Yes.   They shut themselves up in the small oratory, where it was your custom to stay in study and meditation, and upon pain of death, all persons were forbidden to come even near to the door of the apartment."

"No doubt.   No doubt!"

"You do not seem much surprised, my noble master."

"I am not so very much surprised, Jerome, as it would seem likely that I ought to be, but the fact is I know more of this affair than it would be right or prudent of me to disclose, and you may likewise see that it is not from any want of confidence in you that I do no not tell you all, but because it is necessary, I should be able at another time to pledge my honour to the statement, that I had told no one what I knew."

"I understand signor, I am as much pleased by the simple words, 'Jerome, I have confidence in you,' as if you told me all the secrets in the world to prove it."

"You shall not be without your reward, Jerome, and now I may say that indeed am thankful to reach a place of rest and shelter, such as your cottage will afford to me."

The Count Gradunio was crossing the threshold of the humble abode of the gondolier as he uttered these words, and he was soon conducted to a chamber, where he could divest himself of his wet apparel, and take calm and refreshing rest.

The wife of Jerome brought him some warmed and spiced wine, and as she presented to him, she said—

"The girl sleeps soundly."

"Girl!" said the count. "What girl?"

"The young maid who was brought on shore by Jerome, and who was given in charge to him, by you signor."

"You amaze me."

"Is it possible that you did not know, signor?"

"By all that's sacred, I thought I had rescued from the waters of the Adriatic, a young lad who was quite a stranger to me."

The good woman's countenance brightened at this, and she said in a voice of some emotion—

"Oh forgive me signor."

"Forgive you? For what?"

"Indeed I have been unjust towards you."

"In what way?"

"I thought that the young maiden was some light o' love, who had been with you to your knowledge of what she was."

"I trust, dame, that you have not looked coldly upon her."

"No, no! The saints forbid. She was in distress, and that was for me sufficient. But yet it is to me a great joy to find it otherwise."

"Go to," said the count with a smile. "My years of gallantry are long since over. But I have need of rest. You can awaken me Jerome, if anything should happen that requires my presence."

"Most truly, signor."

"And I charge you both to pay more attention to her, whom I have by a happy chance rescued from the water, then you do to me. Who and what she is, we shall learn at some happier opportunity. Do not question her if she awakes."

With this charge to his servants, which he knew they would attend to and fulfil most punctually, the Count Gradunio lay down to rest, and in his exhausted state he soon lapsed into slumber.

But it was scarcely to be supposed that after the heavy occurrences of the past hour, his slumbers would be serene. And indeed they portook of anything, but of that character.

He again fanced himself let down, through the floor of his dungeon into the surging waters, and endeavouring to save the young page, whom he now knew to be a girl.

He found that she ever eluded his grasp, and yet kept crying with piteous accents. "Save me, save me!"

Such rest was not calculated to be very refreshing, but yet despite all these images of the fancy that thronged around him, the count slept on for many hours.

CHAPTER XIV.

THE HORRORS OF A CONVENT.—FLORANTHE'S DANGER.

It will be remembered that when poor Floranthe, completely overcome, and for a time mentally prostrated by the awful sight that had met her eyes in the garden, gave utterance to such incoherent words, as to show how great a mental shock she had received, Gordoni advised her instant removal to the Convent of the Ursulines.

The Count Syracuse had made a faint kind of opposition to this step, on the ground that the Abbess of the Ursulines bore but an indifferent character for kindness, he might have added common justice and morality, but folks were chary in those times of speaking against any one connected with the church.

To do so, might possibly have been almost as much as even the head of the Count Syracuse was worth.

This objection however, had been over-ruled by Gordoni, and it was decided between them, that for a time the Convent of the Ursalines was to be her abiding place.

Bianca was summoned to know what condition Floranthe was in, and in answer to to the enquiries of the count, she said,—

"Floranthe sleeps, I think, signor, for when she reached her chamber, she went at once to a cabinet she has there, and unlocking it she took thence a small miniature likeness of some cavalier, and kissing it repeatedly, she burst into tears, and flinging herself upon her bed she wept herself, as I think, to sleep."

The count looked at Gordoni, and the latter in a low, harsh voice of passion said,—

" Bring hither the miniature."

Bianca hesitated a moment, but a nod of acquiescence from the count let her know that he approved of the order, upon which she left the room and presently returned with a small miniature painted upon ivory.

Gordoni took it in his hand and exclaimed,—

" Yes, 'tis he."

He then handed it to the count, who, after gazing upon it for some few moments, added in a low tone,—

" 'Tis indeed, Stralani, and admirably like——"

" You say it is like," cried Gordoni. " Is it like now ?"

As he spoke he dashed the miniature to the ground, and planting his foot upon it, he smashed it to atoms upon the marble floor of the room in which they sat.

While executing this poor piece of revenge against the miniature, his eyes flashed with quite a demoniac kind of fire, so that Bianca was terrified and shrank back, and even the Count Syracuse half repented him that he had mixed himself up so intimately with a man capable of exhibiting such gusts of violence.

"Listen to me," said Gordoni, after a pause, "it is no matter what we say before Blanca, for money will make her do anything. I propose, that sleeping as she now is,

[FLORANTHE CONVEYED WHILE INSENSIBLE ON BOARD THE GONDOLA.]

the Lady Floranthe be wrapped in a cloak and taken at once in a gondola to the convent."

"The hour is rather unseasonable," said the count.

"Not at all; you will promise a handsome price to the Lady Abbess for her maintenance, and there will be no further trouble in the matter. She can be liberated so soon as she is willing in the convent chapel to become my bride, and not before."

The count hesitated.

"You pause," said Gordoni ; "but let me tell you that to-morrow when Floranthe recovers from the first shock of that matter which has so much affected her, and which we know nothing of, (Gordoni meant these last words as a hint to the count not to take Bianca into confidence regarding the assassination,) she may make so many words that the whole of Venice may be alarmed."

"True, true."

"Who knows what the consequences might be ? depend upon it she is not safe anywhere but in the convent."

"Say no more, I am convinced."

Gordoni instantly rose.

"I will order the gondola," he said. "It shall be ready if you will so quickly as may be, have Floranthe at the garden gate, close to the water steps. Will you proceed with us, count ?"

"Yes," said the count, "I will myself give charge to the abbess concerning her."

Gordoni probably would rather have gone without the count, but he could not very well make any opposition to his presence, and accordingly, while Bianca and the father, who was so unworthy to have for a child such a piece of nature and beauty as Floranthe, proceeded to the chamber of the invalid, he went to get ready a gondola, which should convey her quietly and rapidly to the Convent of the Ursalines.

Floranthe still seemed to sleep, but when Bianca raised her up, it was found that she was in a swoon.

The count affected to be a little shocked at this, whether he was so in reality or not, but after a few moments he said,—

"Perhaps it is as well to get her to the convent, while she is so quiet. Wrap her well up in a cloak, and I will myself carry her to the gondola."

A large cloak was folded round and round the beauteous form of Floranthe, so that even if she had recovered from her swoon she would have found herself perfectly helpless but she did not do so, and the count easily carried her from her chamber.

Preceded by Bianca to open doors for him, he took the least frequented route to the garden, and hastily passing through it, he reached the water steps as they were called, where stood Gordoni, while a gondola reared its black canopy against the night sky.

"Is all right ?" whispered Gordoni.

"Yes, she swoons," replied the count. "It is not sleep."

Gordoni made no reply to that, but stepped at once into the gondola with his lovely burthen.

"Am I to come ?" said Bianca.

"There is no occasion," said Gordoni, "push off gondolier, and take your nearest route to the Convent of the Ursulines."

Bianca made no reply, and the count did not interfere in the matter, so much to her chagrin she was left behind to the dulness of the house, while the gondola was swiftly urged forward in the direction of the Grand Canal, where the Ursuline convent was, and where the unhappy Floranthe was doomed to suffer so much, that without the hope of one day being rescued, death at once under any form or shape, were surely preferable.

But for the present she suffered nothing. The state of insensibility into which she had fallen, precluded the possibility of any mental distress, and perhaps it was a mercy from Heaven that, at such a juncture, she was spared making any useless resistance to the commands of those who would not by any means have scrupled to enforce obedience to the suggestions of their selfishness and cruelty.

The distance to the Grand Canal was not great, and once there, the steps leading to the gate of the Ursuline convent were soon gained.

"Allow me to speak to the abbess," said Gordoni. "I will offer a large sum——"

"A very large sum?" said the count hesitatingly.

"Be under no apprehension regarding the amount," added Gordoni, "I will pay it, you may be assured."

The count bowed his head in acquiescence, and sat in the gondola, while the villain Gordoni went to make conditions for the safe keeping of his child.

Oh, how fallen and debased must such a father have been, to stoop so low, as to barter his beautiful girl, who ought to have been the dearest gift he could receive from Heaven, for gold!

But so it was, the twin demons of gambling and of avarice, had taken possession of him, and under their influence, the Count Syracuse, was capable of anything that was suggested to him by any one who would pander to his vices, and supply him with the means of continuing them.

Gordoni's bargain with the abbess simply was, that the Lady Floranthe was to be kept a close prisoner, and suffered to see no one but himself, and for that service, he desired her to name her own price. This the abbess did, and although the sum was rather startling, Gordoni felt the extreme impolicy of attempting to reduce, so he acceded to it with the best possible face he could assume, and that was not very graceful.

Still in a state of utter insensibility, Floranthe was carried from the gondola up the steps conducting to the gate of the convent, there duly received by the abbess, who from that moment took charge of her.

The gates were closed again upon the count and Gordoni, and they had nothing to do but to get back to the palace of the former.

The count was rather silent, but Gordoni, who considered that he had really been strikingly successful, was rather inclined to be loquacious in his strange brutal way.

"You know the Count Gradunio, I think?" he said.

"Yes, yes," said Count Syracuse.

"Ah his fate was a strange one. Flavius tells me that he must for a long time have supported himself out of the funds of the state."

"But how did he get at them?"

"Ah, that is the mystery."

" And what has become of him ?"

" That nobody knows, unless a dread of losing his head by the pillar of St. Mark, induced him rather to seek death after some fashion of his own in the Adriatic."

" Probably. But you and Flavius are great friends."

" We are tolerably intimate. It is well to be on good terms, in this state of Venice with some one in power."

" Doubtless."

" It gives one two good things."

" And they are——"

" Protection against one's enemies in the first place, and the means of being doubly mischievous to them in the second."

" True enough, Gordoni."

" Yes, and I do not scruple to make good use of my opportunities. When your daughter consents to be mine, I shall then turn my attention to rising in the state of Venice to eminence."

" Thank you she will consent."

" Can she help it ?"

" I know not, I know not. I have my doubts, Gordoni, even although she is immured in a convent."

" And I have none, count. The dim, half dead life which she will there lead, must in time have its effect upon the imagination, and dispose her to the acceptance of any terms which will result in her restoration to the world."

" It may be so."

" It will be so, you may rest assured. This is not the age of violent self sacrifices There is one thing however, which will much assist in bringing about such a compliant frame of mind in her, and it is a thing in your power."

" What is it, Gordoni ?"

" Simply your not going near her at the convent. If you visit her, she will not only weary you with supplications, but from each visit she will gather fresh hopes of a release without conditions."

The count was silent.

" What say you ?" added Gordoni. " Do you hesitate about so trifling a matter as that ?"

" No, no! Not hesitate. I was only thinking."

" Of what ?"

" Nothing, nothing, Gordoni. I am willing to do all that in me lies to forward your wishes, and therefore I say at once, that I comply with your condition, and will not visit Floranthe."

Gordoni smiled to himself.

CHAPTER XV.

THE CONFESSOR OF THE CONVENT.

THE state of insensibility from the overwhelming woe, that else would have swept over her, continued in the pure and exalted mind of Floranthe for some time after she had been removed from the gondola; to the Convent of the Ursulines.

There was a small private room, close [to that apartment which was called the abbesse's parlour, and into which no unauthorised person was ever allowed to enter.

Indeed, there were but two individuals besides the abbess herself, in the whole of Venice, who would have dared to turn the handle of that door.

Those two were a nun named Rene, who might be called the prime minister and accomplice of the abbess, in all acts that were not quite correct, and the father confessor of the convent, who was no other, than the well-known Father Magas, to whom the page of Stralani had made a confession, after betraying to Gordoni the secret of his master's meeting in the garden of the Palazzo Syracuse, with the beautiful Floranthe.

It was into this very private parlour, then, adjoining the abbess's own room that Floranthe was carried, and with respect to the interview and arrangement that had taken place between the abbess and Gordoni, the latter had in effect fairly enough stated the substance of it, to the Count Syracuse.

What inferences the abbess had drawn from the whole affair, was quite another thing, although as regards her, we must start with a full conviction, that she is capable of aiding and abetting in any enormity, for the perpetration or connivance at which she was sure to be well paid.

That she was wealthy beyond the wealth of any one in Venice, was reported and believed, and nothing but the most insatiable avarice could have induced her to heap crime upon crime, for the purpose of adding to stores, far exceeding any amount which she could possibly make use of.

The abbess took but a slight glance at Floranthe on that night, but slight as the glance was, it sufficed to let her see how surpassingly beautiful she was.

That wondrous beauty was at once to the abbess an explanation of the whole affair, and she forthwith hatred Floranthe, with all the hatred that could possess a envious woman, cast in one of nature's most unfavourable moulds, against one who was more than beautiful.

But the abbess of the Ursulines was not one to disturb herself for nothing, and after settling the affair as far as it went, she gave the young girl into the charge of Rene the nun, and retired herself to repose, reserving until the morrow any active operations, by way of proving to Floranthe that she was in the power of one in whose breast gentle pity dwelt not.

The feelings of this nun Rene were by no means placed in a favourable position as regarded Floranthe, for she had been roused from her rest to attend upon her, and however flattering the amount of confidence the abbess had in her might be, Rene would have much preferred a manifestation of it at some more convenient and opportune juncture.

"Just too," she muttered, "as I had taken the small drop of strong waters, without which I cannot sleep, to be roused up. How very provoking. I will be revenged upon somebody."

It was in this amiable frame of mind, that the nun sat down by the couch where lay Floranthe.

"Well," she said, "I have been ordered to take measures to recover her from her swoon, but she may even remain in it, while I try to sleep in this large arm chair by the bed side, for I shall certainly not take any trouble at this time of night."

In the course of a few moments Rene was fast asleep, and unromantic and unlady-like as it may appear to be, she snored at a rate that was enough to awaken the whole convent.

In the room there was but one window, and that was nearly all composed of rich stained glass, so that when the sweet morning light began to gleam upon the city of the sea, it came into that room in many-coloured beams, converting everything within it into beauty, with the exquisite colouring.

Floranthe opened her eyes, and looked confusedly about her.

It was quite evident from the placid expression of her face, that not only had the sudden accession of delirium that had came over her, upon seeing the body of Stralani in the garden, departed from her, but that at the moment, memory had not brought back to her a remembrance of that dreadful scene.

No doubt she thought at the moment, that she was in her own chamber, at the palace of her father.

"Bianca," she cried, "Bianca, is it day?"

A loud snore from Rene came to her ears.

Floranthe half rose and looked about her in alarm. That odd looking figure in the dress of a nun by the bedside, the strange bed, the huge room, the stained glass window, and all the rich gleaming lights of different hues that streamed through it, filled her with alarm.

"Where am I? where am I?" she exclaimed. "Is this some too painfully vivid dream?"

She placed her hands over her face to think, and then with a frightful gush of recollection, there came back to her mind, the particulars so far as she had known them, of the fate of Stralani.

A scream burst from her lips, and she fell back upon the bed in an agony of w oe.

That scream mingled uncomfortably with the dreams of Rene, and awoke her with a start.

"Good God! what's that?" she cried.

Floranthe was weeping bitterly.

"Oh, it's you, you wretch " cried the nun. "Ah, I thought how troublesome you would be—so you have come to your senses, have you?"

"Are you human?" said Floranthe.

"Am I what?"

" Human."

" What do you mean by that? You had better know at once that I am not to be insulted with impunity. I may not have so much power as the abbess, but I have power enough to make any one in the convent feel it, and that most acutely, too!"

" Convent? What convent?"

" Oh, I have no sort of objection to tell you that you are in the Convent of the Ursulines."

" The Ursulines? Oh, no, no."

" And why not?"

" I have heard that the abbess is cruel and unfeeling."

" Have you? Well, she shall know what you have heard, and much good it will do you with her to know that you entertain such an opinion of her."

" No, no," said Floranthe, after a slight pause, " it cannot be—I am quite convinced it is all a dream. From the moment that I left my chamber in my father's palace, nothing is real."

" Please yourself," said Rene, as she rose. " I hear the abbess's bell; you need not attempt to leave this room—others have tried that before you, and all have failed."

" Am I a prisoner?"

" Aye, surely; and likely to remain one."

Rene left the room; and when Floranthe found herself alone, and could no longer cheat herself into a belief that she was dreaming, she joined her hands in prayer, and while the tears streamed down her cheeks, she called upon Heaven to aid and save her.

Somewhat tranquilised by prayer, Floranthe began to look around her, and to speculate more calmly upon her condition.

Gradually the truth dawned upon her. She had a perfect recollection of all that happened up to that dreadful moment when she stooped over what she conceived to be the dead body of Stralani, and dipped her fingers in the warm blood that had flowed from his wound.

After that all was dim and dark to her, and during that loss of thought and recollection, she had now no doubt that she had been removed to the much dreaded convent of the Ursulines.

Well she knew, from what she had heard of that convent, that it was used as a prison house for those who were wished by their friends, and most miscalled friends, to be coerced into an union contrary to all their hopes and wishes.

While Floranthe was thus reflecting, Rene had made a report of her night's proceedings to the abbess, which if it had been a faithful one, would merely have recorded how she grumbled, threatened, slept, and snored, but she contrived to make a very different thing of it.

" Well," said the abbess, " she shall breakfast with me this morning, and thus I shall be able to judge what sort of disposition she has; summon her hither, and leave us alone."

" Yes, madam."

Rene left the room, and proceeded to Floranthe, whom she desired to follow her.

Thinking it useless to resist such a mandate, and unwilling to make a show of resistance, in a matter which was of no importance, Floranthe rose and followed Rene in silence. In a few moments they gained the abbess's parlour, and Floranthe was received with a freezing dignity, which at once placed an insurmountable distance between her and the Superior.

"It is our pleasure," said the abbess, "that you take your morning meal with us, after which we will explain to you the commands of those who have a right to dictate to you."

It will be seen that the abbess of the Ursulines assumed the regal style in speaking of herself.

If anything, however, could have tended more than another to rescue Floranthe from the apathy of grief, it certainly was this dictatorial tone of address, and she replied with far more pride and boldness, than under the circumstances might have been expected of her, loaded too as her heart was with a grief transcending all common grief.

"Madam," she said, " I will do that which is right, and consistent with my feelings, nought else will I do."

The abbess bent her brow upon her.

"Indeed! So bold."

"Yes, so bold, indeed," replied Floranthe. " God knows my heart is now a fountain of tears, but yet I will resist oppression."

"We have means of overcoming obstinacy here."

" Of punishing and persecuting constancy you may have means, but not of shaking it, if it be of the true sort."

"We shall see."

"Amen, madam."

"You openly defy me, then ?"

"Most surely."

" 'Tis well, I will therefore tell you at once, that you never quit the shadow of these walls, except upon one condition."

"And that ?"

"That is as the wife of the Chevalier Gordoni."

"If what you say be true, the shadow of these walls and I, are likely to become most intimate."

"What mean you."

"That upon that condition I shall never leave them.

The abbess instantly rung a small silver hand-bell, that was upon the table close to her, and Rene appeared.

"To the cell of the refractory," she cried vehemently, as she pointed to Floranthe.

Rene smiled her satisfaction, and taking Floranthe by the arm, she cried,—

" Come—come."

" No, I resist."

"Resist!" shrieked the abbess, as she rose and clutched Floranthe by the wrist, with a force that was truly painful. "Drag her to the cell."

Rene reached towards a bell-rope near at hand, and pulled it, upon which several aged cross-grained looking nuns made their appearance, and Floranthe soon found that it would be madness to attempt further resistance to the abbess's command.

THE VISIT OF THE CONFESSOR TO FLORANTHE, IN THE CONVENT DUNGEON.

"I yield," she said, "but I have yet hope, founded upon the justice of Heaven. It will not permit me to perish."

"To the cell with her," shrieked the abbess, stamping with excess of passion.

Floranthe was dragged from the room.

Rene held the young girl with a clutch, that showed how truly delighted she was to execute any orders that had a spice of cruelty and of persecution about them, and two other nuns followed close at hand, in case of their services being required.

A long dismal looking passage was traversed, and at the end of that a flight of stone steps conducted to the chapel. It was with a feeling of hopefulness that Floranthe found herself within that portion of the convent. Surely, she thought, the sight of a place devoted specially to that God who is all justice and goodness, ought to disarm her persecutors.

The nuns, however, dragged her through the chapel with as much unconcern as they would have traversed any other portion of the building, and Rene opening a small arched door at its further extremity, pushed Floranthe into a narrow passage.

This passage was only lighted by a small lamp, which stood in a niche where there was a little statue of the Virgin, but Rene thought nothing of despoiling the shrine, for she took the lamp and having whispered the nuns to hold Floranthe securely, she passed along another dismal looking passage.

This passage terminated in another flight of stone steps, and the pathway they trod upon was only of hardened mould, and a damp, earthy smell pervaded the air. The lamp burnt but dimly in the damp atmosphere of the place.

Floranthe had to do her utmost to keep up any show of courage under the direful circumstances in which she was, and the only thing that enabled her to do so, was a dread that if she betrayed any fears, they would be construed into an indirect encouragement of the suit of Gordoni.

To that she told herself that any death were preferable.

At length Rene stopped at a low massive door in the wall, and producing a key from her pocket, she with some difficulty, as the lock was very rusty, unlocked it.

The door creaked upon its hinges, and then Rene spoke.

"Enter your tomb," she said, "unless you repent you of your obstinacy, for if you do not, you will never leave this place again, either in life or in death."

"As God wills it," said Floranthe.

Rene shook her as she passed into the cell, and then placing the light upon a small stone slab, that was opposite a crucifix let into the wall, she abruptly left the cell.

Floranthe heard the door carefully locked, and as she listened, the retreating footsteps of the nuns faded away upon her ears. She might well be excused at such a moment for bursting into tears and feeling how desolate she was.

In the course of half an hour a loaf of coarse brown bread and a pitcher of water, were brought to her, and placed in silence upon the floor of the cell.

Floranthe disdained to ask a question of the nun who brought such sorry fare, and in another moment the cell door was closed upon her.

CHAPTER XVI.

THE PERILS OF A NIGHT IN THE CONVENT.

FLORANTHE in that dismal cell had no means of comparing night with day, or of discerning when the latter had faded away and merged into the former, yet to her feelings it was a week of suspense and agony before any one came near her.

At length, she heard a footstep in the passage without. The cell door once again creaked upon its hinges, and by the dim light of the lamp, which was now near expiring, she saw a tall figure closely enveloped in a monkish garb.

The figure carried a light, which being held as high as the ceiling of the cell would admit, cast a tolerable radiance throughout its limited extent. Floranthé looked at the intruder with fear and trembling, and yet the ecclesiastical habit ought to have filled her with different feelings than those of dread,

If ever one much oppressed ought to expect help, surely it ought to be from one devoted to the service of that Heaven which rejoices in deeds of mercy.

The monk slowly approached, until near the centre of the cell, and then he spoke,—

"Daughter," he said. "How fares it with you?"

"Alas," said Floranthe. "How can it fare with me otherwise than most ill. Am I not a prisoner, shut out from life, light and joy, in this gloomy cell?"

"Wherefore is it so?"

"To whom do I speak? A friend or an enemy?"

"A friend, I am Father Magas, the confessor of this convent. Speak freely to me, as to a friend."

"Then to speak freely, I call upon you to rescue me from this state of misery and oppression."

"Upon what pretence are you imprisoned in this dreary cell, my daughter. There must be some reason."

"There is an affected reason, father."

"State it—state it."

"There is an endeavour to force me to commit sacrilege and blasphemy."

"Sacrilege and blasphemy! Holy saints, look down upon us. How do you mean my daughter?"

"As thus, holy sir, I am required to call upon God to witness that I will love one whom I hate. I am required to commit sacrilege by desecrating the altar of the Most High, in making it the witness to that which is untrue."

"From all which I gather that an attempt is being made to force you against your will into a marriage."

"Most true."

The monk set down the light he carried upon the stone slab before the cross in the wall.

"Daughter," he said, "you know not into what hands you are fallen. You cannot guess the amount of cruelties and persecutions to which you will be here subjected, until broken down in health and spirits you will become a living wreck, and enfeebled physically and intellectually, you will finally consent to anything demanded of you."

"Oh, no—no—no."

"It has been so."

"But not always."

"And it will be so again."

"Save me—oh, save me!"

"I could!"

She flung herself at his feet, and clung to the edge of his robe. With an half frantic accent she called upon him in the sacred name of that religion of which he was a minister, to save her from a fate which, as he had himself painted it, was far worse to her than any death that could be inflicted upon her.

"Hush," he said, "hush!"

She was silent on the moment, for she thought that there might be some good reason for his caution.

He stepped to the door of the cell, and half crossing its threshold, he, for the space of about a minute, listened attentively. Then returning, he closed the door, and in a low voice he spoke—

"Floranthe!"

"Yes, yes; that is my name."

"I know it is; I have seen you often. Hush!" he cried out, "before you speak to me, I say I have seen you often at the church of Our Lady of Loretto. Your features are for ever more engraven upon my memory."

Floranthe listened with wrapt attention; and, drawing his breath in short gasps, as if powerfully affected, the monk continued—

"I know that I am about to damnify myself for ever."

"Gracious Heaven!"

"Hush! hush! Floranthe! Floranthe!"

"What would you say? This suspense is madness."

"I—I would only say that I can save you."

"Oh, joyful words."

"But—"

Floranthe's heart sunk within her.

"You will not," she cried; "you will not. Some link of superstition or of fear withholds you—you will not."

"No; no superstition—no fear. Floranthe, the worst fate you say that can befal you is to be the bride of Gordoni."

"Oh, immeasurably the worst."

"And the next would be to perish here."

"Yes, yes; that indeed would be terrible."

"Then there is an alternative?"

"Speak it; oh, speak it."

He advanced and grasped her wrist. His words came in hissing and strange tones from his lips. His hot breath fanned her cheek, and she shrunk with horror from him as the words,

"Fly with me," came upon her ears.

"Horror! horror!" she exclaimed.

"Fly with me," again said the monk. "Beautiful being, born to be my perdition. I love you."

"God help me, now!"

"I will help you. God will never more after this hour help me. But you alone shall be the object of my fond idolatry; I will seek in your love a heaven upon earth, as a compensation for that which I have lost all hope of in the life which is to come."

"Help! help!" cried Floranthe.

He pressed close to her. He encircled her in his arms, and rained kisses of fire upon her brow.

"Help! Have mercy, Heaven," she shrieked.

There was a furious knocking at the cell door. The monk at once released her, and folded his habit closely about him, as in a voice of affected calmness he said—

"Who knocks?"

"Open! open!" said a voice.

"Who knocks?" again said the monk, and no doubt he was glad of some delay in admitting the visitor, in order that he might have a little time to recover his own equanimity.

"Help! help!" cried Floranthe.

The door was violently opened, and by the gleams of a torch she saw a cavalier wrapped up closely in a rich velvet mantle.

To rush towards him was the impulse of the moment on the part of Floranthe.

"Save me, I implore you," she cried; "oh, save me from this villanous priest; I conjure you, signor, to have compassion upon me, be you whom you may."

"Beautiful Floranthe!" said the cavalier.

Floranthe recoiled with horror. She had fled for succour to her worst enemy. Too well she knew that voice; it belonged to the villain—the assassin, Gordoni.

"You fly from me," he said.

"As I would fly from perdition."

"And you, holy father, why is it that thus early in your ministrations you have managed to place yourself on bad terms with your penitent? She called you villain, priest."

"Aye," said the monk.

Gordoni bent a curious and searching gaze upon the monk, who, turning to Floranthe, said—

"Daughter, I leave you. Ponder upon my words; we shall soon meet again. Cavalier, a word with you."

Floranthe pale, agitated and terrified, replied nothing; and the monk took Gordoni outside the cell door, and in a low voice of much affected concern, said to him—

"Ah, how much do I suffer for you."

"For me?"

"Yes; have I not been reviled?"

"You have; but—"

"Nay, hear me; you have promised a large sum to the abbess, and a smaller one to me, if between us we can bend the stubborn will of the Lady Floranthe to be yours."

"Well."

"It is well; of course, I pondered much and deeply as to the best and most likely mode of accomplishing your object for you."

"Well."

"Nay, do not interrupt me. It occurred to me that if the Lady Floranthe could be made to fancy herself in a situation much worse to be endured than that of being yours, she would to escape the greater evil fly to the lesser."

"Well?"

"You understand me?"

"I understand the proposition, that to escape a greater evil she might fly to a lesser."

"Well."

"I say well."

"Do you not comprehend?"

"Upon my life I do not. You speak in riddles."

"Go to, my son, go to. The plan I have adopted, must be quite obvious to you. You cannot but guess it. A man of your penetration and abilities, must hit upon it at once."

"And yet with singular dulness I do not, and therefore like the most common of mortals, I would feel obliged by an explanation."

"Of course I made love to her myself."

"You don't say so."

"Yes; was it not capital?"

"Humph!"

"Really my son, you do not seem to see the advantages of the plan."

"I certainly do not."

"Then perhaps you would rather—Eh?

"Do that part of the business myself."

"Yes. Oh, yes."

"Exactly."

"How delightful it is thus thoroughly to understand each other. I shall have the pleasure of seeing you soon, doubtless in the convent parlour. Until then, my son, may the blessing of all the holy saints be upon you, and around you. Amen!"

The monk walked slowly and quietly away, without waiting for any reply from Gordoni, who continued looking after him for a few moments in silence.

"Saintly hypocrite!" he muttered. "It shall go hard with me, but I will contrive some speedy way of requiting you' for the favour you have done me. Villain, and fool! Can you fancy me so weak as to be deceived by your flimsy web of deceit. By heavens! that is the worst insult of all."

The monk was soon out of sight in the gloomy passage, and then Gordoni turned and once more entered the cell, where Floranthe stood pale and trembling.

CHAPTER XVII.

THE STILETTO.—THE NOVICE AND THE DUNGEON.

SEVERAL times during the progress of the brief dialogue, between Gordoni and the monk, Floranthe was upon the point of rushing from the cell into the secret passage, and making at least one bold attempt to recover her liberty.

Had it not been that the murmur of their voices came so distinctly to her ears, as to convince her they were very close at hand, she no doubt would have rushed forth, but the idea of being held by such fiends in human shape, and by force again placed in the cell, retained her, and made her bear the ills she knew of, rather than rush upon those that might be worse.

The time for reflection too was very short, for the conversation between the two worthies did not last many moments, and then she saw Gordoni once more within the cell.

She did not conclude that there was so much to dread from him as from the monk, and therefore it was with more ease of heart that she faced him.

She was resolved not to break the silence, that was maintained for a few minutes between them, but disdaining to complain, she left it for him to speak the object of his coming.

" Floranthe," he said. " This sullen silence ill befits your present condition. Events are thickening around you."

" Murderer!" said Floranthe, " this tone and language ill befits your condition. Much more fearful are the events that are thickening around you."

" Indeed !"

Floranthe was silent.

" 'Tis well," added Gordoni. " I am not surprised or disappointed; your love I did not expect, nor could I expect that a few hours confinement in a convent cell, would be quite sufficient to break your stubborn spirit; I say I did not expect it."

" You were right."

" As I see, but the time will come."

" Never."

" Nay, by this hand it will and shall."

" By this hand, it will not and shall not."

" Now I love you indeed. You have about you something of my own spirit, Floranthe, the spirit of our race; and if before I had at all wavered, which sooth to say, I did not, in my pursuit of you, your present conduct would make me firm as any rock. I say you shall and must be mine. That is settled."

" If you have spoken all that your bad heart can dictate," said Floranthe, " now leave me. Even this cell is by contrast, endurable without you, murderer."

" You will call me by that epithet."

" Yes. Murderer ; assassin ; which you will, or both."

" Girl, you know not what you do. You know not your danger.—You know not the strength of the passions your incautious words may call into existence. The conse- quence be upon your own head."

" Then leave me, Gordoni, while it is in human nature yet to pray for you, and per- chance in time forgive you."

" Pray for me ?"

" Yes ; oh, yes."

" Forgive me ?"

" Are you past forgiveness, or a wish to be forgiven ?"

" Ha! ha! A solemn farce. Floranthe let us cease this idle talk. I tell you that mine you are, even now, to all intents and purposes, and once more I assure you, that you cannot escape me. With a good grace, now, walk out of this cell, as my wife."

"No—no—no."

"You have no friends to aid you. You are as utterly helpless as one wrecked upon a barren coast, where nothing lives."

"My father! oh, my father!"

"Your appeal to him is in vain."

"It cannot be. It cannot be. He will, he must remember that I am his child. Oh no—no.—He has been harsh and unkind, but even he will save me from such as you are."

"Despair of that relief."

"I will not.—I will not."

"I tell you your father has by express agreement abandoned you to me. It is by licence and authority from him, that I am empowered to employ any means I think proper, to enforce you to become my wife. You have no friend on this side of the grave."

"No friend?"

"Not one."

Floranthe wrung her hands and wept.

"Father—father!" she cried, "can this be so?"

"Your own experience with the count," added Gordoni, with a sneer, "points to the strong probability, that it is indeed so."

"Oh that I had a mother."

"Humph. Mothers are troublesome at times. But come Floranthe, take better counsel with your judgment. You will not be the least considered in Venice, by becoming mine."

"Considered ?—Oh what a death were that, to be considered with such as thou."

"A death ?"

"A worse than death."

"Girl, I have power."

"Power! No—no. You may have abundance of wickedness, but in honest, sober, truth, Gordoni, you have no power, but such as fear may give you, and that will not I bestow."

"Do you indeed defy my power ?"

"Rather ask me if I do indeed, rely upon the protection of that Heaven, which hears surely not in vain, such an appeal as I can in this the hour of my distress and danger make to it."

"Superstition!"

"No—no; your's is the superstition that rejects the belief in things so sacred and so true."

"Hear me. You rely on the protection of Heaven ?"

"I do."

"On account of your virtue and your innocence ?"

"Assuredly."

"'Tis well. Now tell me, Floranthe, if in your acceptation and full understanding of those qualities, was not your lover, Stralani, virtuous and innocent ?—and yet he fell."

" O'1, hor r or—horror !"

  " Where was the outstretched hand of the Providence you invoked to your aid when he fell ?"

  " By your hand ?"

  " No; there you wrong me."

  " By the hands, then, of the horrid instruments of your evil passions ?"

"I have already said I know nothing, but by report, of his death. I cannot, of course, force you to believe me."

"No, Gordoni, it would require the word of one greater than now treads the earth, to convince me you were innocent."

"Well, be it so, and yet is all this beside the question; I again swear to you, Floranthe, that you shall not leave this place except as my bride, and if you obstinately persist in your refusal to become such, I will adopt means to overcome your stubbornness. I love you, and as some slight foretaste of joys to come, I will now taste the honey of those lips which, even in the dusky light of such a place as this, shame the rose."

"No—no—no. Oh, mercy!"

"Angel!"

"Hence, thou villain, approach me not."

Gordoni rushed towards her, and tried to clasp her in his hateful arms, and to hold her to his breast.

In an instant, Floranthe wrenched from his side the half-dagger, half-rapier, which he wore, and with it made a sudden thrust at the face of the villain.

That the thrust was effective enough to release her at the moment from the grasp of Gordoni, was sufficiently evidenced by the fact, for in a moment, with a howl of pain, he released her, and staggered back from her.

The opportunity thus afforded her of making good a retreat from the cell was not to be lost, and snatching up the lamp which the monk had left behind him, and still retaining her grasp of that weapon which had done her such good service, she rushed from the place.

In the intricacies and recesses of that convent it could not be said that Floranthe knew whither she was going, and, beyond the general idea that if she pursued the passage in which her cell was situated, turning to the left upon leaving its door, she would reach the chapel of the convent, she knew nothing.

But her proceedings at that time were not so much matters of calculation as of impulse—what she wished was to escape from the villain, Gordoni—and she thought that to accomplish that was much.

It would appear that, if not very seriously hurt, he was at all events either too much alarmed, or too much wounded, to follow her, so that after going for some distance and finding she was unpursued, Floranthe relaxed her speed a little.

She thought, from the distance she had come, she must of a surety be very near the chapel, and she began to look about her for the door of that building.

Suddenly while she was thus occupied, she heard a voice, and from a peculiarity in the tone, she felt quite convinced that it was the voice of the abbess, who, it would appear, mistook her for some other person.

"Hist, hist!" she cried. "Is is you?"

Floranthe drew back, and shading her light from her eyes, she looked in the direction whence the voice proceeded, and saw a small door a short way open.

She felt certain it was the door leading to the chapel.

"Is it you, Rene?" again cried the abbess. "Why do you not speak?"

Floranthe feared an instant discovery and pursuit, and feeling that if unsuccessful in imitating the sharp repulsive tones of Rene, she could not be in a worse position, she made up her mind to the attempt.

"Yes, it is I," she said.

"Ah, I thought so," replied the abbess. Have you heard any noise from the cell?"

"None."

"The cavalier is there?"

"Yes."

"Well, Rene, you will have your reward. Follow me, I would speak with you. Follow me, quickly."

The abbess left the half opened door, and no doubt fully expecting Rene to follow her, walked hastily through the chapel, but Floranthe observing another passage branching off to the left of the one she was in, determined rather than risk an encounter with the abbess, to chance following it, let it lead wherever it might in that dreary building.

Her lamp shed an amply sufficient ray to guide her, and she made her way onward, opposed only by the damps of the place, and the pendant webs of many spiders, who seemed completely to have taken possession of the vaulted roof of that melancholy place.

At another time possibly, and under happier circumstances, Floranthe might have been deterred even by such obstacles as those, but great anxieties and terrors swallow up all lesser ones, and she went on anxiously but fearlessly.

This dreary passage got narrower as she proceeded, and moreover the ground appeared to slope downwards, so that she became under an impression that she was going somewhere far beneath the surface of the earth.

That by proceeding in such a course she should reach light and liberty, seemed to be against all reasonable probability, so af er going a few paces further, Floranthe paused to consider as well as she could, in the tumult of her thoughts, what she had best do.

A low faint groan, or something between a sigh and a groan came upon her ears.

Floranthe trembled, and was glad even to lean against the damp earthy wall of the passage for support.

All that she had ever heard of the supernatural came now vividly across her imagination in startling remembrance, and for the first time she had been in those melancholy passages, she became alive to the impressions of superstition, and indeed, there was a something of so unearthly a character about the sound she heard, that it was likely enough to engender such thoughts.

The strongest minded persons will at times, despite all their better and more mature convictions give way to such feelings, and it is not to be wondered at, therefore, that when the young and inexperienced Floranthe heard again that sad wailing sound of woe she should feel ready to swoon with fear.

Thick coming fancies oppressed, and all she could find strength to do was to call faintly upon Heaven to succour her.

The groan came a third time, and then as nothing followed upon it—as it was the advent of no horrible sight or other horrible sound, she began slowly to gather courage.

She breathed again more freely; and set herself in a posture to listen attentively in case the groan should come again, so that she should be able to come to some opinion of a more rational character concerning it.

It did come again, and then Floranthe said to herself—

"Surely that sound comes from mortal lips, and is the cry of despair from some one, who, perhaps, like myself, has been made subject to the cruelties and the persecutions of this convent."

She felt now as if it was a kind of duty upon her part to take what means were afforded to her of ascertaining the truth or error of her conjecture.

"Protection I have none to offer," she said, "but it may surely be something in the shape of a soothing consolation to some anguished and desponding spirit, to hear but a kind word or two in this world ere it wings its flight to happier regions."

Animated by this feeling, than which there could not be one more pure and exalted, Floranthe hurried now onwards in the direction the groans had proceeded from.

Every few moments she paused to listen if the sounds were repeated, and she had the melancholy satisfaction of finding that she was upon the right track by the greater clearness with which she heard the moans of the sufferer.

As she went on she looked carefully to the right and to the left, in case any door should escape her observation, and as a result of such close scrutiny, she did at length come upon a small gothic door in the wall.

A heavy iron bar across it was its only mode of fastening, it being destitute of anything in the shape of a lock, but that bar looked to be all sufficient.

Floranthe placed her ear close to the rough oaken panneling of the door and listened attentively.

CHAPTER XX

THE HIDING PLACE.

IT was some few minutes before Floranthe felt quite convinced that the groan proceeded from the cell which was closed by the door close to which she stood.

After the sound had been twice repeated from within, she no longer entertained any doubt upon the subject, and accordingly placing her lamp upon the ground, she took both her hands to the lifting the iron bar which secured the door.

She accomplished that with less difficulty than she imagined, from its ponderosity, she would have experienced, and in a moment the cell door creaked upon its hinges.

A faint groan came from within.

"Have you come to kill me? Oh, rather kill me at once. than by degrees thus quench the flame of life."

The voice was full of despair, and yet there was a sadness in it exquisitely musical and sweet. It seemed to Floranthe as if it must be that of some very young girl.

Lifting the lamp from the floor, she entered the cell.

"Courage, courage," she said, "do not abandon all hope yet."

A young and beautiful girl lay upon some straw in a corner of the cell, and as Floranthe held up the lamp so as to cast its rays upon her, she looked the very picture of beautiful desolation. Her attire was ragged and soiled; her own beautiful hair hung in disordered masses about her breast, and the expression of her face was that of one who had long nourished no feelings but those of absolute despair.

Floranthe was deeply affected, and for some few moments after uttering the few words she had, she could not speak again to the fair prisoner.

At length with an effort, she did manage to say to her, in a low tone of deep sympathy—

"God help you."

The young creature looked at Floranthe for a few moments with quite a bewildered air, and then she said,—

"An angel has come to see me at last!"

"No—no," said Floranthe "I am mortal like yourself. Who and what are you, that you are condemned to waste your life in such a place of despair as this?"

The girl burst into tears.

There was something truly dreadful about the hysterical vehemence with which she wept, and Floranthe herself was too much alarmed to say a word to stem the gush of affliction.

Perhaps it was better that she should weep on until her surcharged heart was relieved.

"Be comforted," said Floranthe.

"Oh, God—oh, God!" was all the young creature could say, in reply to the words which Floranthe meant should be cheering to her.

"Nay, you will deprive yourself of all power to act for yourself," added Floranthe. "Remember that you are yet young, and that there is a Heaven above us that sees all."

"It has not looked upon me," replied the girl, "for many a long—long, weary day."

"Until now?"

"Can you save me?"

"I will strive to do so, although my power is small."

"Oh, there is a faint hope, then."

"A faint one. But tell me who you are?"

Floranthe placed the lamp upon the floor of the cell, and sitting down upon the straw by the side of the young creature, she held one of her thin hands in her's while she listened to the words that fell from her lips.

Her voice was very faint and weak, as she spoke to her, who indeed came as an angel of consolation to her.

"I was beloved," she said, "by one whom I loved in return. He was an alien to this land and to its religion, but I would have down with him far away."

You are faint. Have you no refreshment here?"

"Water. I am indeed faint. Will you hold yon pitcher to my parched lips?"

"Willingly—most willingly."

The girl took a deep draught of the pure fluid, and then with more strength, resumed,

"We planned flight, but we were betrayed. What was his fate I know not, but I was brought to this convent, and cloathed in the dress of a novice, and commanded to take the veil at the end of my noviciate."

"You refused?"

"I did. I rather asked for death instead, and so they placed me in this cell, in the hope and expectation of terrifying me as many have been terrified into submission."

"How long was that since?"

"I know not—I have no means of counting the lapse of time here. But it must have been many weeks."

"And your lover. Who was he?"

"An Englishman."

"A heretic?"

"Ah, but so noble and so good. He commanded a ship belonging to his country, and his name was Captain Herbert. I shall never look upon his face again."

"Nay, why should you not?"

"Alas, alas! I am separated from him, I feel assured, for ever and ever."

"He is not dead? You have no surety of his death, and therefore you should not despair."

"Is he not dead to me?"

"Yes, but——"

"Oh, do not seek to tell me I may hope. No one in all the world can be so unfortunate or so unhappy as I am."

"You think so?"

"I am sure—quite sure."

"You do not know me."

The young novice looked in the face of Floranthe, as she said, in a tone of commiseration—

"You, too, have suffered."

"I have indeed ; you are only, perhaps, for a time separated from him who you love but you can nourish a hope of seeing him yet again. I am separated from one who loved me, and I have no such hope."

"No hope?"

"Alas! no—for I am assured that he is dead. I saw him lying in the deep sleep of death. Do not, do not say that you are the most unhappy being in this world of sorrow."

The young novice flung her arms around the neck of Floranthe, and weeping upon her breast, she said—

"Oh, forgive me, forgive that I compared my sufferings with yours for a moment! Are you, too, a prisoner here?"

"I am."

"And have they sent you to share my cell with me?"

"No. Listen to me, and you will precisely understand how much you may hope from me. Perchance we may, by consulting together, devise some plan which shall hold out to us a chance of release at all events."

Floranthe then related her history to the young novice, who listened to every word she uttered with the most rapt attention, and when she had concluded, she said to her—

"We are indeed sisters in affliction. Would it not be some alleviation of our misery if we were suffered to be together ?"

"It may not be," said Floranthe. "There is danger to both of us even now, each moment that we delay parting."

"Must we part ?"

"Yes. Remember that, now I know where to find you, I will go back to my cell, and there in deep meditation I will try to devise some plan of release for us."

"Oh, no, no—do not leave me."

"Hush—it will only be for a time. What if a search was now to be made for me, and finding me here with you, we should each be removed to some distant cells where we should never more see each other ? Have you not named us sisters in misfortune ?"

"Yes, yes."

"Let us continue, then, the interchange of sisterly affection while we can, and that can only be done by our now separating."

"If it must be so ?"

"Believe me, it must. I have an idea of accomplishing something. Farewell for a brief space."

The young novice hung upon the neck of Floranthe for a few moments, ere she let her go, and then the latter hurried from the cell.

She took care to put up the bar across the back of the door, so that there should be no appearance of any visitor having been to the novice, and then she hurried along the passages that led to her own cell.

Her object was to gain it before any general commotion should have been made in the convent. Gordoni, she believed to be, at all events, sufficiently wounded to afford her no annoyance , and indeed she fully expected that by this time he had left the cell.

As she passed the little door leading to the chapel she heard the sound of many voices.

Redoubling her speed, she reached the cell door only a little in advance of those who came to look for her.

The cell was empty, but the key of its door was in the lock, and to possess herself of it and conceal it as well as the dagger of the villain Gordoni, among the straw which lay festering in one corner, was the work of a moment.

It was well indeed that she was so prompt, for the voices she had heard were those of the persons who were in pursuit of her.

The fact was, that although rather badly hurt by the dagger wound that Floranthe had given him, yet Gordoni after recovering himself a little after the first shock of the affair, found strength enough to leave the cell.

It is not to be wondered at, however, that under such circumstances, he should disregard the door, and indeed, as the fair prisoner was absent, the necessity for shutting up the cell was not very apparent.

Bleeding profusely from his wound, he made his way through the chapel and so on to the abbess's parlour, where sinking upon a seat, he gave an account of how Floranthe had wounded him and then fled.

This was amply sufficient to secure the utmost ire of the abbess, who, with Rene and the two aged nuns, who were tolerably deep in her confidence, at once started to discover the fugitive, and lodge her more safely if possible than before.

————

CHAPTER XIX.

THE COUNT GRADUNIO AND JEROME OVERHEAR A PLOT.

FOR a very brief space of time, it now becomes absolutely necessary that we should leave Floranthe in the convent, exposed to all the dangers that can beset innocence and virtue, while we take a passing glance at what is occuring at the abode of the Count Gradunio, who was rescued from the canal beneath the Bridge of Sighs.

It will be recollected that he had placed the most implicit confidence in the gondolier, Jerome, nor was that confidence at all misplaced, for a more honourable man could not exist than he.

The information communicated by the wife of Jerome, that the seeming page who had been so opportunely saved from the canal, was a young girl, had filled the count with amazement, but at that juncture he was unable to take any steps to unravel the mystery.

He felt strongly the absolute necessity of speedily increasing his strength, and for that purpose he willingly deferred anything in the shape of action until he should have recruited himself somewhat by a night's rest.

Although that night's sleep was haunted by all kinds of strange images, he yet awoke much the better for it, and casting his eyes around him, he saw the honest and faithful gondolier seated by his bed side.

"Ah, Jerome," he cried.

"My lord," said Jerome. "How fares it with you?"

"Much better. The page—how is he?"

"The young girl, signor. You forget that my good dame informed you, that you had saved a girl instead of a boy."

"Truly, I did.—How is she?"

"But poorly."

"Indeed."

"Yes, signor; she seems to have some grief upon her mind which spoils all repose."

"I will have an interview with her shortly, Jerome; but now tell me what news you have concerning my affairs."

"I will, my noble master, and speedily too. You must know that neither Flavius nor Gordoni slept here last night, but by an early hour this morning they both arrived and thundered at the great gate."

"The gate facing the square of St. Mark?"

"The same, signor. It was not my business even to hear them, you know, as my

duty," continued Jerome, "is solely confined to an attendance upon the water gate of the palace, which is here."

"Exactly."

"But, nevertheless, being upon the alert to gather what news I could, I made a point of running and opening the gate before Paulo, the regular porter, could get up."

"And you let in Flavius, the grand treasurer, and Gordoni?"

"I did, signor."

"Go on, go on, I pray you."

"They both seemed to be full of spirits, and were talking much more loudly than their wont, but they subdued that as they crossed the court-yard and entered the palace. They ascended the grand staircase and entered a saloon, from whence they betook themselves to the small room that you were in the habit of occupying with your books, signor."

"Ah!"

"Yes; they peremptorily ordered me away, and closed the door and locked it carefully."

"When was that, Jerome?"

"Even now, signor."

"Not an hour since?"

"Not a fourth of the time, signor; I came at once here to see if you had awakened."

"Assist me to rise."

"Nay, signor, would not more rest be of service to you?"

"It might, Jerome, but it is most important that I should be able, if possible, to overhear what those two most notable villains have to say to each other. Will you accompany me?"

"Assuredly, signor."

"There may be some danger."

"Which I would gladly take the whole of, my noble master, but I suppose I can but share it."

"Come with me then, quickly. You shall be a witness to what we shall hear, and I will show you some secrets in the palazzo, of which probably you have no idea."

The Count Gradunio, with the assistance of Jerome, who made a much more efficient valet than could have been supposed, considering his ordinary occupation, was soon ready to leave his chamber, and they together crossed the garden, keeping as much as possible under cover of the shrubbery until they got to the mansion.

They entered by a small door, and found themselves in a suite of rooms, in the eastern wing of the palace.

Jerome was full of interest and curiosity, to know where, precisely, the count intended to go, but when he found that they were proceeding towards the large saloon, which was adjoining the small room where Flavias and Gordoni were conversing, he made up his mind that the count surely intended to listen at the door of communication—a course which he felt confident was fraught with the very greatest danger.

"Let me listen with my ear to the door, master," he said, "I will bring you a faithful report of all that passes."

"Listen at yon door, Jerome?"

"Yes, signor."

"That would indeed, be full of hazard."

"But is there any other way?"

"Have patience for a few moments, and you shall see that there is."

A splendid picture, by the inimitable Claude, hung upon the wall, and from amid the intricacies of the rich carving of its frame, the count took a small key, which had been so securely hidden, that no one who did not know precisely where to hit upon it, could have suspected its existence.

He then proceeded to a part of the room, where some costly tapestry hung in rich masses from the ceiling to the floor, and holding a portion of it aside, he found a small-key hole, into which he fitted the key.

A tall, narrow door, sprung wide open.

"Follow me, Jerome," said the count. "This is a narrow passage, which connects the adjoining small room with this saloon. Come on. Come on."

Jerome followed in wondering silence, for he had no idea that there were [such strange secret places in the palace, but he did not for a moment hesitate in proceeding closely after the count.

The latter closed the door, which shut by a catch, requiring only to be unlocked on its outer side, and then the passage was in a state of the most absolute darkness.

"Tread softly," whispered the count, "but tread fearlessly. You cannot go amiss, and you will touch the walls if you deviate, so that you are sure to come right."

"I follow, signor."

About twenty steps had been taken, when the count stopped, and spoke in a whisper, saying,—

"Now, Jerome, all that will be required of us is the most profound and complete silence, and we must hear all that is spoken in the small room, quite close to which we now are."

"No one shall hear me breathe, signor."

"'Tis well. You will comprehend the full necessity for this amount of caution, Jerome, when I tell you that I am now about to open a door in the wall of the small room, in all respects similar to that in the wall of the saloon, and as a consequence we shall only be separated from those who are our foes by the descending tapestry."

"Yes, signor."

The count having thus fully explained to Jerome his precise position, carefully opened the door, and in a moment a faint light, that made its successful way through the tapestry, illumined the narrow passage.

The sound of voices, too, became distinctly audible.

Flavius was speaking

"You will see clearly, Gordoni," he said, "that it is not merely the getting rid of the Count Gradunio successfully, which rids us of all danger."

"Certainly—certainly. But are you sure you are really completely rid of him?"

"Can there be a doubt? weakened by a long confinement, and loaded with irons, he went last night through the floor of one of the dungeons of the Bridge of Sighs into the canal beneath."

"Well, that seems correct enough."

"Yes. He will be no further trouble to us, so we may dismiss him from our minds, and turn all our attention to a consideration of our own plans."

"Precisely. Go on. I only wish I felt as much at ease about that young gallant, Stralani, as you do about the fate of the Count Gradunio."

" Why, what is your doubt ?"

" I can hardly be said to have any doubt, for I believe that when I see Orcolo all will be explained."

" Oreolo the bravo ?"

" The same."

" He usually makes sure work enough."

" He does. The only thing that puzzles me is that I cannot find the dead body any-where in the garden."

" Oh, that is nothin g."

" Nothing ?"

" Nothing at all. Bravos often, especially if they are in danger of being disturbed, carry off a body to strip it at leisure, and then cast it into one of the canals with a stone tied round the neck. Make yourself comfortable. I have no doubt but that your rival has been so served."

" Perhaps so,"

" I should conclude so."

" Well, Flavius, I know you have experience of these things, so I will give myself no further uneasiness upon such a subject, but look upon it as safely concluded as your little affair with the Count Gradunio."

" The odious villains !" whispered Jerome to the count.

" Hush ! Hush ! Hush !"

" Pass me the wine," said Gordoni.

" Ah, you have a stronger head than I," said Flavius, " I am afraid to drink so soon in the morning."

" It is all habit."

" Well, I suppose it is, but at all events let us to business. Listen to me."

CHAPTER XX.

THE GUILTY CONFERENCE CONTINUED.

THE count and his faithful gondolier listened attentively while the two villains, Flavius and Gordoni, arranged and recounted their diabolical plans and contrivances.

" I think," said Flavius, " with you, that the day will surely come when a discovery of my defalcations as grand treasurer will take place."

" Yes. Yes."

" Then, of course the most obvious policy in the world will be for us to make off before that time arrives."

" Unquestionably."

" Being thus so far agreed, the question arises of where shall we go in order to be in perfect safety."

" I suggest England."

" Well, I don't suppose that any one will look for us there. What do you say to freighting a ship as if for some trading purpose, and getting on board of it all the money and valuables we can, and then being off suddenly when least suspected of such a movement ?"

"I have no objection. We have got rid of the Count Gradunio and of Stralani. Of course you quite understand that I must bring to a conclusion my affair with my uncle and the Count Syracuse's daughter."

"I hear you say so."

"But do not like to hear it."

"I own that I am somewhat surprised and vexed to find a man of your penetration giving way to a mere boyish passion for a girl in her nonage."

"We are not all constituted alike, Flavius. She has taken upon herself to despise me and my suit, and it shall be my care to make her dearly rue the having done so."

"Well, well."

"I am firm as a rock upon this point."

"I shall not seek to turn you from it. Do you mean to run off with Floranthe?"

"Yes, by fair means or by foul, I will do so. Last evening, when she found that her gay gallant had met with a disaster, she treated me and the count with a touch of madness."

"Indeed!"

"Yes; and I took the opportunity of recommending her immediate removal to the Convent of the Ursulines, where she now is, and where to-night I mean to pay her a visit. The abbess and I fully understand each other upon that subject."

"Ah! she is an accommodating abbess."

"When well paid."

"A highly proper condition."

"Well, probably so. I suppose we all have our price."

"All, you may depend. At least it is so in Venice."

"And no doubt elsewhere. But come, Flavius, we seldom visit this room without being the richer for it. Shall we go through the secret panel, and seek the doge's treasury this morning?"

"With all my heart."

"By the bye, you never told me exactly how the Count Gradunio came to discover your defalcations."

"It was a simple enough affair. In times of old this palazzo belonged to the doge himself."

"So I have heard."

"Well, it appears there was a private communication from this room into the vaults beneath the ducal palace, which you know adjoins this, where the treasures in gold and jewels of the state are kept."

"And the count found it out."

"He must have done so, for while I was in the vaults once at midnight he suddenly came upon me."

"You were alarmed?"

"Almost to fainting on the spot."

"What said he?"

"Why, with all the self-possession in the world, he said that as he was sitting in this room of his mansion, he heard the noise of some mice behind the arras, and upon rising to scare them away, and tearing down an old picture, he found a spring, upon touching which a door flew open. He took a lamp and pursued the passage, until he came to the vaults where he found me."

" Do you believe the tale ?"

" I do. For upon accurately examining the gold, I found that not an ounce was missing but what I had myself from time to time removed."

"You will remember that, Jerome?" whispered Count Gradunio, in the ear of the gondolier.

" I shall indeed," he replied in the same cautious tone.

" It struck me thus afterwards," continued Flavius, " that I could make a capital use of the finding of Count Gradunio in the vaults."

" Ah, no doubt."

" I thought that by secretly denouncing him to the senate I could easily transfer all my robberies of the gold of the state to his account."

" No doubt you could."

"I denounced him—I stated to the secret meeting of the senate, that, going as was my custom to the vaults, to take an account of the treasure committed to my care, I found him there. That he tried to escape ; but that I followed him until I saw by what means he had made his way into the vaults."

" That sealed his fate ?"

" It did. He was in the course of the day seized and confined in one of the dungeons of the Bridge of Sighs."

" Well managed."

" Yes. The only annoyance to me was, that although up to that point I had got rid of all my liabilities, the senate, out of a real or an affected regard for me, took an accurate list of all the contents of the vaults, so that all that we have taken since will lie at my door."

" Assuredly."

" For which reason it is that I would fly to England shortly, taking with me what I can."

" Agreed. I hope in a few days to be in a condition to accompany you, and what is more, I am inclined to think that I know of a vessel which will take us."

" You please me much.—Can you trust the captain ?"

" Trust! No ; I never trust any one, except I cannot help it—I can deceive him."

" Which will do as well."

" Much better. But come let us descend to the ducal vaults, and get some treasure at all events ready packed up for deportation."

" Agreed."

Jerome was naturally enough full of curiosity to see by what means these two worthies contrived to get from the little chamber to the vaults, in which were kept the costly treasures of the state of Venice ; but the tapestry, behind which he and the Count Gradunio were, effectually shrouded the room from his view.

" Be patient," whispered the count, who saw he was making exertions to find some place at which he might see through. " Be patient, I will show you all that there is to see at some more fitting time and opportunity."

"Pardon my curiosity," replied Jerome.

"It requires no pardon—it is natural enough. Let them go, and then we can enter the room."

Both Jerome and the count now listened attentively to what was now going on in the little apartment; but they heard no more conversation, and the death-like stillness that ensued convinced the latter that Gordoni and Flavius had indeed descended to the vaults.

Still he was cautious how he moved aside the tapestry, and only took a wary peep into the room at first, in order to assure himself that it was tenantless.

"Come, Jerome," he then said, "we have the place to ourselves at last, and may speak more freely."

They both entered the room, and the count looked about him most curiously and anxiously.

"It is so long a time seemingly," he said, "and yet so short a time in reality, since I have been in this apartment, that I am full of strange feelings, now that, contrary to all my expectations while I was a prisoner in the Bridge of Sighs I again see it."

"It seems new to you, signor."

"New and old at the same time, Jerome; but what have we here, a pocket-book?"

The count, as he spoke, took from the table a kind of memorandum-book, on the first leaf of which were the initials J. J. F., meaning Jacques Justin Flavius. A moment's careful examination of it showed the count that it contained a list of the robberies by Flavius upon the doge's treasures.

"Behold, Jerome," he said, "how by a strange perversity of intellect this man has actually recorded his own villany in this book, and in his own hand-writing."

"Strange indeed, signor ; and yet I have heard it said that no man ever commits a crime without, in some way or the other, providing a means by which it may be found out, and brought home to him."

"I do believe it."

"It would seem, signor, in this instance to be true."

"I think, Jerome, it is always. It is one of those strange providential conditions of our being in this world, and from which man can no more escape, than he can from the penalty of death, that consequential follower of life."

"What will you do with the book, my lord ?"

"Preserve it carefully ; and yet upon second thoughts, Jerome, you shall take care of t, for when I accuse Flavius, as truly I intend to do before the senate, I can and will call you as a witness to the facts of his villany."

"You could not find a more willing witness than I, signor. I shall indeed rejoice when the hour comes that I shall be called upon to depose to what I know."

"Perhaps it would be better that some members of the Venetian senate should actually themselves be witnesses of the conduct of Gordoni and Flavius in the vaults."

"It would indeed."

"Then nothing can be more easily managed, Jerome. Let us retire at present and hear what they have to say when they reappear. In the meantime we can keep possession of the pocket-book, as part proof of the affair."

" A good plan, signor."

" You may depend, Jerome, that they will not separate without making some ppointment for another predatory excursion into the vaults."

" Hush, hush ! They come."

The count listened, and heard distinctly the sound both of voices and approaching ootsteps, so with Jerome, he thought it prudent at once to retire behind the tapestry again.

They had scarcely securely obtained that position, and disposed themselves to listen to what might take place, when Gordoni and Flavius reappeared, loaded with two bags, no doubt containing gold and jewels.

" Let these," said Flavius to Gordoni, " be bestowed somewhere in a place of safety until we make up our minds to leave Venice."

" Trust me for that," replied Gordoni. " Are you sure you have all the ewels ?"

" Certain. Close the secret door. I do hope nothing will happen amiss."

" How can it ?"

" Not easily, certainly; but you know, Gordoni, that when so much is at stake one is apt to be a little fearful or so."

" Pshaw ! Throw fear to the dogs."

" Have you seen my pocket-book anywhere ? I'm quite sure I had it."

" A plague take your pocket-book—what should I know of it, I should like to know ? Let us arrange when our next visit is to be."

" When you please, but not to-morrow. You are aware that from my house about a month ago, my youngest daughter mysteriously disappeared, and to-morrow I am going to visit many places where I offered rewards for her recovery, to find if they have any traces of her."

" Ah, doubtless she has followed some wayward fancy of her heart, and you will one day hear of her with a petition, ostensibly for forgiveness, but really for cash."

" It may be so. To-day is Wednesday — suppose we meet here again on Satur-day ?"

" Agreed ; name your hour."

" Midnight."

" Well, it matters not to me—I am not so scared at midnight as many are. I think it quiet, well-disposed, and gentlemanly hour enough."

" Come away," whispered the Count Gradunio to Jerome. " We have now heard all we wish to hear—come away, and it shall go hard indeed with me if I do not give these two villains a welcome in the vaults, on Saturday next, such as they little wish or expect."

———

CHAPTER XXI.

FLORANTHE'S PERIL IN THE CONVENT CHAPEL.

RETURN we to Floranthe, whom we left in quite sufficiently dangerous circumstances to excite our livliest sympathy, and to induce us to follow her fortunes as speedily as the sayings and doings of the other personages of our story will admit.

"We left her panting, and nearly breathless in the cell, from the door of which she had managed to extract the key, and to hide it.

The trampling of feet, and the sound of angry voices, were every moment coming more plainly upon her ears, and before she could be said to be sufficiently recovered from her hurried flight, a flash of light came into her cell, and through the open doorway she saw come, if not all, her convent enemies.

There was the abbess, and there was the confessor—Father Magas, as well as Rene and the two nuns, who like a body guard waited upon the abbess, in readiness to obey, to, e very possible extent, her behests.

Some vague ideas of danger seemed to possess the abbess, for she certainly held back, pushing on the confessor before her, whose tolerably bulky form operated as a pretty good bulwark.

When, however, she saw that Floranthe did not appear disposed to offer any resistance, she advanced to the front of the party, and in a voice of passion she said—

"How dare you, within the wall of this convent, behave yourself in a manner to scandalize all its blessed and holy inmates ? I say, how dare you?"

Floranthe thought it far beneath her to make any reply to this, and she consequently by remaining silent roused the ire of the abbess to an almost ungovernable pitch, so that she absolutely stamped with rage.

"Minion," she exclaimed, "answer me instantly."

Still Floranthe was silent.

"This conduct, daughter," said the confessor in a hypocritical whining tone, "is most unpleasant and contumacious."

"It is exceedingly wrong," said Rene.

"Oh, very, very," echoed the two nuns, who cast up their eyes as if they fully expected the roof to fall in as a signal judgment upon Floranthe.

"Very well," said the abbess, when she found that no effect was produced upon Floranthe by what was said, "very well, leave her to her silence."

"Certainly," said Rene.

"Oh, of course," said the two nuns.

And added the abbess, with a smile of malignancy upon her countenance, "and I will make it her own act that she suffers by silence."

They all looked curiously at the abbess, for they well knew, by her manner, that some diabolical ingenuity was hatching in her brain.

"What is the hour ?" she said to the confessor.

"It is nine," he replied.

"You hear," added the abbess, turning to Floranthe, "it is now nine in the evening; You shall yourself name the hour when more food and water shall be brought to you. If you persist in keeping silent, you cannot expect any, and your death by starvation will be the result of your own most criminal obstinacy."

The abbess looked exceedingly triumphant as she gave utterance to these words which she thought must have the effect of putting an end to Floranthe's silence.

When, however, she found that it had no such effect, she got quite furious, and boun cing out of the cell, she cried—

"Lock her in—lock her in."

"Yes, lock her in," said Rene.

"To be sure," said the two nuns ; "lock her in."

This was evidently easier said than done, for although everybody looked in the keyhole and upon the ground for the key, it was not forthcoming.

"The Chevalier Gordoni no doubt has it," whispered Rene to the abbess. "But there is the bar."

"To be sure. Bar the door securely, and that will be amply sufficient fastening."

The confessor went close to Floranthe, and in a whisper he said to her, so that no one else heard—

"I can save you."

She returned him no answer.

"Give me but one look of consent, and I will come in two hours' time and restore you to liberty."

The glance of unutterable scorn that she cast upon him was such that he could not mistake, and he drew back muttering between his clenched teeth—

"Be it so—I will have revenge."

Turning then to the abbess, he said aloud—

"I have met with many a hardened sinner, but never one like this. My opinion is that she is a rank heretic, which is the reason why the evil one has such a world of power over her."

"No doubt," said the abbess.

"It must be so," said Rene.

"Of course," cried the two nuns.

"The melancholy conviction that such is the fact," groaned the monk, "has been gaining upon me some time; and experienced as I am in wrestling with the evil one, I can see enough to put it beyond all doubt."

"Dreadful!" said the abbess; and then in a whisper to the confessor, she added, "we must not put our pious threats in execution, for the Chevalier Gordoni would not thank us for a half or wholly starved mistress."

"Certainly not, and yet she is very, very obdurate."

"She is indeed. Let us leave her now, and close her cell door as best we may."

The monk lingered yet a moment to see if upon the countenance of Floranthe he could observe any sign of relenting or faltering in her determination—there was none; and then angrily he closed the door upon her, and put up the heavy bar behind it, which he and the abbess thought would surely be as sufficient a guard against her exit as any lock possibly could, and perhaps much more so.

It was a great relief to Floranthe to be once more alone, even in that cell, for solitude of any character was preferable to the society of those who had just left her, and with whom she had such just and sufficient cause to quarrel.

She set about thinking what it would be best for her to attempt to do.

That she was not dismayed at the fact of the barring put across the door of her cell arose from a very simple circumstance, namely, that she thought she could manage to remove it.

From whence she derived this expectation, we shall very shortly perceive.

Knowing the deep duplicity of those with whom she had to contend, and having seen their evident anxiety to bring her to some sort of terms, she waited awhile for fear either the monk or the abbess should return to the cell, to make another attempt to move her resolution. But while she did so wait, for fear it should be the former who might come, she took care to have the poniard of Gordoni handy to her grasp, and she would not, in the excited state of her feelings, been backward in using it.

Time wore on, however, and no one came to disturb the quiet of her cell.

An hour might have thus passed away before Floranthe arose and prepared for action.

She had noticed that the door of the cell was of very rough materials and workmanship, and, that, when closed, there was a chink or opening left, through which a glare of light from the lamps carried by the two nuns had penetrated. Now the dagger which she had, and which belonged to Gordoni, was a long, powerfully-shaped weapon, and she thought it more than probable that its blade would pass between the door and the wall, so that, if she had strength sufficient for the task, she might be able to lift the bar and displace it.

It was the idea of being able to do this which made her so calm and hopeful.

She thought that if she could leave her own cell and then release the young novice from hers, they might between them, encouraging and assisting each other, be able to devise some means of effectual escape from the precincts of the convent together.

Filled with this hope, dim and indistinct as it was, Floranthe, with hands trembling with eagerness, commenced making the attempt to open the door of the cell.

She found that the dagger would easily enough pass through the clink between the door and the wall; but the bar was so heavy that at the first effort she made to raise it, her heart failed her, and she thought that it was far beyond her power to do so.

She was very disadvantageously situated to bring any strength to bear upon the bar, but after the pause of a few moments, during which she told herself that unless she did succeed in what she was about, all her hopes of escape would be at an end, she renewed her efforts.

The bar yielded—she knew if she could but raise it a few inches it would in all probability fall; and she made the effort. Slowly it gave way, and then with a heavy dull sound it fell from its hold, and the door was free.

"Oh, joy, joy!" exclaimed Floranthe. "I can at least make now an effort for liberty. If I can but gain the chapel I shall surely find some means of leaving it. Perhaps the convent-garden may be reached; and then it shall not be the height of a wall, no, nor the frowns of the portress, that shall keep me within the bounds of this most hateful building."

CHAPTER XXII.

STRALANI'S RECOVERY.—THE FRIENDS.

It will be remembered that some short time after the wounded Stralani had found a refuge in the porter's cottage, in the garden of the Count Syracuse's palace, there came a violent knocking at the outer door of the little building.

This knocking continued for several moments without intermission, and created in the breasts of the porter and his daughter, Pauline, the greatest alarm, for they could not help thinking that it had some relation to the wounded youth, towards whom all their sympathies were directed.

"Oh, father, father!" cried Pauline; "they come to kill him!"

"Hush—hush!"

"Yes. Hark—hark. There again."

Bang—bang—bang! came upon the door of the small abode, and with a force that was really sufficient to break down the frail defence against intruders.

"Open the door," cried a voice from without, "open the door instantly, or dread my anger."

"Gracious Heaven! it is the voice of the count himself," cried the porter. "What is to be done?"

"Father, our guest must be saved."

"But how, my child?"

"I will conceal myself, and you can throw some articles of my apparel upon the bed where he sleeps, and say 'tis I am there reposing. Even the Count Syracuse must respect the sanctity of my chamber."

Bang—bang—bang! came again at the door.

"A happy thought!" said the porter. "Hide yourself at once, my child—hide yourself at once."

Pauline crept into a huge press which was half filled with old lumber, and there awaited, in the greatest possible anxiety, the issue of the next few minutes.

The porter flung upon the bed where Stralani lay various articles of Pauline's attire, and likewise enveloped his head as well as he could in a small cap of lace she was wont to wear. Then casting off his outer garments so as to appear only half dressed, he hurried to the door and opened it.

The Count Syracuse and Gordoni stood upon the threshold.

"How now," cried the count, "why were we kept waiting?"

"My lord, I am old, and slow in dressing."

"Were you not up?"

"No, my lord; I have passed but a disturbed night."

"Ah!" cried Gordoni, "a disturbed night, how was that?"

"My daughter has been sick."

"Humph! listen to me."

"I will, noble sir."

"Did you hear no one in the garden during the night?—Did you not assist some one who was wounded to leave the place? It says in your favour if you did. Answer truly."

"Wounded, my lord? Any one wounded? Goodness gracious, how pleased I should be to assist any wounded friend of yours; but how could any one be wounded in this garden?"

"What do you think?" whispered the count to Gordoni. "He knows nothing, surely."

"I am not so sure. Come, master porter, we must look through your house, if you please."

"Certainly, my house and all I have belongs to the noble Count Syracuse, my master, and if he and any friends of his will cross my humble threshold I am much honoured."

The three rooms in the house were soon looked into, and when they came to the chamber where Stralani lay sleeping, the porter said—

"My daughter's chamber, signor, into which I even do not intrude."

Gordoni just looked in, and then with an oath he took the arm of the count, saying—

"Come away, we only waste time here."

In a short time after they were gone the physician and Pauline sat by the bed side of Stralani, in earnest conversation together.

"Ah," said Pauline, " he will surely die."

"Do you think so?" said the physician.

"Behold him!"

"It is true that blood is upon him, but that will soon wash away; and I say to you boldly, that unless some untoward accident put back the progress of his cure within the next few hours, he shall not die."

"It is as Heaven pleases," said the old porter.

"Amen!" said the Jew. "Heaven is a kind of neutral ground, on which the Jew and Gentile may meet in peace."

"Hush," said Pauline, " what noise is that?"

They all listened, and in a few moments there came the sound of voices and footsteps upon their ears.

"Another search," said the porter, "another search. Hide yourself, Pauline, that we may deceive those who would seek the blood of the innocent."

"What can be done," said the physician; " is that youth really in danger from his enemies?"

"We have reason to think so, sir."

"He is lost!" cried Pauline.

"Why do you say so, my child?"

"Oh, father, you may depend that the wily Gordoni, who looked with an air of so much suspicion into the chamber where you said I was sleeping, has thought that he would have better assurance that it was indeed me. Our guest is lost."

"If it be so, he is lost, indeed," said the porter.

"What is the meaning of all this," said the Jew, as he looked with surprise from one to the other of them, " you speak in riddles to me; explain I pray you, as briefly as you can, what is the nature of the difficulty you are in regarding this affair."

"Hark, hark!" said the porter, "they will break the door. Oh, what will become of us?"

In a few brief and hurried sentences, Pauline related what had occurred to the physician, who at once therefrom comprehended the difficulty.

"It may be," he said, "that the enemies of the poor wounded youth have come back full of suspicion that he and not you occupied the bed, and the way to save him is for us all, with what care we can, to place him in the old wardrobe or press where you hid before."

"I see—I see," cried Pauline, " I will actually occupy the bed where he now lies."

"Precisely."

"Open—open," cried the Count Syracuse, from without—"open, or by all they saints in the calendar, I will smash down your door. Open, I say, open directly, do you pretend now to be sleeping?"

"Never heed him," said the physician, calmly. "Let us carefully remove our patient; I am glad he sleeps soundly. He will continue so for some little time longer."

The knocking continued at the door, but the Jew physician without the least appearance of hurry, and yet with really great celerity, assisted the porter to carry Stralani into the press, where, placing some clothes over him, he was tolerably well secured from observation.

During the few moments occupied by that process Pauline placed herself in the bed, and feigned to be asleep in the posture that Stralani had been.

"Now open the door," said the physician.

The porter, who was trembling with fright and excitement, advanced for the purpose of doing so, but he was spared the trouble, for at that moment the lock was forced, and Gordoni, with frenzy in his aspect, stood upon the threshold.

"What is the meaning of this?" he cried. "I am convinced my suspicions will be confirmed. My Lord Syracuse, I pray you walk in, and convict this porter of yours of lying. My suspicions will be confirmed, I am certain."

"What suspicions, signor?" said the physician, advancing and speaking in a cold, calm, dispassionate tone.

Both the Count Syracuse and Gordoni glared at him with fury in their looks, as he stood so cool and immoveable before them, confronting them with his keen, grey eyes.

"A Jew," said Gordoni.

"Yes, a Jew," said the physician.

"And no doubt alien to the state of Venice. You shall be punished, depend upon it."

"By what authority?"

"Mine," said the count. "I will have you arrested. A Jew may be arrested in Venice, and made to give account of himself."

"Granted. But as I hold an authority from the senate, to practise medicine in Venice according to the law, I apprehend I shall find protection from the laws."

"A physician are you?"

"Ay."

"A sham one. Can you cure all disorders with some quack nostrum? You shall have me for a patient."

"No," said the Jew, "I decline you for a patient; vitiated and rotten hearts and brains I do not cure."

"Villain!"

"Which I am not."

"Now by our Lady!——"

"Peace, peace!" said the count. "If this Jew be a physician, what does he here? That is the question."

"Well," said Gordoni, repressing his anger for a moment,' "what does he here ? That may be the first question."

" Practising my profession."

" Upon whom ?" cried Gordoni with eagerness. " A wounded cavalier, I'll be bound. If so, there is my purse for you, and we are much beholden to you."

" Oh very much," said the count, " and there, too, is my purse."

" What a pity," said the physician, " that I cannot earn two purses, and so many thanks. I attend merely a sick girl."

"'Tis false."

" Very well. As you please."

" This is the tale by which we were before imposed upon," said Gordoni, " but it will not stand the test of a little reflection.   I will satisfy myself who is in yon chamber ?"

" It is my daughter, signor," said the porter.

Gordoni, closely followed by the count, rudely pushed past the old man, and entrd the bed-room, his drawn sword in his hand, fully intending to fini h thelaying of Stralani, if he should find him lying there wounded."

"Is it you, father ?" said Pauline, looking up.

" Confound you all," cried Gordoni, as he dashed past the door of the room. " It is the girl."

" Come away—come away," said the count, plucking him by the sleeve, "we only expose ourselves to further gossip and animadversion, by remaining here."

" Command their silence," muttered the disappointed Gordoni, as he violently sheathed his sword.

" You understand me," said the Count Cyracuse, to the porter. " This affair goes no further."

" Certainly not, my lord."

Gordoni and the count then abruptly left the little lodge. The former muttering as he went the most diabolical oaths against everything and everybody.

In the course of a few minutes, now, the still sleeping Stralani was carefully lifted from the press, and placed in the bed again, while Pauline shed tears of joy at the success of the manœuvre which had been resorted to to save him from those who without a doubt would have triumphed and gloried in his destruction.

" How much we owe to you !" she said to the Jew physician.

" Not at all," he replied, " say no more upon that head. The wounded youth will soon awaken, and I will wait until he does so—or rather, I will walk in the garden, so that if there should be any approach of danger in the next quarter of an hour, I can let you know."

During the absence of the Jew, Stralani opened his eyes, and seeing Pauline hovering about him, was able, after a pause, to tell who he was, as well as to hear from her the particulars of all that had happened to him since his wound.

It was quite wonderful to see how much recovered Stralani was, and when the Jew physician arrived and found his patient looking about him with quite a calm expression, he smiled as he said in kindly accents,—

"Ah, you will not yet, my young friend, make a feast for the worms."

"Thanks to you, no," said Stralani.

"Be still; you made just now an attempt to move. Now, I warn you that any premature getting up will be the death of you."

"Indeed!"

"Yes, I have no sort of objection to tell you that my mode of cure, known only to myself, requires for its perfecting the most absolute rest that can be conceived. You must obey me in that particular."

"I will," said Stralani.

"You will do wisely."

The physician smiled, as he took from his pocket a small bottle, and pouring the contents into a cup that was near at hand, he said, quietly,—

"Drink."

Stralani took the potion, and then, after making a vain effort to speak, he fell back upon his pillow in a deep sleep.

"That will do better," said the physician, than the agitation of such a transcending passion."

<hr/>

CHAPTER XXIII.

FLORANTHE AND THE NOVICE REACH THE CONVENT GARDEN.

We left Floranthe at the moment when, having got from her cell successfully, she was exulting at the newly awakened hopes of freedom that dawned upon her mind. After overcoming many dangers and difficulties, she reached the convent garden, and found out the cell in which Julia was confined. They left the cell together, determined to make a vigorous attempt to liberate themselves, when they heard confused murmurs, as if they came from several persons. This noise was occasioned by the lady abbess and her accomplices, who were preparing to celebrate a forced marriage between Floranthe and Gordoni. After the preparations had been completed, the group left the chapel and turned in [the direction of Floranthe. In endeavouring to fly from the spot, Floranthe trod on the lamp, and fell to the ground. Had it not [been for this unlucky accident, no doubt Floranthe would have escaped; as she fell, she hurriedly uttered "Fly, Julia!" but the young novice chose rather to share the danger of Floranthe, than leave her at such a critical juncture. [The fall of Floranthe quickly brought the abbess, Gordoni, the monk, and the nuns to the spot where she lay. The abbess ordered her to be dragged into the chapel forthwith, and the nuns, with savage joy, did [her bidding. While at the altar she was informed by the [abbess that she would soon leave the convent as the wife of Gordoni; and he told her to look round and see the witnesses that were prepared to swear to the ceremony having been performed.

"As a result of all this," he added "you will be mine, Floranthe."

"Never—never."

"As you say, and as you fancy, Floranthe. There is the altar, there is the priest, and here is the bridegroom."

"Can you be so mad as well as so base, as to fancy that I am to be terrified into the pronunciation of vows which my heart abhors. You know me not, Gordoni."

"Floranthe," he added with an odious smile of triumph, "I have taken my measures. I have set my wit up against your obstinacy, we shall soon see which is the stronger."

Floranthe was silent, and he proceeded.

"You shall be mine, and the choice you have left you is not whether or not you will be mine, but whether you will be so in a manner that will cast no blemish upon your name, or otherwise."

Still Floranthe was completely in the dark as to what he could possibly mean. The abbess showed some signs of impatience, and Gordoni added rather hastily,—

"All here present, with the one exception of that young girl, who hangs upon your arm, have come to be witnesses to your marriage with me in the convent chapel. If you consent and we are duly married by this holy man, Father Magas, all will be well, but if you still presist in your refusal, you will find that the witnesses will do you good, despite your own obstinacy, and will depose to the marriage having taken place."

" No—no !"

" In which case," added Gordoni, raising his voice, as he saw he had produced some effect upon Floranthe. " In which case the laws of Venice will give you to me."

" Impossible !"

" And yet true. Now you know your real position, and may or may not profit by the knowledge as you may think most fit, and proper for your condition.'

" There cannot be such combined baseness in six persons," said Floranthe. " One man such as you, or such as that base hypocritical monk there might steep to such perdition, but I cannot believe that this abbess and her nuns, cruel as they are, dare aid you in such a frightful and unholy business."

" If that be all your ground of hope, 'tis time that you began to despair."

" This young girl's deposition, that the diabolical scheme was declared from your lips will yet defeat you."

" She never leaves the cells of this convent," said the abbess, " with life. I know not by what means exactly you and she are together here; but this I do know, that your escape now, had you not been interrupted as you have, would have been a thing beyond all human possibility. We care not if Julia be or be not a witness. Perchance we may make her yet suffer sufficiently to induce her to add her testimony to that of all others that the ceremony did take place."

" Oh no—no—no," cried Julia. " Do you believe this of me, Floranthe ?"

"Not for a moment."

" I would rather die."

" Do not pain me by avowing so base an insinuation, Julia. We know ourselves that it is impossible."

" Quite impossible—quite—quite."

" We shall see," said the abbess. " Drag her to the altar."

The two nuns made violent efforts to drag Floranthe along the chapel floor, but not until the abbess herself aided them could they succeed in so doing; and even then the task would have been more difficult, if Floranthe had not dreaded that the monk would likewise interpose. And after all, she being dragged to the altar was but a small matter, for when there, no human power could force her to repeat names so repugnant in all respects to her feelings, and so contrary to the remotest probability. Nevertheless, with an impious and a hideous mockery of the ceremony they wished to desecrate, the monk and Gordoni took up their stations, and the former actually began to read the marriage service. This was an outrage of so monstrous a character, that although Floranthe felt, conscious that all appeals either to the fears or to the consciences of those who were about her would be useless, she yet could not resist the utterance of some words in the hope of a protest against the frightful proceedings.

"There must," she said, "come a day of retribution for this desecration of Heaven's altar. Pause, oh pause, while yet there is time to do so."

The monk proceeded with the service. Julia burst into a passion of tears, and flinging herself at the feet of the abbess, she cried,—"You are a woman! and cannot surely be destitute of all feeling. What can you gain by these proceedings, which might not be more than doubled by abstaining from them? Oh, think of your condition in that world which is to come."

"Indeed."

"Yes, and where of those who have been placed in situations such as yours, surely a most exact account of their trust will be required?"

"I do not think," said the abbess, with a sneer, "that you better your condition in this world by any allusions to what mine may be in that doubtful one which is, doubtlessly, as you say, to come."

Julia shuddered, and so did Floranthe, as these words at once indicated the impiety and want of belief of the abbess in the very first conditions of that religion which she professed. Appeal to such a heart must be in vain.

"Proceed with the ceremony," added the abbess.

The monk shook so that he could hardly perform his part in the detestable farce he had undertaken.

"Aye, proceed," cried Gordoni, "proceed with that ceremony which makes me the happy bridegroom of the loveliest maiden in all Venice!"

Gordoni made the necessary responses, but Floranthe, although she was compelled to stand by the altar, and there held by the two nuns and by Rene, who lent a helping hand to the base business, said not one word.

At length, with a trembling voice, the monk pronounced the benediction, and the ceremony was over.

"My bride," said Gordoni, with a sickly smile, "will not refuse one kiss to him who——"

"No, no," cried Floranthe, "do not dare to lay a hand upon me—there is pollution in your touch."

At this moment a loud scream came upon the ears of all who were in the chapel, and then the alarm bell of the convent began to ring violently.

The abbess started, and the whole of the guilty persons there present looked at each other with dismay; Floranthe and Julia alone were glad of any interruption.

CHAPTER XXXV.

THE DOGE'S CHAMBER.—AN UNEXPECTED VISITOR.

LEAVING, for a time, Floranthe and our fair young friend Julia, the enforced novice, in the Convent of the Ursulines, it becomes necessary that we should conduct the reader to a very different scene, indeed, although not a stone's throw from that place.

The ancient Palace of St. Mark, in which resided the then Doge of Venice, occupied a considerable portion of the grand square, and with its white glistening front, and apparently interminable rows of windows, is one of the most striking, if not one of the most picturesque objects in Venice. The residence of the Count Gradunio so closely adjoined the doge's palace, that some of the walls of each were common to both ; therefore the secret passage which led from a portion of the count's mansion to the vaults beneath the doge's palace, where was stowed much of the treasures of the state, need not have been of very great extent. That this secret entrance to the vaults was now well known to the doge, of course we may suppose; but now that, as it was thought, the Count Gradunio was safely got rid of, the secret of its existence was presumed to rest in the bosoms of the doge, the Council of Senators, and the Grand Treasurer, Flavius. It was not thought necessary to dispossess Gordoni, who had claimed the palace by right of kinship, by force, but ever since he had been in possession overtures had been made to him from the state to purchase it. The reasons assigned by the doge and the council for wishing to possess it, was that it was so close to the Palace of St. Mark, that a little alteration would suffice to make it part and parcel of that building. Of course, Gordoni and Flavius both knew well enough that it was in consequence of the secret passage affording so advantageous a facility to any one visiting the vaults and even the Palace of St. Mark itself, which made the state so desirous to possess the building. It would not have done for Gordoni, much as private property and the right appertaining to it, were protected in Venice, to return a rough refusal to the state, but nothing was easier than by one excuse and another, to protract the negociation. It was the policy of him and Flavius to do so until they were ready to fly to England with their booty. Little did they imagine the mine on which they stood, and that the Count Gradunio, whom they supposed safely deposited in the canal, and held down until decomposition should destroy all chance even of recognition of his body, by the weight of his chains, was actually keepng a weary eye upon them both. Little did they dream of the storm that was so soon about to burst over them, at a time when they thought the sky of their fortunes was most serene and cloudless. The Count Gradunio was, as the reader has already seen, a man of the most consummate tact and courage, no enterprise in his hands' was likely to fail from demanding a large amount of coolness and intrepidity. The plan that he now adopted for the purpose of arresting Gordoni and Flavius, and actually entangling them in their own toils, was one which few in his position would ever have dared to think of. He had always been personally and politically opposed to the present Doge of Venice, and something almost in the shape of positive enmity subsisted between them. It was the enmity of men of honour, for the Count Gradunio could not stoop to any unworthy action, and the doge had too much pride of birth and station about him to think of anything even against a foe which savoured of dishonour. So far they were well enough watched, but under the circumstances many would have hesitated to do what the count did. What that was, will best shew itself in the performance which we now proceed with. It was night, and the guard had been, as was customary, doubled outside the palace of the doge. There was but few gondolas about the principal canal of the city, and only now and then, from some small vessel which tarried beneath the window of some loved object, might be heard the faint music of some guitar. The moon, at times only, for the sky was cloudy, shed her silvery ray upon the City of Romance, while in the few spots, where space for walking could be found, there might be seen flitting along the bravo and his victim. A monk too, occasionally would shew himself from out the deep shadow of some door-way, and with a muttered and solemn sounding Benedicite to the chance passenger, he might meet, would pass on to shrive some dying wretch, who would have thought it dreadful to leave this world without the prayers and the absolution of one probably a ten times worse sinner than himself. The pages of honour slept or played lazily at tric-trac in the ante-chambers of the Palace of St. Mark. The halberdiers pursued their solitary march along the galleries, and the guard at the grand entrance beguiled the time as best they might, thinking it hard that they could not eat to a greater extent the bread of idleness than they did. The sleeping room of the doge, was the last one of a suite of rooms on the first floor of the palace—that first floor being the highest likewise for the regal residence has no higher flights.—It was behind, and indeed may be said to be well-known that there were secret modes of quitting the doge's chambers, but such were always in the hands only of the chief magistrates for the time being. At all events there did not appear to be any way of getting to the doge's chamber but by passing through the suite of rooms of which it formed one and the last, so that all the security possible was thrown around the person of the doge. Doubtless he there slept securely enough in his own estimation, for if in one of the chambers adjoining to him, those whose duty it was to watch chanced to sleep, it was not likely that such should be the case in all of them. At rather an earlier hour than usual, the doge had retired to rest. The last person he had given an audience to on that day, was Flavius the treasurer. Probably at that audience the supposed fate of the Count Gradunio had been conversed upon, for as Flavius left the doge's presence, he muttered to himself—

"Strange that he should seem so much to regret the fate of one who was always to him an uncompromising, although open enough enemy."

This was the very reason. It was because the Count Gradunio had always been an open enemy that the doge respected him, and entertained no serious apprehensions of him or his actions. This, however, was a refinement upon animosity which was totally incomprehensible to Flavius and Gordoni, who only looked to the broad fact of a man being an enemy, and then judging of all human nature from themselves, they devoutly believed that he would do anything, either open or secret, to compass some scheme of revenge against his foe. The doge knew the Count Gradunio better, and formed a most just estimate of him accordingly. We will now follow the actions of the Count Gradunio during the evening following the day upon which he had first taken refuge in the humble home of Jerome, the gondolier. When twelve o'clock at night had been given forth from the huge clock in the church tower of St. Olives, the count summoned Jerome to him, and said, "Now, Jerome, I am going upon a dangerous expedition, and it is one upon which you cannot accompany me."

Jerome's countenance fell as he heard these words, and with a dejected air, he replied to them. "Alas, my honoured master, cannot I have the privilege of sharing your danger?"

"Not always, Jerome, although I do hope you may always have the privilege of sharing my good fortune, my safety, and my success."

"Well, my lord, what you please to say must be my law, but am I to do nothing?"

"Nothing, Jerome. It has appeared to me after the whole day's consideration of the circumstances in which I am placed that nothing would be better than a final interview with the doge."

"The doge, your enemy?"

"Yes. But my honourable enemy ever, Jerome."

"Alas! I fear."

"I do not. Come, Jerome, do not think so badly of people, I am quite sure that if the doge will only fairly listen to what I have to say, all will be well; but if he were to make me over to some members of the council, I should not have justice done to me in this world."

"And that is what he will do, signor."

"If he can."

"And how is he to be hindered, my noble master?"

"I hope to be able to hinder him."

"Alas, what power have we?"

"Listen to me, Jerome, I have reason from a variety of circumstances to believe that there is a passage from the vaults where the Doge's treasure is kept into his own sleeping chamber."

"Indeed."

"Yes. And my present intention is to go down into the vaults to-night, and endeavour to find that passage. If I be successful, I will enforce the Doge, as he lies in his bed, to grant me a private audience."

"And may not I accompany you?"

"Well, I see no harm that can result from your going to the vaults with me, but certainly no further."

"My lord, if I can only go one step, I shall think that much better than the not being permitted to go at all."

"Then let us be off."

Jerome was ready at once, but he first went into the house to make inquiry, so as to be sure that Gordoni nor Flavius were there. He heard that Gordoni had not been seen for many hours, and that Flavius, although he had been about ten o'clock in the place, was certainly not there now. So far there the coast was quite clear, therefore, the count and his faithful gondolier made the best of their way to the small apartment where was the secret door leading to the vaults of the Palace of St. Mark. By good fortune they encountered none of the few domestics kept in the mansion, and found themselves safely in the room, having seen no one in their progress whatever. The count had with him a small hand lamp, which, however, small as it was, gave forth a clear bright light, and having locked the door of the room upon the inside, for fear of any sudden and awkward interruption, he proceeded to open the panel leading to the vaults.

"It is rather a long and dreary passage, Jerome," he said, "but it is a fearfully safe one."

"Safe or not safe, so long as I am with you, signor, I am most abundantly content. I don't wonder at the Doge wanting to get this palazo to himself."

"Nor I, Jerome, since it has got now into such bad hands.

They now left the room, and entered upon the secret passage, leading to the vaults. At first their pathway consisted of a spiral staircase, which was so small and steep, that it would have been quite a matter of impossibility for any stout person to have ascended or descended, but as neither the count or Jerome were of that description, they got over very well, indeed. This spiral staircase took them at once, before ceasing, to the very foundation of the Palazo Giadunio. It terminated in a cold damp cellar, which was evidently some short distance below the bed of the adjoining canal, for water was slowly oozing into it, keeping the atmosphere in an exceedingly moist and uncomfortable state.

"Now, Jerome," said the count, "this is our lowest point."

"A good thing, too, signor. We should be swamped, I think altogether, if we were to go any lower."

"Doubtless, but come on. The lamp burns but dimly in the confined air of this place."

The count led the way, and it was evident at each step they made, that they were going up an ascent. This footing, too, was much drier as they went, and soon, from the gritty feel beneath them they were certain they had hit upon a good gravel path. Pursuing this for some few minutes the count then turned to his left, abruptly, and the passage they now found themselves in was perfectly straight. It was of great length and remarkably narrow as well as low in the roof, from which depended in rather uncomfortable proximity, to their faces, many spider's webs. The lamp too, towards the centre of this passage, through which there was only the smallest possible current of air, burnt very badly. Indeed, Jerome thought it was going out for want of oil, but the count assured him of the contrary.

"We shall soon get clear of this place, Jerome," he said, "you will be surprised to find yourself in a much loftier region."

"I shall be pleased as well as surprised, signor, for I have had, I think, some of the largest spiders and their families down my throat, that I ever heard of."

"They attack me, surely first, Jerome."

"No, signor, you disturb them and put them in a sort of pain, but by the time I arrive they get over that, and are only intent upon being revenged upon somebody."

"It may be so, Jerome. But come, that trouble is over, for here we are."

"Where signor?"

The count opened a door—there was a sudden rush of cold air, from which he protected the lamp a moment, and then holding it up at his arms length above his head, he shewed Jerome that they were in a large vaulted room supported upon columns of great strength, and with a groined roof of massive architecture.

"Where are we, signor?" said Jerome.

"We are now exactly beneath the left wing of the Palace of St. Mark," said the count. "These massive pillars will support the super-incumbent structure, Jerome."

The count continued to listen for some few moments longer, and then, suddenly rising, he said,—

"Some one is coming upon our track."

" From the palazzo ?'

" Yes."

" Who can it be ?"

"One of two men. It must be Gordoni or Flavius. I am well assured that no one else knows the secret of the private entrance to the vaults."

"What shall we do?"

"We will, for the second time, Jerome, play the spy upon our enemies; they have played me a worse trick than that. Extinguish the lamp, I have the means of re-lighting it about me."

Jerome glanced around him for a moment, before putting out the light, and the count said,—

"You are right, Jerome. We must have some hiding-place before we leave ourselves in the total darkness of this place. I think that one of those squat Egyptian-looking pillars will effectually hide both of us."

"Not a doubt, signor."

"Come on, then. We shall be completely in shadow, for no doubt, whoever is coming, knows well which is the direct path, and there is little temptation to wander about in such a place as this is."

They both got behind a column that was about half a dozen paces out of the direct path they were pursuing, and then Jerome at once put out the light, and the darkness that reigned around them was of the most profound character that can be possibly conceived.

"They will come this way?" whispered Jerome.

"Most assuredly. There can be but one object in at all visiting this place, and this is the route by which to reach it; we have only to be cautious and still."

Presently, as Jerome bent his eyes in the direction from whence the intruder was expected, he saw a dim ray of light, which gradually increased, and almost at the same time the sound of advancing footsteps came sufficiently plain upon his ears. The person who was advancing, evidently did not think any caution was at all requisite in so doing. No doubt in his own mind he felt quite convinced that he was the only living being in those dreary vaults, and consequently caution would be thrown away. Neither the count nor Jerome now said a word for some time. They each felt how necessary silence was, in order that they might have no doubts or difficulties in the way of ascertaining who the owner was. Besides, in those vaulted subterranean places, sounds were frequently carried great distances, and even the slightest whisper might reach the ears of him who was rapidly advancing. The light increased each moment in intensity, until upon turning a corner made by three columns placed quite close together, there came a man into view bearing a lamp. Both the count and Jerome knew him in a moment, for the rays of the lamp fell full upon his face. It was Flavius, the grand treasurer and senator. As he approached, it was quite clear that nothing was to be apprehended in the shape of a discovery, if they used but the commonest amount of care, for Flavius was evidently completely possessed with an opinion of his own security from all observation. He walked on like a man who had some important task to perform, but who did not for a moment anticipate any danger from it. As he passed the column behind which the count and his faithful gondolier were hidden, he muttered to himself,—

"So—so Gordoni, you think to share with me, do you, in this plunder of the Doge's treasures, but it will go hard if I do not leave you the danger and the consequences, without the gold. There is one already who has found what a very dangerous secret the knowledge of this place is, there shall be another."

Flavius no doubt meant the Count Gradunio when he spoke of one as having found out what a dangerous piece of knowledge that was, and the count was not slow in applying these words to himself. Flavius passed on, and the light he carried had, by the distance he had got, gradually decreased in its brilliancy before the count spoke.

"Jerome," he said, "we are discovering more than we expected by this visit."

"We are indeed, signor."

"You see those two rogues, Gordoni and Flavius, cannot even be true to each other."

"Rogues never are, signor."

" I believe you Jerome."

" I have no doubt, signor, but that Gordoni is even now turning over in his mind how he can best get the better of Flavius, and by leaving him in the lurch in some way, take to himself all the profit of the secret they are both so well acquainted with."

" Nothing is more likely, Jerome ; the probability is, that after all they might be left safely enough to cut each other's throats in their own way."

" Not a doubt of it, signor."

"Nevertheless, we will follow this scoundrel, who is going our own way. Come on, Jerome ; he is at such a distance now that there is no chance of his hearing us, and while we still keep in view the light of his lamp, we shall be quite sure he is not, for any reason, deviating from the track that leads to the doge's treasury."

They both left their hiding place, but the count did not think it prudent to re-illumine the light they had with them, inasmuch as by keeping the reflection of that carried by the treasurer in view, they could not possibly go wrong. Thus they proceeded a considerable distance, until the count whispered,—

" Jerome, he has reached the treasurer's vault—there—he has passed the door, and closed it behind him."

They were now in total darkness, but the count told the gondolier to hold fast by his cloak, and he would lead him right, as he knew the path well. Jerome did so. In a few moments the count paused before a door which could not be seen until the count pushed it open a short distance, and allowed some of the rays from the lamp carried by Flavius to wander into the passage. The door was opened noiselessly by the count, just wide enough for both to peep into the place, so that Jerome was a witness as well as his master to the proceedings of the grand treasurer. These proceedings were indeed well worthy the attention of any one at all interested in ultimately exposing the villany of Flavius.

CHAPTER XXV.

THE DOGE AND THE COUNT.

THE curiosity of Jerome was excited to the utmost pitch as he watched the proceedings of Flavius, and likewise took note of the apartment in which that personage was so busily engaged, in the room, for it merited more to be called a room than a vault, inasmuch as it was fitted up with considerable pretensions to taste. The floor was well levelled, and covered with an oaken boarding ; the walls, if rough in reality, were rendered not so to the eye, by being hung with some of that exquisite tapestry for which Venice was for so long a period famous ; but what gave the place a singular appearance, was a strange kind of erection in its centre, , consisting of broad steps or shelves, growing narrower as they went higher, and upon which, in massive chests, well secured by huge clasps of iron, reposed much of the wealth which the state of Venice, by its arms or its diplomacy, had from time to time continued to collect. The row of chests which was the nearest to the floor consisted of such large ones that they were immovable, and in these were deposited silver coin to a large amount. Above them, again, was a tier of smaller and more portable coffers, in which gold coin and ingots of that precious metal alone found a place. Then again there were smaller chests still, where jewels and rare articles of a costly character were kept, and among these latter vessels was one where the regalia of the doge, only to be used upon rare state occasions, reposed in fancied security. There were several chairs of costly fabric and workmanship, likewise, in the chamber, besides a large oaken table, upon which were scales, and a number of weights for weighing out gold and silver coin, when required for the exigencies of the state. The roof was of the rough material of which the vaults were generally composed. Such was the Treasury of Venice, into which the Count Gradunio and Jerome looked with so much real interest and speculation. Flavius was there in the midst of all this vast accumulated treasure. He had placed upon the oaken table we have mentioned the lamp that he carried, and there he stood, regarding the tiers of chests and coffers with a smile of satisfaction. Presently he spoke,—

"All is well. In some other land I shall be able, indeed, to keep up a princely state ; I shall be able to command the worship of my fellow men, for in all states and in all conditions, man will readily worship wealth. I shall be able to show that 1 have boundless means, and under another name, and with fresh titles, which in Germany I can easily purchase, I shall lead a most royal life."

He took from a small pouch that was by his side several articles, which he laid upon the table. They consisted of a lump of bright green wax—a small coil of taper, and some seals.

"I trust," he added, "that if an inspection of the seals of the coffers of the state should take place before it is quite convenient for me to take my departure hence, that all will be found correct. It would be hard, indeed, if I were not equal to that amount of most ordinary ability and finesse."

He lit the taper, and prepared to set to work. Flavius considered it to be far beneath him to touch silver, or even gold. It was the coffers filled with jewels that arrested his attention, and made him think it worth his while to risk his head by robbing the state treasury. Accordingly, when he had made all his preparations for removing and replacing the official seals, he clambered up to a small box, which he knew contained a number of costly gems, taken from the Turks, during one of the many wars which the state of Venice had had with the Ottomans.

"This will content me," he said. "If I can but carry off one half of the contents of this small chest, I shall be most abundantly well supplied."

The box was heavy; but avarice is one of those passions which lends strength to its victims, and, although he did so with difficulty, yet Flavius contrived to bring it down from its place. He stopped to breathe and rest himself after the exertion, but there was a smile upon his face as he said,—

"Ah, Gordoni, I think you have a subtler spirit to deal with than you think. I shall surely get the better of you, my good friend, in this affair, and while I go off with the plunder, I will see if I cannot leave you to take the consequences of the robbery."

"A pretty scoundrel this, signor !" whispered Jerome to the Count Gradunio.

"Hush ! hush !" said the count. "Listen to all he says, and watch him well, Jerome."

"I will, signor."

Flavius now commenced operations, muttering to himself as he did so,—

"If I can avoid the necessity of using the false seals, it will be much better."

Taking a small narrow-bladed knife from his pocket, he heated it in the flame of the taper ; then wiping it carefully, so that no soot from the flame remained upon it, he slid it under the seals upon the chest, and succeeded in getting them off in a tolerably good condition.

"It will need a closer inspection than will be given to these seals," he said, " to enable any one to see that they have been tampered with, after I have carefully replaced them, as I shall do."

In another moment he had the chest open, for although he had not in his custody the proper seals of the chests of treasure, he had the keys, in his capacity of Grand Treasurer, still in his possession. Neither the Count Gradunio nor Jerome could see into the chest from where they were, insomuch as, when the lid was opened, it effectually obstructed their view, but they could see that the treasurer was filling his pockets from its contents with great eagerness.

"Shall we do nothing ?" whispered Jerome.

"Nothing," said the count.

All was silence for the next few minutes, and then Flavius, finding that he had got as much as he could conveniently carry, closed the lid of the chest.

"One more visit," he muttered, " shall suffice me—I will come on the Saturday, according to arrangement with Gordoni, and then I will make another appointment with him, which I will not keep; but instead of me he shall find the doge's guards in this chamber."

He then proceeded to put on the seal again, which he managed with an adroitness that seemed to show he was no stranger to such despicable acts. The chest was placed in its old position, and Flavius once again placed in his pockets all his materials of robbery, and taking his lamp prepared to leave the chamber.

"We will let him pass," whispered the count to the gondolier. "It is no part of my design to interrupt him now; for not only have I no authority to arrest him, but I want Gordoni to share the same fate."

"True, signor."

"It would be a thousand pities to let such a man as he escape. Stand aside, Jerome, and allow Flavius to pass out; he will not see us."

The Grand Treasurer, with a look of perfect satisfaction upon his diabolical-looking feaures, came forth, and closing the door after him, he, without casting the slightest glance around him, so secure did he think himself, walked away through the vaults, towards the secret staircase in the count's mansion.

"Now let us ascend," said the Count Gradunio.

"With pleasure, signor," replied Jerome. "I am not a little glad that we oversaw and overheard Flavius."

"Yes, Jerome; we certainly have not come here for nothing—but now, remember you are to wait for me here, in the treasure chamber."

"Yes."

"And if I come not within the time I have specified, fill your pockets from any chest you can contrive to burst open, and take your departure from Venice as speedily as you can get any means of so doing."

"You shall be obeyed, signor, I will go——" Jerome added a mental reservation, however, to the words, which signified that he would obey the count, by saying to himself, "Yes, I will go; but not before I am quite certain of your fall, and have done something more substantially and more ably to avenge it, than taking a few handsful of gold, as quits from this place."

He well knew that the count would combat this resolution, so he prudently kept it to himself, lest his master should insist upon his making some solemn and binding promise to the contrary.

"I will leave you the light, Jerome," added the count, "for the path which I now have to pursue is a straight one, and cannot be mistaken.'

Jerome looked at the count in some wonder as to how he intended to leave the treasure chamber; but he was soon set at rest upon that head, for the count removed a portion of the tapestry from the wall immediately opposite to the door at which they had entered, and showed Jerome a small spring, which, when touched ever so lightly, caused a tall narrow door to fly open, disclosing a flight of almost perpendicular ascending steps.

"These steps," said the count, "lead directly to a small council chamber, adjoining the sleeping room of the doge. All you have to do, Jerome, is to be quiet and exercise what patience you can until I return."

"Heaven speed you, signor."

"Amen! I have no apprehensions."

The count at once commenced the ascent of the little staircase. This staircase, however, was only little in width, for in its extent it deserved the appellation of great, inasmuch as it consisted of a hundred steps, making the ascent very fatiguing, winding as they did for the most part round and round a column. The count, however, paused not until he reached the topmost landing, and then in the dark he felt cautiously about the wall until his hand touched a spring, and a door, in all respects similar to the one which was in the treasure chamber, opened.

There was still, however, between him and the room into which it was necessary he should get, a heavy piece of tapestry, and there came directly through its texture a light, showing that some lamps were burning upon the other side. The count now thought it prudent to listen for a few moments, in order to ascertain if any one was stirring in the small council chamber, which he knew was converted into a kind of waiting room for the pages of the doge. All was still as the very grave itself. Not the smallest noise indicative of the presence of any one came upon his ears, which rather surprised him. Cautiously he moved the tapestry on one side, so that he could get a view into the chamber, and there he saw two pages asleep on the large chairs which were used as the seats of the counsellors during the deliberations. A flask of wine and some chessmen were before them, and it would seem that they had been enjoying themselves as best they might upon their watch, until quite overcome by drowsiness. The sleep of the pages upon their post was by no means so reprehensible as it would at first appear to be, for after all it was supposed that no one could approach that apartment without passing through two others, where the doge's guard keep vigilant watch. The only thing that ought to have kept them awake, was in case the doge had required any attendance during the night, but as that scarcely ever happened, they thought they might as well sleep as not. A huge silver branch candlestick, bearing six tall wax lights, was upon a side table, so that the room was brilliantly enough illuminated, and the effect was quite dazzling to the eyes of the count, after being accustomed to the total darkness of the staircase which he had just ascended from the vaults below. The count stepped into the chamber as lightly as it was possible for any one to step. He had no wish to break the slumbers of the pages, although they could scarcely now have impeded his progress to the sleeping room of the doge, but then they might have made such an outcry, as would have brought the guard upon him. So soundly now did they repose, that he might have trod quite confidentially in the rooms, instead of in the manner he did, had he felt so disposed, but that he could not feel quite sure of. A gilt double door admitted to the doge's chamber from the apartment, and towards that the count moved silently. It was possible enough that the doge might be waking, but that was a contingency which Count Gradunio did not dread, for if that head of the state of Venice was slumbering, he must awaken him, and that quickly too, for he had much to say. There was one feeling which made the count wish that the doge might be sleeping, and that was an assurance to that individual that the count came to his chamber with no hostile intent, for if he had done so, it would of course not be his policy to rouse him from slumber. The count opened the gilt door softly, and passed into one of the most magnificent sleeping rooms that the taste and ingenuity of the age could produce. A soft shaded light was upon everything, and the eye was perfectly enchanted by the mellow radiance which invested the decorations of the apartment, such decoration being all of a pale green, inscribed with silver. The Doge of Venice slept soundly beneath a coverlet of green satin, with a silver fringe that swept the floor on all sides of the bed.

CHAPTER XXVI.

RETURNS TO FLORANTHE, IN THE CONVENT CHAPEL.

WE left Floranthe and the young novice, Julia, most critically situated in the chapel of the convent of the Ursulines. The wicked and unscrupulous abbess had evidently made up her mind to one of the most diabolical plans of oppression and of fraud that the most fertile imagination in iniquity could have possibly devised. That was to force Floranthe to stand at the altar, and then to swear that she voluntarily became the wife of Gordoni, so that the latter might be in a position to call upon the laws of Venice to force her into his arms. No doubt the abbess knew, from experience of similar pieces of villany, that she could depend upon Rene and the two old nuns to go to the extreme in aiding in so frightful a piece of duplicity and treachery. As for Gordoni himself, we know sufficient of him to feel that he would have no scruples as to the manner in which he called Floranthe his own, so that he did succeed in compassing that object, which, according to the resistance he had met with, as much as owing to his passion and admiration of her extreme beauty, had become a fixed, unalterable purpose of his wicked soul. It would, indeed, seem that poor Floranthe was now without hope or chance of succour, occasioned by those who were resolved upon her destruction. It will be recollected, however, that at the moment when she was, by force, dragged to the steps of that altar which was about to be so woefully desecrated, there had arisen a fearful tumult, accompanied by screams of alarm from the extremes of the chapel. These sounds could come from nowhere, according to the direction from which they evidently proceeded, but the convent garden which surrounded the chapel upon two sides, and they were evidently such as were calculated to fill all with alarm, excepting Julia and Floranthe, to whom anything in the shape of an interruption to what was going on in the chapel was, indeed, most welcome. To the abbess the sounds of disturbance appeared to be as alarming as they were incomprehensible. She clung to the railings of the altar, and looked quite pale and haggard at Gordoni, as though from him she expected some information concerning the outcries. Gordoni half drew his sword from its scabbard, and looked rather terrified. The two nuns shrieked together, and Rene sat down upon the steps of the altar, and looked as though her last hour had, indeed, come.

"What is that?" gasped the abbess.

"I know not," said Gordoni.

The noise continued for a few moments, and then a nun with a huge bunch of keys in her hand, entered the chapel.

"Help! help! help! Holy Virgin, protect us. Help! help! Oh, help!"

These cries, uttered as they were with frantic energy, caused quite a commotion in the chapel. The abbess herself, with all her diabolical calmness of character, could not forbear uttering a shriek, and the nuns thus encouraged to let their fears have full play, made the place echo again with their cries. Father Magas hid himself behind the altar, and Gordoni, if it had not been for shame's sake, would have followed his example. He had some hope, too, that the affair might after all turn out to be a false alarm.

"Speak, sister Beatrice," cried the abbess, recovering herself sufficiently to make the demand, and seizing the waist of the nun who had the keys, with an energy that must have been painful to her. "Speak! What is the cause of all this tumult and alarm?"

"The—the cause?"

"Yes, the cause."

"Holy Virgin, protect us."

"You said that before, idiot."

"Did I?"

"You know you did. Be explicit. What is the cause of the alarm?"

"Yes—yes, I will tell all, I will tell all. You must know that after shutting the wicket of the great gate, I was going to the vinery to see if the windows were fast, for the cats get in of a night, and set a bad example to the novices, you know, and——"

"How dare you trifle with me thus?"

"I trifle."

"Yes, I ask you the cause of the alarm, and you begin a long story about cats."

"Well, but I was going to say that I was on my road to the vinery, all owing to the cats, when on the top of the high wall by the canal I saw something."

"On the wall?"

"Yes, as I'm a sinner."

"Go on."

"I saw something, and at that moment a dreadful voice said something in an unknown tongue, and a man sprung from the top of the wall right into the garden at my feet, and catching hold of my—my——"

"What?"

"My ancle, he said something else in an unknown tongue, and then I screamed and ran away as hard as I could possibly do so."

"And you left a man in the garden!"

"How could I help it?"

"Are our convent precincts to be so profaned? Father Magas, Signor Gordoni, I call

upon you to slay the intruder upon thesanctity of this holy place.   I am full of horror.
A man here!"

"Madam," said Floranthe, "were he one of the worst and most vicious of the human
race, he would scarcely be a match for those who are even now doing worse than profaning the sanctity of a convent garden, inasmuch as they are profaning the sanctity of this building devoted to Heaven."

"How dare you express an opinion?"

"It was my pleasure."

"Your pleasure?"

"Yes, madam."

Floranthe, with the pride of conscious innocence and virtue, returned glance for glance
at the abbess, who in a low tone, said to herself,—"It will go hard with me, but I will
find a means of subduing and crushing that proud spirit, which seems to grow with the
occasion."

"What is to be done?" said Rene.

"Signor Gordoni, will you help us?" cried the abbess.

"I am wounded and weak, but my sword is at your service, madam," replied
Gordoni.

"'Tis well.   Let us get torches, and go into the garden. Where is Father Magas?"

Rene pointed to the place of concealment of the monk behind the altar.

"Well," said the abbess, pretending not to know what had become of the holy father,
"well, we must do without him."

As she spoke, she contrived to throw over one of the massive silver candlesticks,
weighing about thirty pounds, that was upon the altar.   It fell behind the same place,
and in a moment the monk sprung up, rubbing his head and exclaiming—"The devil
take it, what's that?"

"Oh you are there," cried the abbess. "Some holy saint must have roused you."

"Bless all the saints in the calendar, what is the matter with you, holy sister?"

"A man in the garden, holy brother."

"You don't say so?"

"Yes, and we expect you to arm yourself with some worldly weapon, and attack him,
aided by Signor Gordoni."

"The well-known valour of the noble Signor Gordoni," began the monk with a
bow, "might surely alone ——"

"Be sufficient under ordinary circumstances," interrupted Gordoni; "but at present
I am suffering from a severe wound, and as you are a tall strong man ——"

"I?"

"Yes."

"Oh, you are very much mistaken."

Rene who had left the chapel, after receiving a whispered order from the abbess, now
returned, and placed in the hands of the monk, an antiquated looking arquebus, which
really looked as if it might date its origin in the first year of the invention of
gunpowder.

"What a weapon!" said the monk.

"It is loaded," said the abbess. "Any one who intrudes into a convent garden,
knows well that death is but a part expiation of this offence. Sister Rene, and you two
holy sisters, I charge with the care of these two foolish, and I fear rather heretical young
damsels. See to their safe keeping, while we go in search of the intruder who has so
much alarmed the pious and exemplary portress of our convent."

The abbess, Gordoni, and the monk, preceded by the trembling portress, left the chapel.
As he went Father Magas looked with anything but a pleased aspect upon the old arquebus
which had been thrust into his hands, and he began to wish himself well out of an
adventure, which, after all, might end in by far too much personal risk, to be at all
pleasant to one who liked nothing personal but pleasure.

"It will be sure to burst," he thought.

"Come on, come on!" cried Gordoni passionately, and the chapel door swung
to after them.

Floranthe and Julia were there in the chapel, guarded by R ene, and the two old nuns, who looked at the fair young creatures most indignantly.   Floranthe bent close to Julia, as she said—" Who can this intruder in the garden be? Think you the circumstance has any connexion with your fortunes ?"

" Oh, blessed hope !"

" Hush! hush !"

Julia grasped the hand of Floranthe, and was silent.

" It struck me," said Floranthe, " that your English lover might possibly have made an effort to reach you, especially when it appears the intruder spoke in a tongue unknown to the old portress of the convent."

" Yes, yes. Oh, yes !"

" You really think 'tis he ?"

" My heart seems to assure me of it. What shall I do? What ought I to do ?"

" I do not see that of yourself just at present you can do anything. I have no great idea of the prowess of the foe whom he has to encounter, and as there are lights here in the chapel, he will make his way here if a conqueror."

" Shall we not go into the garden ?"

" I advise not."

" Why—oh, why ?"

" In the first place, recollect that we must have a personal struggle with Renè and the two nuns."

" Alas ! yes."

" You had forgotten."

" I had indeed. I see they are whispering together, and watching us intently Oh Floranthe, if indeed my gallant English lover should come. Oh. what joy !"

" Hush ! I hear sounds from the garden. Let us listen to the purport, Julia, if we can."

CHAPTER XXVII.

ADVENTURES IN A CONVENT GARDEN.

A SMALL boat, at sunset on that evening, had been rowed into the canal basin by two persons. This boat had excited much interest on the part of the gondoliers of Venice, who had chanced to be in the way of seeing it, for not only was it of strange, and to them of foreign construction, but it was not manned by gondoliers, nor was it propelled through the water after the Venetian fashion. One of the occupants of the boat sat at its stern, while the other plied a pair of oars after the English fashion, and not as in Venice, standing up at the stern, and making the strange riot in the water which by some means propels the heavy gondolas lazily along the canals. He who took no part in the propulsion of the boat wore a cap, around which were some golden cords. The rest of his person was enveloped in a huge cloak, which completely wrapped him up. He who was rowing wore the best dress—the shore-going costume of an English sailor of the better class. Blue trousers and jacket, jauntily enough made, set off a robust and powerful figure to advantage, while the straw hat with its bit of flitting black ribbon was worn with quite an air. Nevertheless, his costume, of which he was a little proud, did not by any means prevent him from bending to the oars, and doing his work with all that energy which generally characterises the British sailor, when he has eyes upon him. Many scowling and ungracious glances were cast upon him as he passed the various landing and plying places of the gondolas, but Jack Stevens, for such was his name, gave them look for look ; and when a curse was muttered by some gondolier, Jack, guessing its import, although the language was to him a mystery, replied by a good round English oath. Once or twice, the officer, for officer he was who sat in the boat, said a few words to repress Jack's belligerent spirit, and then lapsed into silence again.

This officer, as our readers by this time have probably guessed, was no other than Captain Herbert, of the British frigate, Wave, which was riding at anchor in the Adriatic sea, and the lover of Julia, the beautiful novice of the Benedictine convent. By what accidents of flood and fortune he became acquainted with Julia, and her family, it is not our present province to state ; suffice it to say, that the mutual attachment was well known to Julia's friends, and they had hoped that, by removing her to a convent, they had placed an effectual and insurmountable barrier between her and her English lover. Their objections to Captain Herbert were many. His country and his religion were both most criminal to the feelings of Julia's friends, and there was besides a certain bold and boisterous manner about the Englishman, that they were far from approving. The denunciations of the family confessor completed the affair, and thus Captain Herbert was formally forbidden to visit the house, and Julia herself was handed over to the tender mercies of the abbess, concerning whom we know quite enough, to believe that she would enter heart and soul into any matter which had for its adjuncts oppression and tyranny.

"Well, Jack," said Captain Herbert, with a smile, after they had proceeded for some distance, for Jack was a special favourite,—"well, you won't be satisfied, I see, until you have had a brush with some of these Venetian sailors."

" Sailors, your honour ?"

" Well, perhaps I ought not to call them sailors."

" Call 'em lubbers, your honour, and it will be nearer the mark. They don't like the sight of us nor our boat, and I can see they would be glad to sink us, if they could, to the bottom of one of these ditches of theirs that we are passing."

" Ditches, Jack ?"

" Aye, your honour, what else are they ?"

" Why, Jack, they are the far famed canals of Venice, a city that has excited the imagination of all Europe. You have no romance, Jack, in your composition."

"No, your honour, I don't think I have, and I hope I never shall have."

" Indeed ? Why so, Jack ?"

"It's something foreign, I suppose, your honour. But only look at that chap with the hearse, just such a thing as they take shore-living lubbers to the churchyard in. How he stares at us ! Should not I like to have a hit at him, sir ?"

" He certainly does not look very amiable, Jack, but pass on, and take no notice of him. You know my object here, is anything but to get into a riot."

" Aye, aye, your honour, all's right."

Jack would, acting under orders, have passed the Venetian boatman quiet enough, but the latter was one of those dogmatical geniuses found in all countries, who have a perfect abhorrence of anything they are not accustomed to, so he could not let Jack go by without making use of some most opprobrious epithets. Now Jack did not understand a word of what he said, but as all over the world there are certain tones belonging to courteous language, so there are certain tones belonging to abuse, and the latter were sufficiently manifest in the language of the boatman. It was too much for Jack's philosophy to pass the matter by, so he retorted with some half dozen English oaths. The gondolier brought the same natural sagacity to bear upon the comprehension of Jack's abuse as Jack had to his, and the next thing the gondolier did, was to put himself into an attitude which all over the world, somehow, is considered contemptuous, and which mainly consists in presenting prominently to an opponent that part of the animal economy which is considered the opposite of the head. This was too much for Jack's endurance, and in vain Captain Herbert cried "never mind him." Jack would not be stayed, but with a vigorous push of one of his oars he sent the Venetian gondolier sprawling.

" Take that," said Jack, " and learn manners, you swab. How do you feel, now ?"

Jack had not contented himself by giving just such a push as would be sufficient for the overthrow of his enemy, and no more, but he had put his whole force into the affair, and the consequence was that while the gondolier lay at the bottom of his gondola howling and helpless, calling upon all the saints in the calendar, the English boat had got a good way on.

" Sarved him right," said Jack.

" It was indiscreet," said Captain Herbert, " although I admit freely enough that it served him right. Pull away, Jack."

" Right a-head, your honour ?"

" Yes, until you get to that large white building near the tall columns. Then turn short starboard and run into a narrow canal you will see."

" Aye, aye, yer honour."

The boat sped on, and just as it turned down the narrow canal remarked by Captain Herbert, he glanced back and saw several gondolas in chase of him. Jack fortunately did not look back, or probably he would not have taken so pacific a view of the matter as the captain.

"Now, Jack,' you have come so far upon a secret expedition."

"Always content to obey orders, your honour."

"Certainly Jack, that I am well aware of, but I hold that it is always better, when it can be done with safety to the service, to explain orders."

"Very good, your honour."

"I let you know at starting that this was a littie piece of privateering of my own. An expedition in which I hope to make a good prize."

Jack shook his head.

"Lord bless your honour, you may depend there's nothing worth cutting out among these lubberly ditches. There's one or two ships lying in the fort that might be worth the taking; but except as a sort of curiosity, your honour, I wouldn't take the trouble to tow out anything that we have seen in these here parts since leaving the port."

"Aud yet I came for a prize, Jack, which I hope to take away with me."

The idea of Captain Herbert takiug away a prize in the shape of a young female, amongst what Jack oalled "illegitimates," was a regular puzzler—and the sailor could not at all comprehend the drift of his captain's intentions. But Jack, seeing that Captain Herbert was fully bent upon carrying out his object, thought it wise not to pursue his inquiries further, but pull away as hard as he could; and in a few minutes the little English boat was safely riding between the high wall of some garden, and the large gondola that was moored to a stake upon the spot. The overhanging trees were so low, that anyone could touch them, but only the slender ends of the branches. Jack looked inquiringly at Captain Herbert.

"This wall, Jack," he said, "bounds the convent garden in which the Venetian damsel is, whom J intend to rescue. Can we scale it, think you?"

"We must, sir."

"Well, we must then, Jack. How shall we set about it?"

There was but a faint light visible from the rapidly retiring twilight, and at that Jack looked with an inquiring eye, and then cast a long and scientific-like glance at the wall and the trees which overshadowed it.

CHAPTER XXVIII.

A NIGHT OF PERIL IN VENICE.

THE difficulties which now beset Captain Herbert and his faithful servant were trivial indeed, especially as the spirits of the former were eonsiderably exhilarated by the suecess which had already attended the enterprise. As regards the latter, he did indeed follow to the very letter the commands of his leader. Aud Jack, who was "all alive," and ready to encounter any danger that might present itself, awaited rather impatiently the further results of the adventure. At last Captain Herbert broke silence by saying,—

"How, Jack, shall we get over the wall?"

"Is anybody looking, your honour?"

"No; I really think we have the spot all to ourselves."

"Here goes, then," said Jack.

From the miscellaneous collection of all sorts of things Jack had in his pocket, he selected a long piece of cord, and tied his knife to the end of it. He then cast it over the branch of the tree that projected over the wall, and managed by such means to pull it much lower, and fasten the cord to one of the seats of the boat, which had sufficient weight, as well as hold of the water, to keep all firm.

"Now, your honour," said Jack, "what's to hinder us climbing up as handily as a squirrel in a hazel tree?"

"Nothing, Jack, nothing. You are the very soul of invention, and the most capital fellow in all the world to bring upon an adventure of this kind."

"All's right, your honour. Now for it. We shall know that the boat's safe too, at her moorings, and that's one comfort. I'll go up, sir, and you follow, when you find that the tackling is all firm and tight."

With an amount of agility that one could scarcely have expected of him, Jack sprung up the bough of the tree. It bore his weight well, and in half a minute he was fairly upon the wall of the convent garden.

"Now your honour," he cried.

"Hush! hush! Not a word," said Captain Herbert, as he ascended. "Silence must be our greatest aim. A chance word might betray us before we have at all reconnoitred the position of the enemy, or found out where our prize lies."

"Mute as a fish, your honour," said Jack.

They both now stood upon the top of the wall, and from thence looked down into the convent garden, where all was darkness, for the night had not only made some progress, but the shade of the tree which had been so great a help to them, enveloped all surrounding objects in its gloom. The descent, however, could not present any difficulties, for there was the tree, the branches of which had been made by Jack so available in gaining their present exalted position; and to seamen the descent of a tree is always an easy matter enough. Jack noiselessly, but steadily, crawled down, closely followed by Captain Herbert, to whom he said in a whisper,—

"You can jump now, sir, when you like. There's a flower bed just below here, and it's as soft as feathers without stalks."

The captain jumped upon the flower bed, to which Jack had previously found his way, and sure enough the softness of it had not been at all exaggerated, for he sunk into it above his ancles, considerably.

"All right, your honour?"

"Yes Jack, all's right. Now come on. Here seems to be a path of some sort, and if we follow it, I suppose we may fairly enough believe that it leads somewhere."

They both proceeded along a path, which was nicely made with sand from the lagunes, intermixed with small broken shells, until they came to a cross path, which went quite at right angles with the one they were pursuing.

The captain came to a pause for a moment, but he resolved then upon following the cross path, as being more likely to lead direct to the convent. He and Jack proceeded for some distance, uninterruptedly, until suddenly there came a flash of light across their eyes, as though from a suddenly revealed lantern, and in another moment an old nun with a lamp in one hand and a bunch of keys in the other, fairly ran into Jack's arms before she was aware of where she was going.

"The devil!" cried Jack, "I'm boarded."

"Help! help!" shrieked the nun. "I'm ruined. It's a male man. Help! help! My Lady Abbess! Help—murder! murder!"

"What did you say," cried Jack, "that I was a merman? Confound you, I'm a British tar, that's what I am."

The nun extricated herself from the rather rough grasp which Jack took of her, and after having, with the bunch of keys, dealt him a tolerably hard blow on the head, she fled shrieking for aid, and making her voice heard as an alarum bell, throughout the whole garden. Thus it was then that so much consternation was spread in the chapel where the abbess would have perpetrated the villany of forcing Floranthe into a marriage, or the semblance of a marriage, with the infamous Gordoni. Thus, then, was it that the proceedings, which were alike so disgraceful to the persons projecting them, and so great a desecration of the building in which it was proposed for them to take place, were suspended. It will be remembered that Gordoni and the monk had sallied forth into the convent garden to ascertain the cause of the alarm.

"Confound her! she has escaped," cried Jack.

"Then," said the captain, "I fear the convent will be alarmed prematurely, and we shall be unable to accomplish our object. Nevertheless, what man can do, that will I do. Come on, Jack, come on."

"I tried to hold her," said Jack, "but she had as many claws as a crab, to say nothing of the keys. I'd rather board an enemy's frigate any day, than a convent full of old women—if they can, like this one——"

"Hold—some one comes."

Jack and the captain hid themselves behind a large myrtle bush, as Gordoni and the party which was with him advanced, carrying lights.

"There is no one," said the monk.

"We cannot yet come to such a conclusion," replied the abbess. "But a small portion of the garden has been searched as yet; let us proceed. I trust, Signor Gordoni, you will not scruple to inflict death upon any one who has, with unhallowed feet, dared to desecrate this place?"

Gordoni growled out some unintelligible reply; and Jack whispered to the captain—

"Lord bless you, sir! there's no fear; we can go in upon them, I should say, with a flowing sheet, and take the ship as easy as looking at it—shall we do so, sir?"

"I think it would be best, Jack."

"The very best, sir; only say the word, and it's done."

"There are two men."

"And a she-dragon!"

"Well, we will not meddle with the dragon; you take one of the men and I'll take the other, Jack."

"Very well, your honour—only let me have the fellow with the sword. I somehow feel as if I should like to have a little tustle with him. He's just the sort of fellow for me."

"Take him then, Jack, and I will silence, by fair means or by foul, yon stalwart monk, who looks about him with so strange and sinister a glance."

Gordoni was thrusting his sword into the thickets and evergreen bushes, in search of any one who might be concealed, and the monk was in an attitude of listening. Probably, low as they spoke to each other, some faint sound of the voices of Jack and Captain Herbert had come to his ears, and he was endeavouring to discover from what direction precisely the voices came. The abbess was standing in an attitude expressive of haughty anger; while Rene stood trembling at a few paces distant from her most arrogant mistress,

"There is no one hidden," said Gordoni, as he thrust his sword up to the hilt in a flowering shrub close at hand.

Jack sprung upon him, and pinioned his arms to his sides, crying—

"Stop a bit, old fellow: you may chance to do somebody a hurt with that cheese-toaster of yours."

At the same moment, Captain Herbert darted forth towards the monk; but as he approached him, he saw something gleaming in his hand, which he rightly enough guessed was a stiletto. He did not give the villanous ecclesiastic time to use it—for with one straightforward blow in the face with his foot, he sent him head over heels among the flowers in a cultivated border close at hand.

"Hurrah!" cried Jack, "the ship's our own. Hurrah, hurrah!"

Gordoni seemed to be petrified at the suddenness of the attack upon him, and not able to come to any conclusion with regard to the strange animal which had hold of him so effectually. He, however, made an effort after a few moments to regain his liberty.

"Avast, mounseer," said Jack, "you'd better be quiet, or it will be the worse for you,—won't you?"

Captain Herbert sprung forward, and wrested the sword from the grasp of Gordoni, saying,—

"Let him go, Jack, he is harmless now."

"There you are," said Jack, and with a terrific kick he sent Gordoni flying after the prostrate monk, and they both lay rolling over each other upon the flower bed, shouting for help.

Jack and the captain now certainly had all the field to themselves, for the abbess and Rene, during the brief and conclusive contest that had just taken place had completely disappeared. The object of that disappearance boded no good to Captain Herbert, for in another moment the alarm bell of the convent, which was never rung except in case of fire or some peculiar emergency, commenced ringing furiously.

"We shall have the whole city upon us," cried Captain Herbert; "confound the women, do you hear that infernal bell, Jack?"

"Rather, your honour, what do they make it now?"

"Follow me."

Captain Herbert now felt that the next best thing to accomplishing his object upon that night, was to leave himself at liberty to accomplish it on another, and he meant, now that all idea of secresy was at an end, and a general alarm was given, to leave the garden as quickly as he could. He would have missed his way, however, to the tree by which they had descended, had it not been for Jack, who pointed out the right path, but they had proceeded already far enough upon a wrong one to come in sight of the chapel windows, from one of which streamed something white, which catching in the breeze, floated close enough to Jack for him to catch it, and thrust into his pocket. The alarm bell continued its rapid reverberations, and they gained the tree just as some other bell attached to some other religious establishment began to answer its iron summons.

"Better luck another time, Jack," said Captain Herbert, "come on and let us now regain our boat."

He clambered up the tree, and Jack followed him. They had something of a view of several of the canals as they stood on the top of the wall of the convent garden, and they could see lights flashing on board of vessels, gondolas, and upon the few dry spots to be found in the city, while a general rush seemed to be making towards the convent.

"We are just in time," said Captain Herbert.

"Hush!" said Jack.

"What's the matter?"

"Cast a cat's-eye into our boat, your honour."

The captain looked carefully through the branches of the tree down into the boat, and there he saw crouched up close to the gunwale, a man in a brown cloak, evidently on the watch for something or somebody.

"Who in the name of all that's uncomfortable," said Captain Herbert, "can that fellow be, Jack? He is a most villanous looking rascal."

"Yes: it's the mounseer of a boatman, that I upset in the queer craft as we came along. He's waiting for me, I'll be bound."

"Then, Jack, you had better be careful, for these fellows are all assassins, and think no more of a cool-blooded murder than you would of a proper stand-up fight. We must think of some way of circumventing the rascal."

"Aye, aye, your honour. We'll manage him. Will your honour make a rustling among the boughs, and attract his attention, by pretending to come down on that one the cord is not fast to?"

".Yes, Jack. Certainly."

Captain Herbert did as Jack required, and the dark eyes of the gondolier were fixed most relently upon him, while Jack stepped glibly down towards the boat. When he got about twelve feet only from it, he disengaged his feet, and held on for a moment only with his hands, then timing his distance well, he jumped upon the back of the gondolier with a vengeance enough to knock all the breath out of his body. As it was he knocked him into a state of insensibility, and then flinging him overboard, poniard and all, for the fellow had one in his hand, Jack cried, cheerily, "All's right, pull away, and hurrah for the Wave!"

CHAPTER XXIX.

THE COUNT GRADUNIO'S INTERVIEW WITH THE DOGE.

THE situation in which we left the Count Gradunio was a most critical one. It will be remembered that he had made his way to the bed-room of the Doge of Venice, and only paused as to the most eligible mode of awakining him, to listen to the important conversation he had come with a firm resolve to make to him. Only for a few moments did he look around him at the gorgeous trappings and decorations of that chamber; and then observing a vacant chair close to the bedside of the doge, he flung himself into it.

"There," he said to himself, "sleeps one whose death would convulse the state, and perchance plunge Venice into anarchy. But time is precious to me, and I must awaken him."

The count laid his hand heavily upon the gorgeous coverlet of the bed, and said, close to the doge's ear, "Awake! awake!"

The effect was instantaneous. The doge opened his eyes, and half sprung up in the bed. He would have made a cry of alarm, but the Count Gradunio held up his hand, and said, "Hush!"

There was something in the very pronunciation of that one word that had an effect upon the doge, as though some physical force had been used to make him still. He glared at the count like one under the fascinating influence of a magic spell.

"Hush! Doge of Venice," said Gradunio. "There is safety absolute in stillness and in patience, and there is danger as absolute in impatience and alarm; never yet was the Doge of Venice so safe as he is now."

"Safe!" cried the doge. "Who—who are you?"

"Time and sorrow have changed my features, although there was a time when the Doge of Venice gave me ever a smiling recognition. As for your safety, noble sir, it is doubly assured."

"Doubly assured!"

"Yes, your arm will protect you as well as mine. You still look upon me with eyes of suspicion. You, perchance, think me an assassin. If I were such I could have done my unholy work while you slept."

"I must call my attendants."

"Not so."

"Ah, you coerce me!"

"For your own good, doge, and not for mine, listen to me.' Your object in calling your attendants, would be to make head against me. That you can yourself do. I see but this one weapon in the chamber. Take it, sir, and feel that you are armed while I am defenceless."

As he spoke, the count reached a magnificent sword from off a side table, and handed it to the doge. There was some nobility—some natural feeling of dignity in the character of the doge, which made him not like to be outdone in courage and generosity of feeling.

"Replace the weapon from whence you took it," he said; "I fear nothing at your hands. Tell me what it is you wish, and how you came into this chamber."

"As yet you do not know me, sir."

"By the saints I do not, and yet there is a something in the voice familiar to my ear."

"It is difficult to fancy that those whom we think with the dead are by our sides in our very chambers. It is rare for the dungeons of the Bridge of Sighs ever to yield up a living victim. Ha! you know me now."

"The Count Gradunio, by all that's sacred!" exclaimed the doge.

"Yes, I am the Count Gradunio."

"Gracious Heaven! How 'scaped you killing? Have you come to tell some wondrous tale, of how Heaven having spared you, man should now do so; or come you for some refined revenge upon those who condemned you because of your exceeding guilt?"

"Guess again, Doge of Venice—guess again."

The doge was silent, and his eyes wandered to the sword. The count saw the movement, and instantly reaching the sword again, he placed it on the bed by the side of the doge, saying, "Are you now better satisfied, my lord?"

The doge looked vexed, as again he pushed the sword away from him.

"If I have failed to guess it, my Lord Gradunio," he said, "your coming must have some meaning."

"It has."

"I pray you explain it."

"Amid the guesses you were pleased to make of my motives, sir, you forget one, and

that was the true one. I came not here to avenge my wrongs—not to ask for clemency, but to prove my innocence."

"Indeed. If wrong at all has been done you, it has been most grievous wrong."

"It has been most grievous wrong. Upon the accusation of the grand treasurer and senator, Flavius, I was seized and conveyed to the dungeon, from which it was expected and believed I should never again emerge, but to instant death."

"He brought so clear a charge against you?"

" So seeming clear."

" Well, perchance it was only seeming clear."

" It was, indeed, only seeming clear; by accident I discovered a small opening door
in the wall of one of my apartments, I opened it and pursuing the passages and most
mysterious staircases to which it leads, I found myself, as much to my surprise
as aught can possibly be, in the vault beneath the palace of St. Mark where are kept
the treasures of the state."

" Go on—go on."

"I saw there a man loading himself with gold, and glancing ever and anon about him
with all the aspect of a thief; that man was the grand treasurer Flavius; I spoke to him,
shewed him the secret passage from my house to the vaults, and discoursing fairly, he
left me, affecting to have been engaged in the treasury by virtue of his office, and an
order from you."

" 'Twas false."

" Aye, but greater falsehood was to come, my lord. Within two hours, I was
seized by virtue of an order from two members of the council, and cast into a dungeon in
the Bridge of Sighs."

" I know you were."

" From whence I was precipitated into the canal beneath."

" As I likewise know. The treasurer reported, that upon making an official visit to
the treasury he heard a noise, and that upon extinguishing his own light, and concealing
himself, he watched you filling a bag with gold. That how you got there, he had not
the most distant idea, but that your style of life, your liberality to the arts, and
your sumptuous entertainments, were no doubt all paid for by your robberies of the
state."

" The villain."

" An order was signed for your imprisonment, and another at his solicitation."

" For my death ?"

" Yes. It was found that the robberies in the treasury had come to so large an
amount that no mercy could be shown to you. With regret I admit I consented to your
death."

" Whence is seen how fallible is human judgment,"

" It may be so."

" It is so, my lord."

" If injustice has been done you, Count Gradunio, and you can make it appear to me
that such is the case, the best blood in Venice shall not screen any one from just punishment. If we err in judgment we will at least meet out as even handed justice as we
may."

" I am satisfied. It is perhaps known to your highness that a bad, and too well
known kinsman of mine, named Gordoni, has seized upon my house and there resides."

" Yes, but this secret of the private entrance to the vaults he knows not."

" Indeed, my lord ! and yet the last time these eyes looked upon Gordoni was in the
vault."

The doge started.

" You are susprised, but perhaps you know that Gordoni and Flavius are intimate
friends, if such men may be spoken of in connection with so sacred and holy a word as
friendship."

" Of that we know nothing."

" Nor that together they visit the vaults, possessing themselves of gold and
silver."

" Is this possible ?"

" Nor that each go alone, thinking to outdo the other in the career of peculation,
while not many hours will elapse, before the time when they will with their ill-gotten
spoil, attempt to sail for England."

The doge was evidently strangely moved.

" I will rise at once, Count Gradunio, and consult the council. As I understand you,
what you mean to assert is, that to screen himself, Flavius accused you, thinking
that at all events up to that date, all his defalcations would fall upon your
head ?"

" Precisely so."

" And that since he has been carrying them on, and intends flying with Gordoni from Venice, despairing of such another opportunity of making an innocent person suffer for his own delinquencies."

" That s my case, my lord."

" It sha ll be seen to, count. When do you say they propose going."

" After the last final robbery of the state's treasure upon Saturday, at one of the clock, when they will meet together in the vaults."

" The villains. If this be true, Count Gradunio, your honour will stand upon a high pinnacle in Venice."

" No sir."

"No ?"

" I say no. I will remain in Venice so long and no longer, than will amply suffice to expose this monstrous ɟpiece of villany, and then no longer will I trust myself in the keeping of a state, which condemns, unheard, even her noblest sons to a terrible and ignominous death."

" We shall hope count, to make you think better of this resolve."

The doge had risen, and having thrown around him an ermine robe, he advanced to the door of his chamber, and called aloud—" What ho ! Without there ?"

One of the pages hastily awoke, and stumbling over some article of furniture that lay in his way, he came into the doge's chamber, when his astonishment at beholding a stranger seated, was ludicrous in the extreme.

" Have you kept good watch ?" said the doge.

The page threw himself upon his knees, for he thought now that his doom was sealed.

" Rise, fear nothing. Take this signet ring, and hie thee at once to the houses of the senators Caltili, Romano, Mercandante, and Julius. Bid them come hither with all convenient despatch."

" Yes, my lord, yes."

" Go, go, at once."

The bewildered page departed upon his errand, and then the doge, turning to the count, said—" Remain with me, Count Gradunio, and we will hold a secret council, which will, let us hope, circumvent those who are your enemies."

" Give me a pass, my lord, and I will return within the hour by way of the proper entrance to St. Mark, I have an urgent necessity to say some words to one, who waits my company."

" Take this," said the doge, as he hastily wrote an order, for the admittance of the count, to his private council chamber. " Take this. It will pass you to us freely. Do not be beyond the hour, count."

" Your highness may depend upon me. This affair sits too near my heart, to be at all neglected."

" Will you leave by the public road ?"

" No, as I came let me go, your highness. I have my reasons, and upon my head be the truth of that which I have told to you. An examination of the state coffers, will soon prove the recent proccedings of Flavius and his associate."

" They shall be made public examples of."

" Aye ; your highness punish publicly, and let those who are accused of wrong-doing face their foes and accusers, and not be murdered in the dark, because they may have deserved death in the light."

" Such shall not be the case with our grand treasurer. The tortuous policy of taking the lives of criminals in secret, has always been opposed to my own feelings. The matter is worth considering. It is long since the head of a noble has fallen between the pillars of the square."

" It is, and the people think that death is only dealt to the commonalty, and that a criminal noble is smuggled away to some other land. But these are matters not germane to our purpose. In an hour your highness may be sure to see me."

" In an hour be it."

The Count Gradunio bowed to the doge, and left the apartment by the secret door.

He hurried onwards, for much he feared he had remained beyond the time he had specified to Jerome, as that after which he was to wait no more, but conclude that something had happened amiss to his master. He called him with a loud voice, and to his great joy, received an instant and joyous response from him.

CHAPTER XXX.

THE BRAVO'S HAUNT AGAIN.

"HA! ha!" shouted Orcolo the bravo and bandit, as he drained the glass to the dregs, "Ha, ha, ha! Let Pietro float out to the lagunes, and feed the crows and the fish. He was always but a bungling hand."

"We earned our gold dearly on that night, in the garden of the Count of Syracuse," muttered the companion of Orcolo, "two of our fraternity killed, and a third badly hurt."

"Bah!"

"Bah! yourself. What do you mean by saying 'Bah!' you great idiot?"

"What. Will you be always flouting at me, and teazing me, Marco. Some of these odd days, my dagger will drink your blood."

"If I thought that for one moment, Orcolo," replied the other, "I would plaster that wall with your brains."

"My brains!"

"Aye, true, I beg your pardon. You have none, but I would knock that great chuckle head of yours to pieces, and smash it against the wall as food for the infernal beetles that abound here, so that to walk about they go off cracking like nuts beneath our feet."

"Ha! ha! You are merry."

"I am not."

"I say you are."

The abrupt entrance of the lad who served as a guide to customers, put an end to a colloquy, which was certainly becoming anything but harmonious.

"A cavalier," said the boy, "is close at hand. A job for you both, I daresay. Give me my wage."

"Give you what?"

"My half scudi that I am entitled to, for showing the way to a customer."

"There take it, but it's shocking to see one so young giving his mind to avarice. Shew in the cavalier. We shall find some old friend, Marco."

"I don't care if we do."

"Oh, you brute, nothing will please you."

"What's that to you."

"Well, who said it was. Hold your riot. Here is a worthy cavalier come to throw a few gold pieces in our way, I'll be bound."

It was Flavius, the grand treasurer, who made his appearance now at the haunt of the bravos. He was enveloped in an ample cloak of grey cloth, and wore a very plain velvet cap without a feather. He smiled after a strange fashion, as he said, "A good day to you, gentlemen, I trust I find you sufficiently disengaged, to earn a few gold pieces in the way of your vocation."

Orcolo grinned, as he replied, "Signor, we are never above business. All we want to know is the name and the price."

"As for the name, it is Gordoni. The price you shall yourself set upon your work so soon as you have done it."

"Gordoni? He who occupies the Palazzo Gradunio?"

"The same."

"Humph!"

"You know him, I may perceive by you conduct."

"Oh, yes. Lately we had a little job from him on hand, that is all, signor, but that is of no consequence, for business with us takes precedence of all other considerations. If we do the deed, may we name a hundred pieces?"

"Yes, and half down."

"Half down, according to our usual practice, signor. You may then consider that your wishes are accomplished."

"There," said Flavius, as he laid a heavy purse upon the table. "There is more than you require. We can reckon when I again see you. Farewell, I will call to-morrow."

"Adieü, signor; you know how to transact business with men of honour. There, now," added Orcolo, when Flavius had gone, "that's the sort of fellow for my money. He settles the affair in a trice, making no dispute about the terms. Was there ever such a cool comfortable job now? Hilloa! what now?"

"Another customer," said the boy. "Give me my wage."

"Why, you young rascal, you will be as rich as Anabob the Jew, if you go on in this way. There's a whole scudi for you, and it will stand good for the next time any is due to you."

"All's right. This way, signor."

"I know the way well enough, boy," said a stern voice, and in a another moment who should make his appearance, looking very pale and ill, but Gordoni himself! The bravos started and looked significantly at each other. Gordoni was in evident pain as he spoke to them.

"Do you chance," he said, "to be acquainted personally with Flavius the senator, and Grand Treasurer of the State?"

They shook their heads.

"What manner of man is he, signor?" said Orcolo, "and how does he go about attired in Venice?"

"He is a suspicious man, and adopts many costumes. To-night he wears a large grey cloak, and a velvet hat without a feather. I parted with him only an hour since near the canal Orsini."

"Il diavolo!"

Marco was fearful that Orcolo was going to spoil the market by letting him, Gordoni, know that Flavius had actually been there to pay them for his assassination, and he gave him a warning kick under the table.

"Ahem!" said Orcolo. "What price did you think of paying, signor?"

"Why, if the affair be not bungled, like the last you had in hand for me, I care not what you ask me—so that it be at all reasonable. I am aware that such a man as Flavius should be paid for better than one of the mere bourgeoise."

"Right, signor, right; we will do it for a hundred pieces down in advance."

"The half down as usual."

Orcolo looked puzzled; and beckoning Marco aside, he whispered—

"You were wont, Marco, to have a good wit and a clear head at figures. How can this affair be managed? Here are two hundred pieces to earn, and if we take fifty from Gordoni to slay Flavius, we miss Flavius's fifty for slaying Gordoni!"

"As how—can't we slay both?"

"Yes; but, stupid, how are we to get the fifty from a dead man? How is it to be managed? Come stir up thy wit."

Marco looked fairly bothered.

"Take Gordoni's fifty," he said at length, "and we will talk the matter over together, and perhaps find out some way of managing. Let us make sure of the fifty from each first, and then we will consider over a bottle."

"Good; then you would let Gordoni go now, because we might comfortably enough then do Flavius's little job, you know?"

"Oh yes, let him go now, he is sure to come to us to-morrow."

"True, true, and most likely he has no more than fifty about him, so we will even take it, and let him go in peace as you say; oh, Marco you have a wit."

They returned to Gordoni who had felt a little uneasy during the progress of the wispered conferance and Orcolo said to him,—

"The half down then signor, and we will do your work."

Gordoni counted out the money with care, and then after stating that by that same hour on ' the following evening he would call with the other fifty, he took his leave.

"All's right," said Marco, "I have it."

"Have what?"

"An idea."

"Hold it fast, then, stupid, it may be a long while before you have another."

"Hark you, Orcolo, I know that's not your own wit, but to utter it is your own folly, and if business of importance was not now on hand you should repent of it most bitterly."

"Bah!"

"Exactly, that is the full amount of your eloquence. But as regards this affair, what is to hinder us from doing the job for Gordoni if he comes first, and Flavius if he comes, and so pocketing the money which each will bring to pay for the other's murder, and we will behave like men of honour, by feathering a stiletto into both of them."

"I said you had a wit," cried Orcolo, as he dealt his thigh a blow; "I always said you had a wit, I could not see my way through the difficulty, and here you now have made it as clear as a glass of old Cyprus."

"Which would be no bad thing just now Orcolo."

"Good again."

The two bravos sat over their Cyprus wine, and while they are enjoying themselves after such a fashion, we will take a glance at Gordoni and Flavius who were each so intent upon the destruction of the other It happened that Flavius walked very slowly after leaving the haunt of the bravos, so that as Gordoni happened to be taking the same route which was homewards, he overtook him.

"Ha! Flavius," exclaimed Gordoni, full of meditation are you."

Flavius started.

"Yes Gordoni," he replied "are you better from your night's adventure in the convent, when Floranthe let you know that every rose has its thorn."

"Thorn, indeed. Had it gone a little deeper it might have reached my heart. As it is, I have only a flesh wound, but yet an awkard and uncomfortable one. I would not wish an enemy such a wound."

"No, because you think it will heal."

"Perhaps so. But we shall fear no enemies in England, where we can live in as perfect good fellowship as may be."

There was a pause of some few moments duration, which was broken by Flavius saying,—

"Have you carefully packed your share of the plunder from the vaults?"

"I have, and you, where have you bestowed yours?"

"In my chamber ready for removal. I hope the English ship will take us, after we have taken the trouble to go out to her in a boat with our valuables. It is a chance, but I hope for the best."

"No chance; I have known it to be done often. Whither go you?"

"I have some business."

"And I."

"God bless you. Adieu!—You will be a corpse soon I hope."

"The saints hold you in their holy keeping. Adieu!—I think you will not have breath for many hours longer to say, adieu."

Then these two villains of the first degree separated from each other, each anxious to do so in order that the bravo's might find an opportunity of executing the frightful purpose.

And in the midst of all this lay poor Stralani, in all the fever of his wound, and the worse fever of his anxious thoughts. Oh how he wished to be up and about that he might fly to the rescue of Floranthe, for he could but perceive by the manner of his kind entertainers that something was amiss. The opiate that the physician had given him, certainly did its duty in inducing sleep, but it had the after effect of all opiates, namely, in leaving behind it a sense of confusion which the brain in vain tried to struggle against. He looked earnestly at the gardener's daughter, and when she did not speak, but only looked tearfully at him, he said, "Ah, there is bad news from the palazzo."

"No, no."

"Have you seen Floranthe?"

The young girl shook her head, and uttered a faint negative. It was at once responded to by Stralani with a groan. He could not and would not divest his mind from the feeling that something very serious must have happened to Floranthe. Far better would it have been for those who were around him, to have told him at once what had became of Floranthe. Suspense was to him worse than certainty. When the Jewish physician again made his appearance, he looked hard at Stralani, as he said "You are suffering from an amount of anxiety which will much retard your cure."

"Yes, yes. I admit so much."

"Will you confide in me?"

"I will most freely. It is anxiety concerning the fate of Floranthe, the only child of the Count Syracuse, that sits so heavy at my heart."

"If to know precisely what has occurred to that young lady will in any way compose you, I can tell you."

"Oh, speak! speak!"

"By accident I chance to know that she is in perfect safety in the convent of the Benedictine nuns."

"I breathe again."

"It must be obvious to you that there she had better remain until your recovery, and if you would wish note or message sent to her, I have a means of accomplishing so much."

Stralani could only look his thanks to the the Jew physician for this most signal service.

———

CHAPTER XXXI.

THE FURTHER ADVENTURE OF FLORANTHE AND JULIA IN THE CHAPEL.

WHILE Captain Herbert and his faithful follower, Jack Stevens, were doing their best to effect the rescue of Julia the novice, that much persecuted young girl was in the chapel with Floranthe, guarded by the two old nuns, who grinned and chattered together about the probabilities and the possibilities of what was occuring in the convent garden.

"What can it be?" said one.

"Perhaps a man," said the other.

"Impossible! A man in the precincts of this holy place. When did you ever hear of such profanation."

"Never, except when the lady abbess has had important affairs to settle with some one. He! he! he!"

"Ah, then, indeed. He! he! he!"

"You will choke yourself, sister."

"Not I—not I. Only sometimes when I laugh I have a slight cough, which when I am old ought to leave me, seeing that it has attacked me while I am quite young."

"When you are old, sister?"

"Yes, yes."

"Why, what do you call yourself now, my dear sister?"

"Middle aged, my dear sister."

"Oh, pho! I am middle-aged, and I am fifty; I'm sure you are sixty at the very least."

"Sixty?"

"Yes, sixty to be sure. Don't think to deceive me, dear sister, you know you are now old and aged."

"Aged?"

"Yes aged, and if you are respectable when you are aged, I don't see why you should make such a riot about it."

"Oh, that I should live to be so insulted."

"What can these two hags be talking of," said Julia, "oh, Floranthe, perhaps even they may listen to the voice of avarice and aid us upon promise of an ample reward for so doing."

"The attempt cannot make our position worse," said Floranthe ; "make it Julia, try what your eloquence can effect upon them ; who knows but this may be an opportunity that may enable us to do more towards our deliverence than we have yet had a chance of doing."

Julia walked up to the old nuns. She did not think it at all necessary to make any long preface to what she had to say, but at once proposed the matter to them, saying—

"We have friends who are without the convent walls who will pay you well for aiding our escape."

"Escape," cried one of the nuns.

"Escape," cried the other.

"Yes," continued Julia, "we both wish of course to leave the convent, and if you wil aid us so to do, we will take care your reward shall be ample."

"And pray damsels, children, infants almost I ought to say, why do you want to escape from here."

"Oh, to some odious men," cried the other, "to be married."

"Well," said Julia, "There's no crime in that."

"Yes, but there is though, and if you were to offer us all the money in the world you should not escape for such a purpose ; we hate men, we hate to hear of young children like you being married, and we will go through fire and water at any time to stop you."

"So that's both your answers ?"

"To be sure," cried the other, "we are both ashamed of you."

"Hark," said Floranthe, "do you hear those sounds from the convent garden, Julia? what do they portend."

"My heart tells me," sighed Julia, "that an effort of some kind is being made to save me."

"What shall we do ?"

"Strive to second those who would rescue us from this dismal place ; do you not see Floranthe, yon flag in the corner with a spear handle to it ; it was presented to the convent by a victorious general of Venice. Suppose we see how far the use of such a weapon will frighten the nuns who are guarding us, if we could succeed in overcoming them, and locking them in one of the confessionals we might go into the garden."

"With all my heart," said Floranthe.

"Do you fear."

"Not I, and as I think, Julia, I am the stronger of us two, I will make the demonstration with the flag."

"I will second you."

"Come, come," cried one of the old nuns, "we object to all this whispering in the chapel of the convent, it must not be ; the Ursulines was always a quiet and a pious place."

Floranthe went to the corner where the victorious trophy in the shape of a flag was kept; without any hesitation she seized it, and advanced with the formidable looking spear head directed towtids the nuns.

"Any death," she said, "is preferable to the thraldom in which we are now kept, and any desperate deed, may be a forunner of death ; your two lives will at least in some respects satisfy our vengeance."

The old nuns were for the moment, too thunder-stricken at this attack, to say a word or to move, but the shriek they simultaneonsly gave utterance to when they did recover a little, almost made Floranthe let fall the weapon, which a very slight share of resistance would have disarmed her of. They then set off at great speed towards the chapel, and as the first open door they chanced to come to was the door of a confessional, they both rushed in, fighting, tearing, scratching, and jostling each other for precedence. The moment they were both in, Floranthe fastened the door by a bolt which was upon the outside.

"We are now comparatively free, Julia," she said.

"Yes Floranthe, and limited as our freedom is, we must try to make some use of it. The door of the chapel is open, let us make four way into the garden, and endeavour to find friends, even if it should end in our confronting foes."

Floranthe needed no second bidding, and the two young girls who were so unjustly deprived of their liberty in the convent, at once hastened to the door conducting to the garden. A short flight of six steps, conducted them to one of the gravel paths, and then pausing to listen a moment, they heard the voice of the abbess crying in loud shrill notes—" Help, help."

This was at the precise juncture, when Jack and Captain Herbert had attained so signal a victory over the villains, Gordoni and the monk. To hasten in the direction of the sounds of tumult, was of course the impulse of Floranthe and Julia, and they reached the flower bed, where Gordoni and the monk sat looking at each other, as well as the faint light would permit them, with woeful countenances, which would have been quite a study for a painter.

" Herbert, Herbert !" cried Julia. Are you here ?"

" Help, help !" shouted Floranthe.

Gordoni struggled to his feet, and seized Julia by the wrist.

" And so," he said, " it is a friend of yours who has desecrated the garden of the convent; let him beware."

" Off villain," cried Floranthe, disengaging herself from his grasp; " there is contamination in your touch."

" Herbert! Herbert!" again called Julia, and with the hope of attracting the attention of her lover if he came near at hand, she waved a handkerchief in the night air.

A branch of a tree caught it from her grasp, and afterwards, as we know, it came into the possession of Jack Stevens. Gordoni was about to make another attempt to seize upon Floranthe, when the rapid sound of many approaching footsteps, and the flash of numerous lights came upon his senses, and he desisted. In another moment the abbess accompanied by all the force of the convent made her appearance, while the alarm bell which continued tolling was sure shortly to produce plenty of aid.

" This way," cried Gordoni, " this way, your nuns have deserted their trust, madam, for here are your prisoners at large."

The abbess was astounded to see Julia and Floranthe in the garden, and for a few moments she could not speak to then. Then stepping close to Floranthe, she said, How dared you leave the chapel without my orders so to do ?"

Floranthe's heart swelled within her, as she replied, " And how dared you seek to detain me there contrary to my inclination."

" This is well," said the abbess. " Open defiance; I like it much better than a weak covert resistance to my power, and an affected submission. We shall know how to deal with you, Floranthe. Seize her."

Some half dozen nuns laid hands upon Floranthe.

" Carry her," said the abbess, speaking slowly, " to No. 3."

What or where No. 3 was, was a mystery to Floranthe, but she could not help observing that even the nuns gave a shudder as they heard the words.

" No—no," cried Julia, stepping forward. " I was the instigator of this proceeding, and upon me and me alone should the consequences, if any, fall."

" As for Julia," said the abbess, speaking in the same composed tone, " conduct her to No. 4."

The nuns shuddered again.

" I believe," said Floranthe, as she glanced around her, " that some thirty women and two men have power sufficient to perpetrate any diabolical act they please, upon those who are defenceless, but I tell you, madam, that a day of mortal retribution will come."

The abbess smiled.

" A day when you will be asked to account for every word and look that you have made use of towards me, since my imprisonment in this most sinful and unholy place."

" She calls the convent sinful and unholy!" exclaimed Rene.

" It matters not," said the abbess. " Carry them away."

" I will visit them shortly," said the monk, " and exhort them."

" Is not the interrupted ceremony to go on?" whispered Gordoni to the abbess.

" Not now. There are too many spectators. An alarm has been already given which will soon bring some of the eclesiastics of the city to the convent."

" The bell has ceased."

" Yes, but it has been tolling."

"What then would you have me do?"

"Leave the convent now as quickly as you can, and come to-morrow when I will take such measures as shall insure you no disappointment, I feel now personally aggrieved and interested in these matters. My authority has been braved, and I have endured much personal contumely and insult."

"Yes, yes, you have."

Gordoni was delighted to find this feeling in the bosom of the abbess, for it served to ensure him a kind of partisanship, which otherwise he would have found it difficult to purchase, even at any pecuniary sacrifice.

"Yes, yes," he added, " your authority has been scoffed at, and you yourself have been insulted."

"Concerning which," said the abbess, "I need no prompter. Leave the convent now."

Gordoni had nothing to oppose to the suggestion, which came quite in the shape of an order, and he bowed and left the building. He did not fail, however, to cast a threatening glance upon Floranthe, whom he still believed would be persecuted into becoming his, before she ever again crossed the threshold of the Ursuline convent. The abbess made a sign to the nuns, that she would have the orders she had given concerning Floranthe and Julia, obeyed forthwith.

"At least," said Julia, " if we are to be imprisoned, let it be together."

"No," said the abbess, " that may be a gratification, and therefore it is denied to you. It will not again happen that you are able to break out of the place in which it is my pleasure you should remain."

"Ask no favour Julia," said Floranthe, "of those to whom cruelty is nature. Farewell, and may Heaven bless you!"

Julia sprang forward, and clung to Floranthe. It semed to her as though the time had arrived to bid her an eternal adieu. She clung to her, and spoke despairingly saying—" No, no ! we will not part. We will not part, Floranthe. In joy—in sorrow —in despair or in hope, let us be now together."

"Part them," said the abbess.

With a savage sort of joy, the nuns sprang forward, and with much more than necessary violence tore them asunder. The abbess made an impotent gesture with her arm, ad they were hurried across the garden, and into the convent again, by a low small doorway which led into one of the long narrow passages, from which branched the cells, which were devoted to the night lodging of the nuns. It would seem that where ever the places in which they were by the command of the abbess to be imprisoned, were, that they could not be very distant from each other, for the nuns who held Floranthe, proceeded on the same course with those who held Julia. At the further extremity of the long corridor in which they were, was a wooden door of ordinary enough rm, and the abbess said to Rene—"! You know where in my private parlour to lay your hand upon the key we shall want. Go quickly, and we will wait your return."

Rene hastily departed. It was during her absence, that Floranthe made one more effort to obtain her freedom.

"Lady abbess," she said. "Listen to me. It may be true that my father, the Count Syracuse, instigated by Gordoni, has placed me in your hands, but if he is capable of deserting me, I belong to a large and noble family; enquiries will soon be made of him concerning me, which he will be compelled to answer, and then you will be called upon to account for these most scandalous outrages."

"Which I am perfectly willing to do," said the abbess.

Rene came back with the key that the abbess had sent her for at this moment, and began opening the wooden door at the end of the passage.

Julia and Floranthe looked on, fully expecting that the door when opened, would lead to some subterraneous thoroughfare; but such was not the case, for immediately behind the wooden door was another, but of very different appearance. This was a door of massive iron, studded with huge knots, and having altogether more the appearance of some fortress than a door in a convent. One of the keys that Rene had brought fitted the lock of it, and with a creaking sound it moved on its hinges. Beyond all was darkness, and a strange close, damp atmosphere came from within. The lights carried by the nuns burnt but dimly, as they came into contact with the vitiated atmosphere.

"Pass on," said the abbess.

"Whither does this lead?" said Julia.

"Pass on."

"Better to die here," exclaimed Floranthe, "than be immured in such a place as this."

"Hope!" said a voice.

The abbess looked about her in amazement. The most eager inquiry was made, but no one could ascertain from whom the sound had come. Floranthe and Julia were dragged onwards.

CHAPTER XXXII.

THE BURIAL VAULTS OF THE URSULINES.

AFTER passing through the doorway, Floranthe became aware that the bare ground only was beneath her feet, and that that was, in places, extremely damp, while a putrid sort of exhalation pervaded the atmosphere, making it most difficult and noxious to breathe. That it was very impure was sufficiently testified by the state of the lights, for they moved considerably, and one or two of them even showed symptoms of approaching dissolution.

"If," said Julia, "our death is a thing determined upon, cannot we be murdered by some more quick method than by incarceration in such a place as this? Even your own myrmidons evidently shrink aghast from so unheard-of an amount of cruelty."

"Forward!" said the abbess.

The nuns trembled, and some of them audibly repeated prayers. All their superstitious feelings began to be excited, for the passage they were in led to no other a place than the vaults where the dead of the convent were interred, and left to sleep that sleep which knows no waking. Suddenly the abbess paused, and when Rene, who was following her closely, came up to her, she held out her hand and had some more keys delivered to her. With one of these she opened a low-arched door, and before Julia could even make an unavailing opposition, she found herself thrust into some place in which she could plainly hear the plashing of water. The door was immediately closed upon her, and locked by the abbess, who again commanded the cortege to proceed. Floranthe was half maddened by observing the fate of Julia, and she, hopeless as the task seemed, resolved that she would make one more effort to be free. The abbess had just paused before another door similar to that through the opening disclosed, by which poor Julia had been so noiselessly thrust, when Floranthe, snatching one of the lights from the foremost of the nuns, made a rush down the passage. For the moment she outstripped pursuit, and probably she might have got further, but that she ran against some one, who said to her in a low but friendly tone,—

"Hush! for Heaven's sake. By offering resistance you only provoke more coercion. Be calm and hopeful. In less than half an hour I will come to you."

"Oh, do not deceive me," said Floranthe.

"God hears us," was the brief, but emphatic reply from the nun, for such she was Floranthe had no doubt but that it was this same nun who had so astonished the abbess by pronouncing the word "Hope!" which had certainly had some effect in calming the fears of Floranthe and Julia. This short colloquy did not take above a couple of seconds in taking place, so that by the time the abbess and the nuns rushed upon Floranthe, there was all the appearance as if she had been stopped by the nun who had spoken to her the few consoling words.

"Thanks," said the abbess.

The nun bowed her head.

"This service shall be remembered, and set against some instances of contumacy which we have recorded against you."

The nun bowed again, saying,

"May I have leave to pray to-night in the chapel, Madame?"

"Yes."

The nun did not allow the abbess to see the satisfaction that irradiated her features, but passed on, with her face partially hidden in the veil which she wore. Floranthe was more reconciled to her position—a position which she could not alter even by force, and in the course of the next two minutes she was alone, and in perfect darkness, in a place, which, for horrors of fact and of imagination, transcended anything which she had thought could be found in the whole of the convent. Darkness certainly adds to some terrors, and takes away from others; the probability is that it now, so far as Floranthe was concerned, had both these effects. She heard the water was either actually within the place where she was imprisoned, or so close to it, as to give all the effect, in the dark, of its being there, and she heard or fancied she heard, every now and then, a splash, suddenly coming upon the ear, and suddenly subsiding, as though some reptile was swimming or disporting in a stagnant pool. Floranthe shuddered, and it was quite a quarter of an hour before she could gather courage sufficient to try to make any researches in her dungeon, or even to remove from the spot upon which she stood. Then, however, she slowly moved forward, stretching out her arms as she went, so that no unexpected obstacle should come in her way. She had not proceeded far in this fashion, when she touched something soft, and, upon feeling it more minutely, she was convinced it was velvet, but for what purpose, or how it came there, she was completely at a loss to conjecture. Had she but known that she was touching a velvet pall which was over one of the coffins of a deceased abbess of the convent, she would have shrunk back with horror. There is, even to the young, something so terrible in death, that there are few indeed so callous to the presence of the destroyer, who will not feel more than the tongue can tell, at any enforced contact with the sad remnants of mortality. Floranths, however, had no such feeling, and continued her examination of the vault, without a suspicion that she was really among the dead. Such, however, was really the case. The next object which she encountered was a something near to the floor, which she at first thought was a table of some sort, and then a bench set up for some purpose—at all events, it afforded to her a place whereon to rest, and she gladly availed herself of it. She little thought it was a coffin raised to a certain height upon a strong framework of timber, covered with black cloth.

"An hour," said Floranthe to herself, "an hour—I was promised aid in an hour. Oh, what a length of time one hour is to those who watch each moment as it slowly passes into eternity, never to return! An hour! What, to some in Venice now, is an hour? A few fleeting minutes of gaiety, a laugh or two, some sparkling words—perchance a sigh that time flies so swiftly, and the hour is gone!"

But the longest hour must have an end; and even that which the poor persecuted Floranthe watched in the vaults of the Ursuline convent came at length to an end. Suddenly Floranthe started to her feet, for she had heard a faint sound outside of the dungeon door. She was for a few moments at a loss to come to a conclusion as to what it was; but she felt almost certain that some one was making an effort to force the door. That it could be any other than the compassionate nun, she could not think; and yet she feared to commit her or herself by saying anything, or by even taking any notice of the efforts making without; yet, as may be well supposed, she listened with the most intense interest to all that was passing. The efforts were not all unavailing. The door was very old, and in a few moments it shook, and with a cracking noise began to give way. A faint gleam of light shot into the dungeon. Floranthe's expectation was on tiptoe. She hastened forwards, and, no longer able to command herself to silence, she cried—

"It is you, my friend, who whispered hope to me; it is you!"

All was still. She fancied that her voice had not penetrated so far as the outside of the cell, and she spoke again—

"One word! Speak to me one word, that I may call to my aid all the hopes you have implanted in my bosom."

The door burst open with a crash. Floranthe rushed forward, and could hardly save herself from falling into the arms of—the monk!

In one hand he carried a lamp, and in the other a small iron crow-bar, by the aid of which he had succeeded in forcing open the door of that dismal habitation. There was upon his countenance an expression which, to Floranthe, was inexpressibly terrifying. He bent his gaze upon her for a few moments in silence, and then he said—

"You thought it was another?"

Floranthe was too much choked with terror and indignation to answer him, had she felt inclined to do so, and, after waiting for some few minutes, and finding she was silent, he added—

"It matters not. Floranthe, I am prepared to stake soul as well as body upon the issue of my love — my wild, uncontrollable passion I should call it — for you!"

Still Floranthe said nothing, she only shrank back with a look of such absolute horror and abhorrence, that even he could not but be able thoroughly to translate it. Blended indeed, by passion must he have been not to feel how hopeless it was for him to attempt to light up the flame of affection in such a breast as Floranthe's, and yet so far had what he called his wild love controlled his judgment, that he persevered.

"Floranthe, angel sent to bless, tempt, or curse me," he said, "you made me love you, I demand love in return. Perhaps, 'tis well before you answer, me that you should hear me out."

"No, no, no. I have no answer but what is contained in one word."

"And that?"

"Is—begone!"

"I expected this—I looked for this—yes, I looked for scorn, contempt, reproaches, maledictions; but yet I love. Floranthe, I will, I can rescue you."

"Better death."

"No—oh, no—do you know where you are?"

"Anywhere becomes endurable alone when contrasted with your most loathsome presence"

"Oh, Floranthe, have pity upon me, I will be your slave—the humblest slave that mortal ever had, if you will but pity me. I will wait upon you as ever fawning dog waited on an imperious master for a look or a smile; but do not say you loathe me; and, oh! let me save you from all the countless horrors that in this dreadful place surround you."

CHAPTER XXXIII.

THE PARTIAL ESCAPE.—GORDONI'S ERROR.

FLORANTHE now, indeed, felt that she had more than ample need for all her courage and presence of mind. Should either fail her at such a juncture as this, what horror might next be in store for her! She spoke in a tone of confidence that was belied by the tears that were really struggling at her heart as she said,—

"Base man, you see all things through the clouds of your own passions. Once more I bid you begone. I am not so helpless as you imagine. Gordoni, your vile associate and accomplice! has already felt that I am not defenceless?"

"You wounded him."

"Beware yourself."

"And do you, can you, really think, Floranthe, that I am not far past all dread of consequences. In my visit now to you I have proclaimed war with Heaven; however, I am content to trample upon all my vows; and think you then that after so much I shall be deterred by personal danger? No, I have said you are mine, and you shall be."

"No—no—no!"

"Yes, I say, yes; and let heaven or hell stir to prevent me, I still will clasp you in my arms, and in one last embrace."

He advanced as he spoke, but at that moment the door of the vault was opened, and a figure all in white, the face of which was covered, presented itself to the monk, and to the rather startled Floranthe. A cry of terror came from the lips of the monk. The figure slowly moved aside, and pointed to the door of the vault—with bowed frame and trembling limbs the monk obeyed the order, and crept slowly from the place.

"Mercy ! mercy !" he moaned, "do not follow me! I think I know the disturbed spirit, you are she who last perished in these vaults. Mercy ! mercy ! Oh, do not follow me, and drive my soul to madness."

Still the figure pointed to the door, and in another moment the monk was gone. Floranthe heard him fly, shrieking down the long passages as though he were driven absolutely mad by the apparition he supposed he had seen. Floranthe by no means shared in his fears, but she did look with some amount of curiosity upon the truly spectral-looking appearance that had so effectually scared away so unwelcome an intruder. She had an idea that it could be no other than the compassionate nun who had promised to come to her, and the moment the veil was removed she saw that she was right.

"How can I sufficiently thank you," said Floranthe.

"Do not thank me at all; I only rejoice that I arrived so opportunely to rescue you from that monster.

"A monster indeed!"

"I overheard all that he said to you, and now, having that power over him, I think I can terrify him from ever attempting such acts for the future."

"And poor Julia, where is she?"

"I intended to have brought her to you, but seeing a light gleaming from this vault in which you had been placed, I forced the door of the one in which she was a prisoner and came to you."

"Oh, fly to her rescue," cried Floranthe, "she must be suffering much if her temporary abode be like this."

The lamp which the monk had left behind him in his terror, as well as one which the nun had with her, enabled Floranthe to see now that she was in a vault consecrated to the dead and that what she had been resting upon was a coffin.

"You shudder," said the nun, as they left the vault together. "but the serenity and companionship of the dead in this place is far better than that of many of the living."

"That I truly believe," said Floranthe.

A few steps brought them to the cell of Julia, and the nun, assisted by Floranthe, soon succeeded in opening the door.

"Julia, Julia!" cried Floranthe.

The young girl who had shown such noble courage, and such true vitality of soul, sprang forward with a cry of joy and flung herself into Floranthe's arms.

"Oh, you have come to save me," she said—"you have come to save me."

"Nay, do not thank me," said Floranthe. "This," turning to the nun, "is our friend and preserver from the continued horrors of these dreadful places."

Julia embraced the nun, and loaded her with expressions of gratitude, which she in vain tried to stop.

"I pray you say no more," she said. "Recollect that time is precious, that each moment may bring danger with it."

"Oh, yes, yes. What are we to do?"

"That is what has engaged my most earnest thoughts; and if you can carry out in safety what I propose, all will yet be well."

Both Julia and Floranthe were eager to hear the proposition of the nun, which they knew would be dictated by the highest regard to their feelings, and interests, situated as they were.

"There is a suite of rooms at the west wing of the convent, in which two young novices long ago committed suicide.'"

"Alas!" said Julia.

"They found their condition so intolerable that they resolved to die in each other's arms, rather than continue to endure it, and they did really so die in one of those rooms. Since then, the apartments, which are five in number, have been reported to be haunted by the spirits of the two novices. What say you to hiding there?"

"Oh, with pleasure," said Floranthe.

"Anywhere is welcome," said Julia.

" You have no fears ?"

" None, none. Surely if there be really the spirits of those poor young creatures, haunting those rooms, they should feel compassion towards us, rather than aught else.'

" Doubtless."

" Oh, we shall have no fears."

" I hope that your stay there," continued the nun, " will not be long. It shall only last until some good opportunity occurs of getting you past the convent gates, which just now are guarded with double strictness."

" Yes, no doubt," said Julia, " such will be the case, after the alarm that was given, while we were all in the chapel of the convent. Can you tell me any particulars of that alarm ?"

" Yes."

" Oh, speak, speak !"

" It appears there were two men actually in the convent garden ; and when the whole place was in the confusion of such a circumstance, they maltreated Gordoni and the confessor, and then escaped in a boat that was moored, as we hear, close to the wall in the canal, to the eastward."

" It was he !" said Julia.

" Your English lover ?"

" Yes—oh, yes. He knows that I am here, and it was an attempt of his to rescue me; you may depend that it will be renewed."

" In that case, I will be upon the watch," said the nun, " and try and assist him. But come, we must close the doors of these cells, and then, when the lady abbess does condescend to visit them, she will be not be a little surprised to find them, to all appearance, as she left them, but the prisoners gone."

The doors of the two vaults, were then carefully fastened, and the nun preceded Julia and Floranthe to the upper portion of the building. Oh, what an exquisite relief it was to bid adieu to that festiferous region, and breathe a purer air! Floranthe felt her spirits rise proportionably, and so did Julia, so that they really looked like two different beings. The nun, notwithstanding the conventual life she had led for many years, had by no means divested herself of human sympathies. On the contrary, it gave her the most sincere pleasure and gratification to notice that the two young girls were so well pleased with even the partial change that had taken place in their condition. Tears started to her eyes, as she said—" I do hope I shall be able to free you."

" And if not," said Julia, " you are, for the attempt so to do, entitled to our eternal gratitude and love."

" Most truly so," said Floranthe.

The nun, in her progress of conducting them to the suite of apartments she had made mention of, stopped more than once to listen if any one was stirring, but no sound broke the stillness of the convent. At the end of a long gallery she paused, and opened a door, which had evidently not for some time moved upon its hinges.

" This," she said, " leads to the rooms, I mention."

An ascent of about twelve steps of polished oak, with a balustrade of curious carved work, led directly to the haunted rooms, which certainly were as pleasant ones as the convent could afford. Indeed, they had been formerly used as lodging chambers, for any distinguished guest, who might wish to remain, during her stay in Venice, beneath a religious roof. All the antique furniture and rich hangings remained just as they had been before the catastrophe occurred which had given the room so evil and fearful a reputation.

" Oh," said Julia, " this is heaven in comparison with the odious place we have just left."

" It is indeed," said Floranthe.

The lamp was placed upon one of the antique tables, and the two young prisoners of so barbarous a policy as was adopted by their friends, looked around them with intense interest upon the dust-covered, and faded glories of those once magnificent rooms. But it was time their guide should leave them, in case her absence should be noted by any of the sisterhood.

GORDONI CAUGHT IN THE ACT OF ROBBING THE DOGE'S TREASURY.

"Now you are safe," said the nun. "Depend upon me finding some means of visiting you, and bringing you refreshments shortly. Until then farewell! and Heaven hold you both in its holy keeping. You shall be rescued from this place, if I can find a means to do so."

CHAPTER XXXIV.

THE REVELATION OF THE PAGE.—THE COUNCIL OF VENICE.

The Count Gradunio could not but be well enough pleased at the turn affairs had taken, and the manner in which the council had supported him, in his justification of himself. He looked forward with intense satisfaction to the punishment of Flavius, who had to such an extent added the sin of false-witness to his other crime. When he left the council at the Palace of St. Mark, he did not take the same precaution to conceal his face as he had hitherto done, since his escape from the dungeons of the Bridge of Sighs. Probably he did not feel that there was the same necessity for that particular concealment, and probably, if there had been, his spirits just then were in too great a state of exultation for him to think of such minor matters at all. Certain it is, though be this how it may, he walked with a free step to one of the numerous quays, and ordering a gondola, he determined upon having an airing by going a round-about way home to the lodge of his own rightful home. The gondola soon pushed off into the stream.

"Now, at all events," thought the Count Gradunio, "justice will hold sway in Venice, and right will most surely be done."

He folded his cloak around him, and retired somewhat beneath the canopy of the gondola, for many boats were on the grand canal, and he did not wish yet a recognition, even from those who might have been quite delighted to see him. The gondolier having received orders to go leisurely, commenced a song with a low melancholy cadence to it, and to the tune of which he paddled on his gondola, which gradually left the Palace of St. Mark behind it. At the lazy pace the gondolier was going, one would hardly have supposed that any accident would have occurred, nor, indeed, would it, if he had not, in the most flagrant and pertinacious manner, insisted upon continuing the song he had began. Now this song had about it such a slow movement, that it quite took an effect upon the man, the consequence of which was that he had not such command of his gondola as would otherwise have been the case with him. From one of the cross canals there suddenly shot out a boat going at great speed. Of course such a circumstance ought to have been sufficiently common to be well guarded against, but, in this instance, a collision took place, and the two gondoliers commenced abusing each other in the most approved fashion of their class. The Count Gradunio thought it would be better for him not to interfere in the matter, so he rather drew back, than otherwise. The passenger in the other gondola was by no means, however, of a similar opinion, for he came forward, and added his threats and menaces to the abuse of the gondolier. The voice struck upon the ear of the Count Gradunio familiarly, and a glance assured him it was no other than Gordoni.

"Another word," cried Gordoni, to the gondolier, "and I will come on board your boat, and sacrifice you to my resentment."

The gondolier laughed aloud at the threat. Gordoni was so aggravated at this, that he stepped from one boat to the other, and was upon the point of drawing his sword, when Count Gradunio, fearing that something serious was about to occur, thought that he was bound to appear upon the scene. He suddenly slipped out from beneath the canopy of the gondola, and confronted Gordoni. The manner of the sudden appearance of the Count Gradunio, and the imposing appearance of his tall figure, half enveloped in the folds of a cloak of great richness and value, would at any time, and under any circumstances, have attracted attention, but when, superadded to all that, Gordoni looked upon the well-known and unmistakeable features of the count, he was truly petrified.

"Gradunio!" he gasped.

The count looked sternly at him. For the space of a few brief moments he withstood all the terrors of that gaze, from one whom he believed numbered with the dead, and then he fell back into his own boat.

"Go on," said the count to the gondolier, who had charge of the boat he had hired, "go on."

The gondoliers were, however, both of them so stunned at what had happened, that it was a few moments before either of them could move away. The sudden surprise, and natural feelings of curiosity, made them friends in a moment.

"Let us forget that we quarrelled about nothing," said Gordoni's gondolier to the count's.

"Certainly, as you please."

"What, in the name of all the saints, is your master?"

"Master! I have none."

"Pardon me. I ought to have noticed you were a free gondolier. But who have you in your boat?"

"That I know not."

"It must be the devil himself; for did you not see how the noble signor, whom I carry, fell before him?"

"Aye, did I; but that is no good reason why my signor should be the devil himself."

"Nay, how else would mine have so shrunk before him?"

"Perhaps yours is the devil, and finding by the looks of mine, who may be holy as a saint, that he was discovered, he sunk before him in the way we both saw."

"Go to—go to."

"Go to yourself."

The quarrel between the two gondoliers would probably again have been renewed with more virulence than before, but the Count Gradunio put a stop to it, by saying,—

"Forward, gondolier; I cannot be delayed."

Making some contemptuous speeches to each other, the gondoliers now separated, and the Count Gradunio was not sorry to increase his distance from Gordoni, for he had no wish yet for that infamous person to know exactly that he was among the living. Fearful that Gordoni might recover from the state of surprise into which he had fallen upon the unexpected appearance of the count, the latter now urged the gondoliers to speed. The slow song was no longer sung, and the gondola shot rapidly through the water. In the course of five minutes the Count Gradunio was landed at the garden entrance to his own house, where Jerome was waiting for him with some anxiety.

"My lord," he said, "the young girl who was in the disguise of a page, rescued by your lordship from the canal, expresses a wish to have some conversation with you."

"Oh, certainly. Is she much better?"

"Oh, yes. My wife tells me now that she is quite recovered, but that it is evident something is pressing heavily upon her mind."

"I will go to her at once."

"Is all well at the council, my lord?"

"Quite as well as even you could wish, Jerome."

"Then it is well indeed!"

"Yes, Jerome. You will now live to see me in Venice as once I was, but not for long."

"Not for long, signor?"

"I mean, not for long here. I shall seek some other land, where there is more rational liberty, and more justice than in Venice. Jerome, you may share my fortunes, if you will."

"Signor, I would follow you to the end of the world," said Jerome, and the tears that involuntarily started to his eyes sufficiently testified to the heartfelt sincerity of his words.

"You shall, then, Jerome."

"How can I thank you, my lord?"

"Rather the question is, Jerome, how can I thank you sufficiently for your generous and chivalrous devotion to me? But we will say nothing of thanks just now."

"A good master, my lord, makes a good servant."

"Well, well, we will look upon that as settled—that you go with me, Jerome, to England."

"Anywhere, my lord."

The count now took his way to the apartment where he was told he should find the young girl whom he had so opportunely rescued from a watery grave. She was kneeling as if in prayer, and he drew back a moment, for he had no wish to interrupt her in her devotions. She had heard his footstep, however, and rose to meet him. A deep flush overspread her countenance as she said,—

"Signor, I owe you my life, but—"

"But what? Speak to me freely as a friend."

"Dare I do so?"

"Indeed you may."

The tone and manner of the count was cheering and assuring, so that she was able to say,—

"My history is in a few words summed up. I love,—"

"Love is a holy passion."

"Yes—yes,—I love, but am not loved."

"Then a hopeless passion it was that induced you to attempt your life."

"It was."

"Ah, you will live to look back with wonder at the motives that then actuated you. Doubtless you have friends in Venice?"

"Not one."

"Is that possible?"

"It is. I have relations, but not one friend."

"Then what do you purpose doing?"

"Taking the veil in some other country. It is to you, signor, who have kept me in life, that I can look for aid to carry out my projects."

"I will be a friend to you ; but will you not tell me your name and condition?"

"Oh, do not ask me until we are far away."

The count was much puzzled to know how to act for the best, as regarded one who was evidently now not in a frame of mind to act for herself. He adopted, under these circumstances, the best course he could do, for, after a few moments' consideration, he said,—

"I can have no possible desire, but for your happiness."

"I know that—I feel that," she said hastily. "All that I hear of you is good, although no one will tell me who you are."

"Will you exchange confidences with me, telling me who you are, if I, in return, tell you who I am?"

She hesitated a moment and then shook her head.

"Not yet, not yet. Oh, no—no—do not ask me, signor. You shall know, but not yet—oh, not yet. I feel that I cannot yet ; it would kill me."

"You speak," said the count, "mildly but kindly, as though I had the will and the power to force you to a confidence with me."

"Oh, forgive me."

"There is nothing to forgive. Believe me, that I should prize your confidence, but to be prized it must be freely given. It never will be extorted."

She was silent for some few moments, and then, when she spoke, she said in a wailing tone—"I am a poor weak girl, and my conduct must appear to you full of all sorts of follies and inconsistencies."

"Not at all."

"Nay, I feel that it must be so. I—I have one request."

"Name it!"

"It is that in Venice you would try to get me news of one person, in whose fate I am interested."

"I will do so."

"At once? Oh, can you at once seek for the blissful tidings, that I have not destroyed him."

"It is impossible for me to proceed upon such scanty knowledge, or to interest myself at all in your service.   Nay, do not look dejected or disappointed—I have one who in all faith and diligence, even as I would myself, will make the inquiries for you. What is the name of the person ?"

It seemed as if to pronounce that name would choke the young girl, but by an effort she did at last succeed in saying—" Signor Stralani !"

The count merely bowed, and made no remark about the name, nor did he pain her by attempting to draw any inference whatever from her wish to learn news of a cavalier. Ah! how warmly in her heart she thanked him for such forbearance.   The count sent for Jerome, and said to him in the presence of the page, so that she might be assured that he was not in any way trifling with her, in respect to her request—

" Go, Jerome, and make all the cautious inquiry that you can concerning the fate of a Signor Stralani."

" Yes, signor."

" Whatever news you bring will interest this lady first, so that, if I be not in the way, you will communicate it direct to her."

" I will, signor."

The young girl, who had played to Stralani so successfully the part of a page that he had never for a moment suspected the imposition, was much pacified by this means, which the count adopted of bringing her some news of Stralani. If, however, she had only been a little more explicit to him, she might have furnished him with a far better clue to the inquiries which Jerome was commanded to make. The mere mention of the name of Gordoni, would have been a circumstance that would have put the count in a better position to satisfy her ; but as it was, when each might have hushed each other's feeling, they were both going a little at cross purposes. We can scarcely wonder, however, at a young girl, situated as this one was, making but a very partial sort of confession of what was her real situation, and what were her real thoughts and wishes. Indeed, it was only the ingenuous manner, and the age of the Count Gradunio, which had got from her so much of her story as she had chosen to reveal. With him, it was quite clear to her that she would find a kind as well as an indulgent critic of her conduct.   After this the Count Gradunio found that it was time for him to attend, according to the promise he had made to that effect, the private council of the doge.   Of course, satiated as he now was, all other considerations must give way to the one of proving the guilt of Flavius, for it was from the proof of that guilt that he, Count Gradunio, was to pick his own triumphant justification from what had been alleged against him.   It would be needless to detail what passe at the council.   The signet ring of the doge procured the Count Gradunio ready admission to the Palace of St. Mark, and his appearance in the council chamber had quite an electric effect upon the two noblemen who had been summoned by the doge.   They both of course, in common with all who knew anything about his fate, or thought they knew—imagined him to be quietly sleeping the sleep of death, in the canal beneath the Bridge of Sighs.   The doge introduced him.   While absolute confusion sat upon the countenances of the two councillors, the Count Gradunio, at the request of the doge, related his story to them, just as he had related it to him.   At its conclusion, one of them said,—" Can you forgive us, count ?   There is an air of truthfulness about what you say that at once convinces me of your innocence."

He held out his hand as he spoke, but the Count Gradunio did not take it, but, fixing his eyes upon the councillor, he said,—" This is your old fault, my lord."

" Old fault?"

" Yes.   It was by too readily believing what you were told, that made you vote for my imprisonment and death upon the mere word of Flavius. Be so kind as to allow me to prove what I assert."

The councillor, as he might well be, was considerably abashed at this reproof, and the rest of the sitting was consumed in arranging the best mode of apprehending Flavius and Gordoni actually in the fact, that is to say, robbing the doge's treasure in the vaults beneath the palace.

CHAPTER XXXV.

GORDONI'S MISSION TO THE ENGLISH VESSEL.—RAPID EVENTS

THE English frigate "Wave," of which the lover of Julia, the young and beautiful novice, was the captain, had taken up a station in the gulf of Venice, as close to the city as a vessel of such size could find a secure position. It was the opinion of the officers of the vessel, that their captain had some political mission to Venice, which he was not at liberty to disclose to them. He certainly had a secret mission, but that it was the very reverse of political we happen to be well aware, as likewise is the reader. Jack, whom he had taken with him to the convent garden, with the hope of, by his assistance, carrying off Julia, was of course bound to secresy in the matter; and a very important personage Jack accordingly became among his messmates. To be sure, any extravagant notions of delicacy did not prevent many of the crew plainly putting the question to Jack, as to what he was about when he went on shore with the captain. Jack's reply, although exceedingly euphonious, and adapted to the comprehensions of his hearers, was such as we do not feel exactly at liberty to set down, but must leave it to the imaginations of our readers. Suffice it to say, that it was considered quite conclusive. By the grey light of morning on the Saturday, which was to be so eventful a day to Gordoni and Flavius—for they were to visit the vault for the last time, and to load themselves with treasures, always provided the bravos did not put a stop to the career of each—the watch upon the main deck of the "Wave" gave notice of the approach of a small boat in the direction of the ship.

"Hail it," said the officer of the watch.

"Boat ahoy!"

"They don't understand that, sir," said the sailor. "Perhaps they have only come out of curiosity to look at the ship."

"Very likely."

The boat, however, if impelled by curiosity, was not very scrupulous, for it came close alongside the vessel, and Gordoni—for indeed it was he—stood up in it, and in French asked for the captain. The officer of the watch happened to speak French, and he replied at once, that he would not disturb the captain, unless he knew what for, and that the cavalier had better come on board at once and be explicit. Gordoni was by far too intent upon his project to refuse this invitation, and he now stood upon the quarter deck of the "Wave."

"Well, signor," said the lieutenant, "what is it?"

"It is a private affair of some importance, signor," replied Gordoni, "and, by your leave, I should much prefer communicating it to Captain Herbert, which I hear is the name of your gallant commander."

Now it struck the lieutenant all at once that this must have something to do with the captain's nocturnal visit to the city, and he thought that by prying into the matter any further he might not be thanked for his pains, so he made up his mind to at once communicate with Captain Herbert, whom he knew would be stirring, although the hour was an early one. He accordingly descended to the captain's cabin, and to the no small surprise of Herbert, told him that a gentleman from the shore was upon deck and had some important private matters of which to tell him. Captain Herbert at once thought that it was some one from Julia, and he ordered that the visitor should be shown at once to his cabin. Gordoni, with every demonstration of respect, made his appearance, and bowing to the captain, who invited him to be seated, said,—

"Signor, will you name your own price for taking two passengers to England?"

"Sir," said Captain Herbert, reddening with anger, "do you take this frigate for a packet boat?"

"No, signor; but I had a hope that you would not refuse a passenger, who—"

"Damn your hopes!"

"Signor!"

"Nonsense, sir, nonsense! We don't take passengers."

"Myself, signor, and a young lady from a convent, whose mind is seriously affected, surely could not much incommode so gallant a signor as yourself in so spacious a vessel as you so ably command."

"Young lady from a convent ! What convent ?"

"The Benedictine convent, commonly called St. Ursula.''

Captain Herbert was staggered. It was of course the very convent in which Julia was a prisoner.

"Sir," he said, " if this be anything in the shape of oppression or wrong done to the young lady, I then might——"

This was quite a sufficient hint to Gordoni.

"Ah, signor," he said, "I see you have a feeling heart. There is much oppression —much wrong, I assure you, signor. It is only by securing a passage in this vessel that she can be rescued from all the horrors of conventual imprisonment. You will indeed, signor, be doing a worthy act, which you will never regret while you live; your consent will make me the happiest of men."

"Who," said the captain, in a faltering tone, "is the young lady ?"

"Her name is Floranthe!"

"Floranthe ?"

"Yes. Such has been the rigour with which she has been treated, that I, who am her best and indeed her only friend, she suspects to be her enemy ; and I dare say even to rescue her, poor thing, I shall have to use some degree of force ; but how gratified she will be when her reason is recovered ! We have been privately married, signor, so there can be no scruples upon that head, and if you consent to aid me, I shall send on board in the course of the day some chests belonging to myself and the young lady."

All this while Captain Herbert had been looking very hard at Gordoni, and listening to his voice and wondering where it was he had heard it somewhere before, until it struck him that it must have been in the convent garden, upon the occasion of his visit there with Jack.

"Signor," he said, " if you like, I will certainly assist you, but if the young lady is to be taken by force from the convent, I——"

"Oh, no—no—not exactly by force; I only suspect that pious motives of cupidity and dread of losing a victim, the abbess, and such friends as she may have about her, might object. But—but—"

"Half a dozen of my crew," said Captain Herbert, "would soon put all that to rights, sir."

"Might I then indeed count upon such valuable assistance ?"

"Oh, certainly ; we think nothing of such little adventures."

"Signor, your goodness most sensibly affects me; I know not what to say to you to express my grateful feelings. If, at the dusk of the evening, you would lead your men, I could conduct you quietly to the convent garden, when, if you once effected an entrance, the rest would be easy."

"You may depend upon me," said Captain Herbert. "If you keep a look-out, you will find me with a good boat's crew at any landing you name."

"There is an obscure one by the Dalmatian wharf. It is called Ursula's Gate, in consequence of conducting to a water-gate of the convent garden."

"Depend upon me, I will find it."

Gordoni was quite delighted. He had made up his mind that, by force or fraud, Floranthe should be the partner of his flight ; and it would suit the views both of himself and the Lady Abbess that it should seem that the abduction of Floranthe was accomplished by foreigners, which would completely divert pursuit from him, Gordoni.

But if this plan suited Gordoni, how much better it suited Captain Herbert, who, when once he should get into the convent, determined not to leave it again without possessing himself of Julia. It seemed as if fortune cast into his hands, without trouble upon his part, the richest possession he coveted—the hand of the fair Venetian girl whom he loved with so much devotion. Gordoni was perfectly satisfied ; and after making some minor arrangements with the captain, he took his leave. On the quay where he landed he met Flavius, to whom he said—

"I have arranged all with the English captain. Send on board during the day as much gold as you can. He will take us both off at nightfall. You will surely before this," thought Gordoni to himself, "fall into the hands of the bravos, and I shall go alone with Floranthe!"

"My dear Gordoni," said Flavius, "what a manager you are! We will go to England, and be princes. Surely! the bravos will settle this rascal before long," added Flavius to himself, "and I shall go alone, having all the gold and jewels to myself, which is much better than sharing them with him."

"Another boat!" announced the watch on the main deck of the frigate.

"A pest take these Venetians, with their intrigues!" said the officer of the watch. "I suppose we shall have no peace now, on board the 'Wave.'"

"Boat ahoy!"

A white handkerchief was waved from the boat, as a sort of signal that its destination was the frigate, and when it was alongside, a tall, distinguished looking man, asked in a polite tone for the honour of an interview with the captain. He was invited upon deck, and once more the lieutenant proceeded to Captain Herbert's cabin, to tell him that he was wanted. This new arrival, upon the report of the lieutenant, was considered quite worthy of the same amount of courtesy, at all events, that Gordoni had received, and he was admitted to the cabin. The Count Gradunio, for it was no other than he, descended, and, with a grace of manner peculiarly his own, introduced himself to the captain, adding,

"Signor, the favour which I come to ask of you, is one that ought to be prefaced by an entire confidence in you. Are you disposed to listen to rather a long story?"

"I am quite at your service, sir," said the captain.

The Count Gradunio then, without the least reservation, put Captain Herbert in possession of the full particulars concerning himself, Gordoni, and the Grand Treasurer Flavius, which are already so well known to the reader, adding, to the end of his narration,—

"I have watched Gordoni pay you a visit, Signor, and I thought it was but proper to put you in possession of the real facts concerning him."

"You astonish me," said Captain Herbert.

He then rapidly related to the count what had passed between him and Gordoni, and he did not stop short of informing him of the promise he had made to land at sunset with a force and surprise the convent.

"What do you tell me?" cried the count. "Are you really so far deceived by this man, whose looks, I should have thought would have awakened all your caution, to entertain the idea of really assisting him in his most rascally and infamous proceedings?"

"Certainly not," said Captain Herbert, with a smile.

"And yet you promised him?"

"I did; but, as he came to deceive me, I thought it but right that I should turn the tables upon him, and make use of him for the advancement of my own views. Listen to me, sir. Since you have given me your confidence so frankly and unreservedly, I feel that I cannot do better than return the compliment."

The Count Gradunio was all astonishment while Captain Herbert related to him his acquaintance with, and love for Julia, and the attempt he had already made to carry her off, and the hopes he now had, through the instrumentality of Gordoni, of fully succeeding in doing so upon that very evening.

"The monstrous villain!" cried Count Gradunio.

"Bad enough, no doubt, signor," said Captain Herbert. "But have you any idea of who this lady, named Floranthe, really is?"

"Yes. It must be the daughter of the Count Syracuse. I have heard some confused story of an attempt to patch up an union between her and this Gordoni, who is her cousin, but could not believe it of Syracuse, who was once a brave and honourable man. However, this information that you give me, Signor Capitano, will enable me to defeat in all ways the villain Gordoni."

"But oblige me, signor, in one thing."

" If it be in my power to oblige you in anything you may command me; nay, you may command all the influence I possess in Venice, only make me your confident, let me know your request."

" Then do not in any way spoil my expedition to the convent this evening, from which I am determined to wrest the Lady Julia."

" I wil most assuredly not put any obstruction in the way of your accomplishing an act which is so humane. I am directly opposed to the arbitary proceedings of the church and its mercenaries, therefore you may calculate upon my aid."

" Then I am easy."

"No doubt every facility will be offered to you to make your way into the convent. All that will be arranged between Gordoni and the abbess ; but I think, long before you land for that purpose, both Gordoni and Flavius will be prisoners of state; and now, signor, for my special request. Will you take me to England?"

"If you wish it. But as all this villany, from which you have suffered so much, will be discovered, what can you have to fear?"

"Nothing to fear, but I confess myself to be much out of conceit with Venetian laws and Venetian arbitrary powers. I wish to live in a more free country, notwithstanding I am credibly informed that in England you are taxed almost for the air you breathe, to support a lazy and knavish aristocracy, and a state church."

"Humph!" said Captain Herbert. "There are certainly taxes in England, but as a public officer it is not my province to talk politics ; so if you wish to go with me just say so, and there's an end."

"Most cordially then do I wish it."

"Very good. Come on board when you please."

"Upon that point, then, I am quite easy. When I have fully exposed the villany of Gordoni and Flavius my mission in Venice is over, and I shall turn my back upon it for ever."

The count rose, and cautiously took leave of Captain Herbert, who was certainly rather astounded at the rapidity of the events which occurred to place his own affairs in so very different a light. He was overjoyed at the prospect of rescuing Julia from the horrors with which he felt certain she was surrounded in the convent, and he waited with the greatest amount of impatience for the evening to come. Gordoni and Flavius little imagined the precipice upon which they stood, each being that day surprised to find the other untouched by the bravos. The fact is, that the secret of their preservation consisted in the fact that the assassins were waiting for either of them to come to their haunt, when they could have immediately despatched him, and then waited patiently for the other, so that they would have, in their opinion, properly and honourably earned the money of both. The frequent meetings of the two villains prevented either of them from running into such danger, as neither thought it worth while to call upon the bravos until the assassination was done. We will now follow the footsteps of the Count Gradunio, who, after he left the frigate, went upon a most important mission indeed, and one pregnant with immense results.

CHAPTER XLVIII.

THE COUNT GRADUNIO'S INTERVIEW WITH COUNT SYRACUSE.—AWAKENED CONSCIENCE.

WHEN the Count Gradunio had heard of the imprisonment, for it could be called by no other term, of Floranthe in the convent, he recalled to himself the sort of confession that he had heard from the young girl whom he had rescued from the canal, immediately beneath the Bridge of Sighs. That young girl had told him, that for love of Stralani, she had disguised herself in the costume of a page, and attended upon him, and that she had found the Lady Floranthe, daughter of the Count Syracuse, had all the affections of Stralani. She had, however, refused to state who she was. Nevertheless, from what she had related, the Count Gradunio had no difficulty in coming to the conclusion that it was by Gordoni's means that the young Stralani had been assassinated, for the girl-page fully believed that he was no longer among the living, having no information of his preservation at the gardener's lodge, or of his rapid recovery under the care of the Jewish physician. This belief she had likewise impressed upon the Count Gradunio, so that taking all the circumstances into consideration, and scarcely being able to believe that any father could be so utterly regardless of his daughter's feelings and happiness, he came to the conclusion that the Count Syracuse must be the dupe of Gordoni. There was no danger now to be apprehended from showing himself to any one, upon the part of Count Gradunio. He was fully protected by the doge and the council, so he resolved upon paying a visit to the Count Syracuse, whom he had formerly known quite well enough to warrant him in doing so.

"I may awaken him to the villany of Gordoni," thought Gradunio, "and get him to remove his child from that atrocious convent; or, if he be really an accomplice of Gordoni against the happiness of his own daughter, conscience may not be altogether so dead within him, but I may succeed in fanning some small spark of it into a flame, and so saving him from greater wickedness, and the fair Floranthe from further suffering."

Such were the feelings and wishes with which the noble and chivalrous Count Gradunio started at once for the Palazzo Syracuse. There was really something now quite strange and new to the Count Gradunio, in passing through Venice without the necessity of any amount of personal concealment. He felt as one might feel who was restored from death once again to walk among the living. He had availed himself of the services of the faithful Jerome to carry him along the canals that lay between his own and the Count Syracuse's residence, and the gondola was soon moored at the gate of the palazzo where Floranthe had been born, and in the small garden attached to which she had listened to the voice of Stralani. The Count Gradunio was in doubt at first, whether or not he should give his name to the page who made his appearance to receive the visitor, but after a few moments' consideration, he determined that he would not do so, and merely desired the page to announce that a gentleman wished for an interview with the count upon important business. Count Syracuse was rather alarmed at the eagerness of this message. The guilty are alarmed at everything that they do not at once and readily comprehend, and he hesitated about giving an interview to one who refused even the solitary satisfaction of his name. But yet, fearful that he might miss some important intelligence, and feeling that if he let the visitor go without seeing him, he should be upon the well of curiosity to think what it could possibly be he had to say to him, he made up his mind to see him. The Count Syracuse gave the necessary orders, and Gradunio was shown into an apartment of luxurious appointments, and told that the Count Syracuse would be with him immediately. When the Count Syracuse entered the room, Gradunio's face was much muffled up in his cloak, but advancing towards the window, through which came a bright strain of light, he let his cloak fall from him, and said in an earnest voice—

"Do you know me, Count Syracuse?"

This apparition, for such indeed it seemed to be, of the Count Gradunio, filled Syracuse with horror. He stood for some few moments as if stricken with so much surprise, that all his faculties, both mental and physical, were suspended, and then in a tone of horror he cried,—

"Off—off, spectre. What have I done to thee, that thou shouldst haunt me? Off—off, I say. Oh, this is horrible."

"And can you really be so weak," said Gradunio, "as to think me an apparition?"

"Are—you—not?" gasped Syracuse.

"Look well at me. Feel my hand. Are you now convinced?"

"Gracious Heaven, Gradunio, by what miracle are you restored to life? Gordoni told me you were—"

"Aye, Gordoni told you—that villain of villains."

The Count Syracuse trembled, and tottering back, sunk into a chair.

"Is it your wish," said Gradunio, "that your only child should be sacrificed to this Gordoni? Is it—can it be with your connivance that this night he is going to carry her from the convent, and take her with him by force to England?"

"Good God!"

"Count Syracuse, I came to warn you. No spectre from another world could possibly speak more prophetically than I do now. I come to warn you, I say, that you stand upon the brink of a precipice from which you have now but barely time to retreat. One step forward, and you are lost—lost for ever."

"Spare me!"

"Spare others."

"What mean you, Gradunio, if you be really the living, breathing Gradunio? Oh, I have suffered much, and there are times when I look into my own heart, and see there such frightful and despairing images that gladly would I purchase oblivion by death, if I were sure it could be so purchased."

"Aye, if you were sure."

The Count Syracuse trembled, and Gradunio added—

"Were you privy to the assassination of the young cavalier, Stralani?"

"Ah," cried Syracuse, "now I know you cannot be human, or else you would not know that dreadful secret."

"Alas, then it is true?"

"Off,—off, spectre. Off, I say. Do not torment me while yet I live. Time enough when I am no more, will it be for you to horrify me by those dreadful looks and more dreadful accusations. I know well that I am lost—lost—lost. There is for me no mercy."

"There is for you much mercy."

"No—no—no."

"I say yes, but inasmuch as you strove to earn perdition, so much do you strive to earn mercy. Endeavour now from this moment to do what you can to undo the mischief that you have done. Endeavour to do what good now lies in your power, and most of all, I ask of you at once to release your child from the convent, where such cruelties are practised, as must have reached your ears."

"Yes, yes—I will, I will. But there is one crime which in its consequences cannot be recalled."

"And that is——"

"The murder of the Cavalier Stralani. Oh, horror—horror, if I could but see him in life, and place my child's hand in his, Gordoni might do his worst, I could smile at his most deadly malice."

The door of the apartment opened, and the old gardener appeared upon the threshold. Agitation was visible upon every feature of his face, and for some moments he could not speak; when, however, he gathered power to do so, he said,—

"My lord, I did not come to listen.—I did not, indeed; but as I passed this door, I heard some words which tempted me to pause. Oh, my lord, do you really mean that you would be glad to hear that the Cavalier Stralani lives? because—because,—

"What! What?"

"Because—"

"Speak, old man, speak, I say. Do not torture me by these half sentences and inuendos, speak, I charge you, fully, or you will drive me mad."

"Dare I? Dare I?" cried the old man, as he fell upon his knees. "Oh dare I ask? Yes, he lives, he lives! The young and noble cavalier Stralani, lives in my humble home. He is sorely wounded, but I took him bleeding and insensible, from the foot of the flight of marble steps, where he had fallen beneath the dagger of the bravo!"

"Oh joy! joy!" cried the Count Syracuse. "I—I am saved from that dreadful crime. Now Gordoni, do your worst; I am no longer your creature."

The Count Syracuse appeared to be about to faint, and Gradunio threw open the casement, to give him air. In a few moments he recovered, and turning to the old man, he said, with a voice half-choked by emotion—

"I—I will visit Stralani. Will he—can he see me?"

"Yes, my good lord. Yes, he is so much recovered that he can almost leave his bed, and I am sure, if I may judge from his sweet and Christian temper, he is not one who will refuse to hold out the hand of forgiveness to any one."

"I—I will go to him. Yes, I will go to him. Oh, Gradunio, what a mercy this visit of yours has been to me. Go, old man, and prepare the Chevalier Stralani for my visit."

"Be cautious," said Count Gradunio, to the gardener, "be cautious; you are now in possession of a secret that would much compromise your master, therefore, keep it locked up in your own bosom, for now, his means of doing good must not be paralysed by any thoughts of personal danger."

"No—no," said Syracuse. "Even Gordoni's power of mischief shall not stir me, and he has indeed powers of much mischief."

When the old gardener had retired, the Count Gradunio said to Syracuse—

"You may rid yourself of all fears of Gordoni. It is now eight o'clock; before five more hours have expired, you may dismiss Gordoni, and all that in any way concerns him, from your mind completely. You need wish even for no revenge against him."

The Count Syracuse looked puzzled, as well he might, at these words. He begged for an explanation of this, and Gradunio added—

"The secret is not wholly my own, and I dare not say more to you, than that he will be by one o'clock, or some short time afterwards, a state prisoner for practices against the republic. His crime is of sufficient moment to ensure his death."

"Then, indeed, I shall feel that I am free," said the Count Syracuse, as he drew a long breath, "but you have awakened new thoughts and feelings in my heart, Gradunio, and I long to embrace my child, Floranthe."

"Upon consideration," said Gradunio, "she must still continue where she is for some hours. If she was taken from the convent before Gordoni were in custody, he might, and doubtless would, hear of it, and if his suspicions were once in the smallest degree awakened, he would take to flight. For my own part I should care little for that, but it is necessary he should fall into the hands of justice, and that his criminality should be clear and apparent, for my own vindication from false accusation. I will leave you now, Syracuse, to make your peace with Stralani."

The Count Syracuse over and over again thanked his old friend, Gradunio, for thus coming to him, and when he was gone, he, Syracuse, with trembling steps sought the lodge where Stralani lay, still but partially recovered from his wounds. It must indeed have been a deep humiliation to the count, to be thus making his way to the bedside of the man whom he had so much injured, for the purpose of asking his forgiveness; but it was a thing that had to be done, and after all it was worth doing, if to purchase the peace of mind that would be sure to follow it, and the serenity of conscience which had been for long now a stranger to the breast of the proud, haughty, but weak, Count Syracuse. He hoped the old gardener had well prepared Stralani for the interview, and, indeed, such was the case, for upon entering the room the Count Syracuse saw a smile upon the lips of Stralani, and his out-stretched hand towards him. Oh! how pale, thin, transparent was the hand, and how languid and bloodless was the face of the wounded cavalier.

"Can you forgive?" began the Count.

"Hush—oh, hush my lord," said Stralani, "let the past be forgotten."

"But, you know me now as——"

"As the father of Floranthe, and as nothing else, from henceforward—let us never for one moment look back."

"Am I dreaming of so much generosity? Oh, Stralani, although you will not speak of what has happened, your thoughts will be busy, and, as you look upon me, you will shudder to think that you behold him who——"

"Why will you thus distress me, my lord?" said Stralani. "The mistakes—the remorse—the passions of the past, should never be raked up from their ashes to make the present hideous; no more, I pray you. Let us speak of Floranthe."

"Yes, yes," said Syracuse; "she shall be yours, and yours only. Stralani, from my hand you shall receive her, and may you be happy."

These words had an almost magical effect upon Stralani. The colour came back to his cheeks, and he felt as though at that moment he could have risen from his bed and rushed himself to Floranthe to tell her how happy they would now be, and with what an unchanging and dear affection he had loved her. The count, however, insisted upon his remaining quiet, and succeeded in inducing him to do so, by a solemn promise that he should see Floranthe before the day was gone.

While all these events were taking place in Venice, poor Floranthe and Julia still were filled with feelings almost approaching to despair, as the difficulties surrounding them seemed to be upon the increase instead of diminishing. They little imagined that so remarkable a change had taken place in their destiny. But we must leave them for the present, to turn to more turbulent scenes in this history—scenes which rapidly drop the curtain upon some of the personages who can be spared from the body politic of Venice. Who will regret such men as Flavius and Gordoni? Mutually watching each other, and mutually surprised to find each other free from the bravo's poniards, they passed the morning. Each had thought that it would be his good fortune to visit, for the last time, the treasure vaults of the State of Venice alone, and so enrich himself with spoil; but, as it happened, they both met in the chamber where was the secret pane, just as the great clock from the belfry of St. Agatha struck the hour of one! It was that appointed for their last visit to the vaults beneath the doge's palace.

CHAPTER XLIX.

THE ARREST OF GORDONI AND FLAVIUS IN THE TREASURE VAULTS.

THE two villains looked at each other with some degree of surprise; but of course each of them forbore to say anything to the other concerning the likelihood of either coming not to the rendezvous.

"Let us be quick," said Flavius. "The sooner we get the chests, in which we have packed our vast treasure, on board the English frigate the better."

"Certain y," said Gordoni. "Remember, we take nothing to-day from the vaults but precious stones, and gold of the highest value."

"Of course. Come on."

With hasty steps, in which there was no caution whatever preserved, for they had not the most distant idea of any interruption, they descended and reached the vaults. Gordoni had with him a sack, in which the precious stones were to be placed, and, as he glared around him at the vast treasures which the vaulted chamber contained, his avaricious heart prompted a sigh that he could not take all away. The idea struck each of them that it might be possible enough to make away with his companion before leaving the vaults; but it was not sufficiently matured to be, by either, carried into speedy effect. It was indeed a strange sight to see those two men conversing and acting together, while the mind of each was full of anxious thoughts as to the best and safest mode of murdering the other. And they were seen, although they little suspected such to be the case.

"Now," said Gordoni, "from your knowledge of where the greatest valuables are kept, let us proceed. We need have no scruples now as to what seals we break, and what locks we open. Where are the personal diamonds of the doge?"

"Here!" said Flavius, as he climbed upon two chests and pointed to a third, which was sealed up with two massive seals of yellow wax.

"Could we not take that small chest as it is?"

"We might, indeed. A rare booty it would be, if we took nothing else from these vaults, which are so crammed with riches. The plunder of some half dozen Eastern campaigns is here, Gordoni. By the Mass I think it but a small matter to rob the State of Venice."

"But the state of Venice would think something of it," said Gordoni; "and I suppose, if the poor doge and his myrmidons had been cunning enough to catch us, the only favour we should have had a chance of receiving, would be that we should, on account of our noble lineage, have our heads chopped off by the pillars of St. Mark, instead of being hanged like dogs, or drowned in chains from the dungeon of the Bridge of Sighs."

"That favour is granted!" said a deep, stern voice; and from behind one of the massive columns supporting the arched roof, out slipped the Doge of Venice.

The light which Flavius was carrying dropped from his hand, and he uttered a shriek of terror and amazement. Gordoni, even, with all his natural effrontery, staggered back as though he had been shot.

"What, ho! guards! guards!" cried the Doge.

In an instant, from every available place of concealment, from behind boxes, columns, and from dark corners, there appeared the doge's guards and the councillors of state, all fully armed. The soldiers hastily, by the aid of lanterns, which they had about them concealed, began to light some flambeaux.

"Seize those robbers!" cried the Doge.

"Mercy! mercy!" shrieked Flavius, and he fell from the chests upon which he was standing, and grovelled upon the floor of the vault.

Gordoni drew his sword, but it was beaten down, and he was on the instant made a prisoner and bound.

"Lost!" he said, "the game is up! Do your worst, Doge of Venice, I am beaten. Ha! who art thou—off, hideous spectre. Once before have you crossed my path. Off, I say. Do not blast me with that dreadful look."

The Count Gradunio had made his appearance from amid the soldiers of the Doge, and now he stood confronting Gordoni.

"Villain!" he said, "if anything can add to the bitterness of this moment, it will be the knowledge that I escaped your treachery."

"Escaped.—Confusion!"

"Yes, confusion! I escaped, and in concert with the doge and the council of Venice, I planned your capture here, with your miserable accomplice.

Gordoni shook.

"You are doomed," added Gradunio, "for your crime merely. I could pity your fate but for your base treachery; I have no feeling but abhorrence."

"Remove the prisoners," said the Doge. "Count Gradunio, it is the unanimous wish of the council and of myself that you accept the office of grand treasurer."

"We will speak of that another time," said Count Gradunio, bowing.

"Be it so. March, soldiers."

Gordoni walked with a sullen air from the vaults, but Flavius was dragged, shrieking for mercy, by two soldiers along the long dreary passages. When the party reached the rooms in Count Gradunio's house, for they went that way from the vaults, to the surprise of all, they found a page standing there, looking pale and haggard. It was the young girl who had been rescued from the canal by Count Gradunio.

"A dream! a dream!" she cried, "I saw the block and the sword of the headsman. I saw a grey head, and it was my father's. Where am I—oh, where am I?"

"God of Heaven!" said Flavius, "that is my lost daughter's voice."

With a shriek the young girl threw herself among the soldiers and embraced Flavius. She was indeed his daughter. In another moment her arms relaxed their hold, and she fell to the floor. The Count Gradunio rushed forward and raised her tenderly. He held in his arms a corpse. The shock had killed her, and Flavius found himself childless at the moment when he had most need of consolation.

"Justice is disarmed," said the Doge with a shudder, "Heaven has taken away the reason of this man. Let him be placed in an asylum for such melancholy objects, and stoutly guarded. It would be murder now to take his life. To-morrow Gordoni dies Away with them both."

CHAPTER L.

THE CONCLUSION.

As was fully expected by the Count Gradunio, Gordoni had arranged matters with the Abbess of the Convent, so that no real resistance was offered to Captain Herbert in taking Floranthe away, but the abbess was not a little surprised when Julia was demanded. She demurred; but a vigorous search through the convent soon found the young novice, and with a cry of joy she rushed into her lover's arms.

"Come, Julia," said Herbert, "we will away now; my mission here is accomplished."

"But there is another here who must be rescued," said Julia. "The Lady Floranthe Syracuse. Ah, I cannot leave her to the horrors of this convent."

There is one here who has a better claim to rescue her than I," said Captain Herbert.

He stepped aside, and from the group of armed men by which he was accompanied, out stepped the Count Syracuse.

"Abbess," he said, "I demand my daughter."

The abbess was astounded.

"Oh, certainly, count I—I—Rene—"

"Yes, madame."

"You will fetch the Count Syracuse's daughter."

Rene departed on her errand, and soon returned with the wondering Floranthe, who, when she saw her father, made sure that he had come to enforce the tyranny of the abbess; but when, with tears in his eyes, he said,—

"Floranthe, can you forget the past, and be my own child again?" she flung herself upon his breast, saying,

"Oh, yes, yes, father. Oh, joy, joy!"

The convent was soon left by the now happy party, and while Captain Herbert repaired on board the "Wave" with Julia, the Count Syracuse, with Floranthe hastened homewards. When they got near to the Palazzo, he said to her,—

"Floranthe, you saw a sad sight once in the garden, at the foot of the marble steps."

"Father! father!" she exclaimed, bursting into tears.

"Come, my child," he said, "you shall once more descend those steps and show me the exact spot whereon you found Stralani."

In vain Floranthe implored her father not to expose her feelings to so grievous a trial. He persisted, and in half an hour's time, by the light of a brilliant moon, she was once again with trembling steps descending those steps at the foot of which she had before met with so terrible a surprise. Ah! what a new surprise awaited her.

"Floranthe! my Floranthe," cried a voice, and in a moment she was clasped in the arms of Stralani.

Joy overcame her for the moment, and she could not speak. When she did, however, recover sufficiently to utter a coherent word, she cried,—.

"If this be madness, Heaven keep me so."

"No, my Floranthe, it is not, my own, my beautiful. I am yet weak from my wounds, but I am rapidly recovering. Your father consents to our union, and we shall be happy."

"Happy! happy!" cried Floranthe; and she wept tears of extacy. "Oh, Stralani, what have I not suffered since that dreadful night when I saw you lying here with blood upon you, and so—so still."

"Hush, dear one, no more. Promise me one thing."

"Anything, Stralani."

"Then never, to your father, allude to the events of that dreadful night."

"I will not, Stralani."

"The future shall be to us full of sunshine, we will not dim its radiance by summoning up the shadows of the past."

They then ascended together the steps—those marble steps which it was almost a miracle to think would ever be pressed by the footsteps of Stralani.

*   *   *   *   *   *

The Frigate "Wave" sailed out of the Gulf of Venice with speed. Three persons stood upon the deck taking a last view of the city of the sea. Captain Herbert and Julia stood side by side, and a little distance from them was the Count Gradunio, who was quitting Venice for ever. Jerome was amply provided for by Count Gradunio efore his departure. The Ursuline Convent was suppressed stoutly, for it was found hat if it had not been so put down, the indignation of the populace would not have left one stone of it standing upon another, as many of the villanies carried on within its walls came to light. Gordoni was executed between the pillars of St. Mark, in presence of a large concourse of spectators. Within one month from these events, a bridal party approached the altar of St. Mark, and with a smile of joy, Stralani whispered to Floranthe,—

"Dearest, how I have longed for this—"

"Appointed hour," said Floranthe.

FINIS.

THE SEQUEL.

OLD FRIENDS.

THE period of six months has elapsed since the gallant "Wave" flew like a bird southward of Venice, leaving behind it the waters of the Adriatic; but during that six months how much has happened! We will take a brief glance at those in whose fate

we have felt so great an interest, and whose fortunes, through the wiles of Venetian intrigue, we followed with our readers. In a southern county of England, the shores of which are washed by that restless piece of water called the English Channel, at about half a mile distance from a pebbly beach, stood a mansion which no one could look at without more than ordinary curiosity, or leave the neighbourhood of without an inquiry concerning it. It was not the palatial style of the building—it was not an appearance of any cumbrous state or dignity about it that attracted the gaze, but it was a something truly singular and un-English in its architecture that made it a prominent object in the surrounding landscape, and yet a more thoroughly English house than the one which the whole neighbourhood remembered well as standing, a very short time before, upon that spot, could not have been imagined. The change that had been wrought consisted in this: Projecting a distance of about twenty-five feet from the house, upon three of its sides, was a glass roof supported upon slender columns, between which were windows and jalousies after the Venetian fashion, so that the whole space thus covered could be enclosed at pleasure, making a covered and protected garden of large dimensions. Within this favoured spot, protected by artificial heat, was to be found one of the rarest collections of exotics that the county could boast of, and even in the depth of winter that place bore promise of eternal summer. This was the abode of Herbert and Julia. The gallant captain, for that was a piping time of peace, had found now that he had so fair a face to look upon, and such pouting lips to kiss, that it was indeed

"Stale flat and unprofitable"

to be beating about the Mediterranean at the caprice of some gentleman in a snug room at Whitehall. Like a man of sense, therefore, he had given up the command at sea, to enjoy such an empire on shore as few mortals are blessed with. The empire over youth, devotion, and beauty. The winter had fairly set in, and there had been some nipping winds, and blusterous days around their fair domain, but the one upon which we introduce Captain Herbert and his Julia again to the reader, was the worst that had yet occurred since the beautiful Venetian had found a home beneath our more northern skies. She and Herbert were walking together in the delicious conservatory, and as Julia hung upon his arm with both her hands clasped around it, she said—

"And shall we indeed witness to-day one of the commotions of sea, and air to which the rugged shores of England are subject?"

"I have lost faith in the weather," said Herbert, "if by sunset we don't have as pretty a gale as any one would wish to see."

"But you do not wish it, Herbert?"

"No, no—not exactly. Only you see, Julia, it is a great advantage being so near the sea, that when there is anything of the kind, one does see it, and know all about it. Only listen to that, now?"

They were silent for a few moments, and then Julia said—

"All I hear, is something like a faint whistle a long way off, or a sigh!"

"Ah, that's it!"

"What is it, Herbert? Is it danger?"

"Oh, no. That's the gale coming—that's all. I only hope our friend the Count Gradunio will not let a little rough weather prevent him from making us his promised visit. But as he comes over land it will hardly stop him. We must endeauour to make him stay as long as possible, for there is a melancholy yet clinging to him, which I would fain see him fling off."

"Ah! he suffered much in Venice."

"He did, indeed, poor fellow. Hilloa! There she goes! Storm-sail there! Hard a port! What the deuce am I saying? Its only a squall burst into one of our windows and blinds here. Really for the moment I fancied myself on ship board again, the whistle of the wind is so familiar a sound."

"Will it be worse than this?"

"A little," replied the captain with a smile. "But come, Julia, it is too dark now for you to see even your bright and favourite camelias, so let us get in doors, and I will peep out of the little window at the top of the house to see how the storm gets on. The channel will froth a little to-night, and woe be to the ship without a skilful captain, or a good offing between now and the day dawn to-morrow."

Julia shuddered as still leaning upon the arm of Captain Herbert, she with him sought the house. The dinner hour had arrived and no Count Gradunio had made an appearance, but Herbert, whose habits were punctuality itself, ordered the king meal of the day to be served, and the night crept on until they gave up all thoughts of the arrival of their friend on that day. The wind had now become furious. The squalls of wind that had about sunset come every few moments, had increased to a gale, and that gale was sufficiently furious to be called a hurricane. Captain Herbert had frequently been "aloft" as he called it to a little window that opened on to a portion of the roof of his house to notice how the weather went, and he had each time made a sort of report to Julia, as though she had been admiral of the fleet, not that she understood above one word in ten of the nautical language in which he couched his statements. At length, she became evidently so much alarmed at the roaring of the wind, that she prayed him to remain with her, which he did, making an ineffectual attempt to calm terror, by talking of old times in Venice.

"Shall we ever see Floranthe again?" he said.

"Oh! yes, yes. We must hazard going to Venice even, rather than not look upon that brave and noble girl once more."

"Well, I should like nothing better, and a yatch would take us nicely in the sweet summer time. It will be a good satisfaction to me, to take the gallant Stralani by the hand again. Ah! what's that?"

Captain Herbert sprung to his feet.

"What? Oh, what is it, Herbert. You terrify me. To what are you listening so intently?"

"Hush—hush! There again. Hear you nothing?"

"Yes, a dull, heavy sound apparently far off."

"Yes. You are right. To your preception, Julia, it is but a dull heavy sound far off, but to mine, it is a signal gun of distress from some ship at sea. Often amid the storm have I heard those minute guns telling of danger and of suffering, and now I am confident some ship in sore distress is driving upon the coast. Hark! There again. Those guns come at regular intervals. Oh, Julia, you do not—you cannot know how such sounds fall upon the breast of a sailor."

"Herbert—Herbert! What would you do?"

"What you would wish me to do, Julia," he replied. "What you would command me to do. To fly to the relief of those who are perhaps each moment driving on the rocks, and looking for aid where aid there is none. Some one is always wanted upon these occasions to direct the movements of many who know not how to do the least work in such trials, and I, from my experience, am calculated to be that person."

"But you will be careful of yourself, Herbert."

"Not very, and yet enough. Farewell until you see me back again with a wet jacket, Julia, which, I think, will be the extent of my sufferings."

Captain Herbert hurried from the dining-room, and collecting all the men servants, with what lanterns and ropes the premises afforded, he hurried down to the beach, resolved at any personal hazard, to render aid to the unfortunate vessel. The moment he got upon the sands he caught sight of the lights of a large vessel in the offing, not more than a mile from the rocks, and drifting each moment in shore. She fired another gun, and the flash of which was distinctly visible amid the howling of the storm. A number of persons was collected on the beach. But as he, Captain Herbert, fully expected, they were there without order or any one to direct them what to do to succour the unfortunate vessel, which it was quite evident to his experienced eyes must inevitably come on shore. There was but one spot where the ship might ground without a probability of going immediately to pieces, it was towards that spot that Herbert wished to direct her. He collected all the laterns at the head of that place, which was a little sandy cave and then waited the result. The ship drifted on, a heavy sea struck her and cast her upon the beach. Her mizen mast, which had hitherto stood, broke short by the deck, carrying with it a host of top hamper that the storm had reduced to ribbons, and the ship was a perfect wreck, lying wedged among some rocks, which held her forward, while aft she was lifted by each rush of waves some twenty feet, and then let down again with a blow upon the sandy shore that was enough to dash her timbers from each other. In fact she was just going to peices, when Captain Herbert having lashed a rope round his waist, and given the end of it to some fishermen on the shore, dashed boldly into the surf with the end of a hawser in his grasp. The task he had set himself was one of no ordinary difficulty, but he did, after a frightful struggle with

" The wild rush of angry waters"

succeed in establishing a connection between the shore and the stranded ship, by which one by one the mariners and all on board escaped to land. Scarcely had the last of the ill-fated crew been received in the arms of the fishermen, than with a cracking noise, the wreck went to pieces.

"To my house with every one!" cried Captain Herbert. "To my house at once. There all wants shall be attended to. Forward!"

"Here is a lady, sir," who has fainted."

"Where is she?"

"Here—here, Captain Herbert, " she lies upon some of our jackets, this way."

They led Captain Herbert to the spot, and without a word, or so much as looking at the face of the lady, he took her up in his arms and carried her to his house. The fishermen brought all the others who had been saved from the wreck. At the door of his own house, Captain Herbert met Julia leaning upon the arm of Count Gradunio, who had arrived in his, Herbert's absence.

"Ah, count," cried Herbert. "You are late, but welcome. Julia, here is a lady who has been rescued from the wreck."

Herbert at once walked into the dining-room with his charge, and laid her upon a sofa. The light of the chandelier fell upon her face, and Julia uttered a shriek, as she cried—

"It is Florathe!"

At the same moment the two gentlemen knew her, and the count cried—

"Good Heaven! where is Stralani?"

"Here! here!" shouted some one, rushing into the room. "Who calls upon the bereaved Stralani? Oh, Floranthe, are you lost to me for ever. During my aggregate fears the rude buffeting of the ocean has robbed me of you."

"Behold!" cried Count Gradunia. "Behold!"

He moved aside so that Stralani could see Floranthe, and in another moment they were in each others arms.

Our tale is now over, Stalani had endured so much persecution in Venice from the friends of Gordoni, that he and Floranthe had resolved upon coming to England in search of Captan Herbert and Julia, and had been wrecked as we have seen within a couple of hundred yards of his house. Of course the Herberts warmly coincided with Stralani and Floranthe in settling in England, and not many weeks elapsed ere they found a home in the immediate neighbourhood, and a more happy family-circle was not to be found in England than that composed of the Herberts and Stralanis. The Count Gradunio was a frequent visiter, and when a happy group of fair children surrounded them all, many a winter's evening was robbed of its weariness by tales of Venice and of the Bridge of Sighs.

[END]

www.ingramcontent.com/pod-product-compliance
Lightning Source LLC
Chambersburg PA
CBHW080832250626
47160CB00008B/2907